A lover of storytelling in
worked for major film stu
novel, which won *RWA*'s Gc
in Northern California with her husband and a very
spoiled but utterly delightful cat.

LOVE AND OTHER *Hollywood* ENDINGS

SUSANNAH ERWIN

All rights reserved including the right of reproduction in whole or in part in any form. This edition is published by arrangement with Harlequin Enterprises ULC.

This is a work of fiction. Names, characters, places, locations and incidents are purely fictional and bear no relationship to any real life individuals, living or dead, or to any actual places, business establishments, locations, events or incidents. Any resemblance is entirely coincidental.

This book is sold subject to the condition that it shall not, by way of trade or otherwise, be lent, resold, hired out or otherwise circulated without the prior consent of the publisher in any form of binding or cover other than that in which it is published and without a similar condition including this condition being imposed on the subsequent purchaser.

® and ™ are trademarks owned and used by the trademark owner and/or its licensee. Trademarks marked with ® are registered with the United Kingdom Patent Office and/or the Office for Harmonisation in the Internal Market and in other countries.

First Published in Great Britain 2025 by
Afterglow Books by Mills & Boon, an imprint of HarperCollins*Publishers* Ltd
1 London Bridge Street, London, SE1 9GF

www.harpercollins.co.uk

HarperCollins*Publishers*
Macken House, 39/40 Mayor Street Upper,
Dublin 1, D01 C9W8, Ireland

Love and Other Hollywood Endings © 2025 Susannah Erwin

ISBN: 978-0-263-39745-1

0225

This book contains FSC™ certified paper and other controlled sources to ensure responsible forest management.

For more information visit: www.harpercollins.co.uk/green

Printed and Bound in the UK using 100% Renewable Electricity
at CPI Group (UK) Ltd, Croydon, CR0 4YY

For Tahra, Charles and Errin, the wonderful Afterglow Books editors I've had during my journey so far, for believing in me and always being delightful to work with (and who have made me a much better writer)!

Dear Reader,

This book is set during the filming of a Hollywood studio movie. Themes explored include sexism and favoritism in the workplace and internet harassment campaigns that spill into real-life harassment. The novel also touches on the death of a loved one in the past, a child who was orphaned in the past and growing up with parents who are physically present but emotionally absent. And if this book were a film, it would be rated R for containing sexual situations. There is a more extensive list of potential triggers on my website, susannaherwin.com. Please don't hesitate to always put your mental well-being first!

xo,

Susannah

One

EXT. THE VASTNESS OF SPACE—ETERNAL NIGHT.

PAN across an unfamiliar star field to a bright orange-and-white planet. The camera tilts down, zooming in at a million miles a second, piercing the atmosphere until we see:

EXT. THE DESERT WASTELAND OF KARTH—DAY

The Quantum Wraith is no more. The once-proud spacecraft, a sleek corvette that sliced through the heavens controlled by the Maro Empyreal, now lies in shards scattered among the tall cacti and sharp red rocks of the hostile planet Karth.

The wreckage glints in the hot golden rays of the sun. One piece, larger than the rest, still smolders—the former cockpit of the *Wraith*. Amid the gray smoke, a hatch suddenly pops open and a human figure emerges, coughing, sputtering, their movements slow with pain but also with urgency as they free themselves from the wreckage. They attempt to stand on the roof of the cockpit, but their left leg gives out and they tumble to the harsh sand below. Their face hidden by the full visor of their helmet, they look up at the cockpit looming above them, and then they start scrambling away from the wreck, using their hands, elbows and knees as best they can, their movements frantic. The reason for the haste becomes evident when the smoke appearing in the background begins to build, turning black and oily. Then flames lick at the hatch—

KAPOW!

The remains of the cockpit ignite. The human throws their arms over their head to protect themselves from the flames and debris (to be added in post-production). When the imminent danger is past, the human rolls over onto their back, pushing a button that retracts the full visor.

The camera pans in to reveal LYS AMARGA, the pilot of the *Quantum Wraith*. She's alive. For now. Because Lys, wincing, presses her hand to her side, then holds her palm to her eyes, and we see the bright blood dripping between her fingers.

LYS: Still beats prison—

"Oh, shit, I said the wrong word again, didn't I?"

"Cut!" The command came immediately.

Xavier Duval took his gaze off the video monitor and exited his folding chair. His barked order caused an entire village of people, who previously had been silent and frozen in place, to go into quick but practiced action. The large Arriflex camera, suspended on a long metal gimbal programmed to follow Lys's escape from the crashed ship, returned to its original starting position. The scenery crew jumped in to examine the still smoking escape pod, ensuring that the expensive prop was still in good working order and could be used for the next take. Walkie-talkies buzzed as different departments checked on what they needed to do to prepare to repeat the scene again. The set up was a complicated one, with many moving parts that had to coordinate with flawless rhythm, but Xavier was determined to capture the scene in one continuous take without any edits.

He ignored the commotion swirling around him and strode across the packed sand toward the set, accustomed to the heat of Arizona's Sonoran Desert by now. He had eyes for one person only: his leading actress, Contessina Sato. This had been the seventh take. The first two takes were cut short when the smoke didn't appear. The third take was stopped when the helmet visor wouldn't retract. But the last four were scrapped because Contessina flubbed her line. And since *The Quantum Wraith* was based on a cult comic book that had a rabid fan following, Lys needed to say, "detention hold"—a key setting in the comic—not "prison." As the screenwriter and director of the film, Xavier had carefully considered every word in the script.

Contessina slowly rose to her feet, assisted by her makeup artist, who also helped remove Lys's helmet. She took a long sip of water from the bottle held for her by a production assistant before meeting Xavier's gaze. "Sorry," she said. "I'll be good to go again whenever you're ready. And the Friday beers are on me."

Xavier regarded her. His leading actress looked tired and

defeated. He was hard-pressed to find the spark that had lit the camera on fire during her screen test. "The crew would appreciate not holding the usual raffle to buy drinks. What's going on?"

She sniffed, and to his horror, tears appeared in the corners of her eyes.

"Are you okay? Is it the armor?" He'd worked with the costume department to design garments that would look like scavenged pieces of metal haphazardly pieced together to create battle suits but were crafted of layers of moisture-wicking material to ensure the actors would stay as cool and as comfortable as possible under the desert sun.

"I'm fine. Costume is fine." She visually composed herself. "I just… I was distracted. Won't happen again."

Xavier caught a blur of motion out of the corner of his eye and managed to sidestep in time to avoid a collision with Tori, Contessina's personal assistant. She held out a cell phone to Contessina with one hand while clutching her side with the other. "It's your wife," she said between gasps of air.

Contessina grabbed the phone. "Sorry," she said to Xavier before turning away to give herself a semblance of privacy. "Juliana? How are you doing? Are the police still there?"

Police? Xavier turned to Tori. "What's going on?"

Tori was still struggling to bring her breathing under control. She glanced at Contessina, who gave Tori a nod over her shoulder before returning to her phone conversation. "There was an intruder at Conti's home. Scared Juliana. And the guy was rambling about this movie, so we're pretty sure it's tied to the hate campaign—"

"Wait. Hate campaign?"

Tori exchanged glances with Contessina. "Y'know. A bunch of angry people on the internet. They're mostly harmless if very loud comic book fans—"

"What are you talking about?" He was genuinely drawing a blank.

Tori stared back at him. "The terminally online people who are upset Contessina is playing Lys? Because Lys is a blonde with a 40D chest in the comics?"

For the past eight months, Xavier had lived, breathed, slept and ate *The Quantum Wraith*. The film had occupied his every waking thought and nearly all his dreams. When he closed his eyes, he saw space battles and scrappy warriors and aliens battling to establish their place in a universe that sought to steal their individuality and subject them to a bland sameness. His walls were covered in storyboards, his only form of entertainment was watching reels of work from the VFX studios auditioning to add the final digital effects. He thought he knew every aspect of the production inside and out, forward and back.

He knew the original comic book had a loyal following. But angry fans organizing online? A wholly foreign concept. But then, he didn't use social media, as he found keeping up with the lives of strangers via two lines of text and a carefully edited photo to be a waste of time and energy. His producer, Pauley Robbins, and their shared assistant used the film's official account to post cheerful updates that revealed nothing about the actual filming, hoping to keep the story a surprise for as long as possible.

Contessina glanced up from her phone conversation, holding up her index finger in the universal sign to wait a minute.

"Yes, love, I'm still here… Are you sure? Because I can— But are you— Okay. No, I said okay. Why won't you believe me— Fine. I love you." Contessina handed the phone to Tori. "Thanks. It's been a rough day, but it's almost over. Why don't you take the rest of it off?"

Tori shook her head. "You need me."

"I need to go home—" Contessina pressed her lips together, then turned to face Xavier. "I don't suppose we can change the schedule so I can go to LA for a few days." Her tone was flat, her expression resigned to the negative answer she anticipated. "Juliana can't leave her patients to come here."

Xavier held his expression still. Contessina was asking the impossible. Nearly every scene slated to be filmed while the crew was in Arizona featured Lys, and they'd already blown past the original schedule two weeks ago. He and Pauley had tried to account for as many things going wrong on location as possible and built in extra time to accommodate them. But the reality of filming in a semi-remote location full of sand, dust, heat, bright sun and high temperatures exceeded even his usual pessimistic outlook.

He needed this film to work, to be considered a financial *and* artistic success. He would accept no alternative. He couldn't. His future, and the future of the people closest to him, depended on it. While he knew ultimately the audience reaction was out of his hands, he was determined to control what he put on the screen, to ensure the film met his high standards.

That was one of the reasons why he pursued directing. Life was chaotic and rarely responded as he wished. People left without warning, or wouldn't respond as he wished. But the world on-screen? He was in charge of every aspect. "The schedule..." he began slowly.

"I know. Sorry I asked. I'll get my head together. I promise." Contessina tried to smile, but it was the worst acting he'd seen from her yet. "It's been..." Her voice trailed off as her gaze became distant. "I miss Juliana."

"I understand. Your home was broken into." As far as he was concerned, as an actress Contessina should realize relationships were usually collateral damage when pursuing success in the film industry. That was a lesson he learned early in his career and never had to repeat. Especially when it came to actors. Or a smart, perceptive would-be screenwriter, but that was a particular regret he had long tried to submerge. An intruder, however, was a criminal matter. "Does the studio know?" he continued.

She nodded, her shoulders hunching forward, appearing almost to collapse into herself. "Yes. And Monument offered to provide protection, but Juliana says she would feel like she was living in a prison. We had a big fight right before I left for location so I'm worried this will..." She shook her head as if to clear her brain, and then drained the water bottle. "Never mind. I apologize for bringing my personal life to work." Her smile was determined, but her eyes remained distant. "The set is well guarded. I'm fine."

She didn't seem fine. He glanced over his shoulder. A large knot of crew members was gathered under the canvas awning that protected the video monitors and other electronic equipment from the elements. Jay Watkins, his trusted cinematographer and longtime collaborator, caught his attention and signaled, asking if they were going to attempt another take. Xavier shook his head slightly. Even if Contessina were one hundred percent ready to film another take, the sun was no longer in the right position in the sky.

Another day lost on the schedule. He had a sinking feeling he would lose more. But Contessina needed to be at the top of her acting game, needed to sparkle and seduce onscreen. The story required audiences to fall in love with Lys, which would make the terrible choices Lys had to make hurt that much more.

And her desire to make sure her family was okay after a traumatic incident? He understood that. Intimately.

"The schedule's tight," he said, taking out his phone and sending a quick text to his producer. "But I'll talk to Pauley, see if we can rearrange it so there is time for you to go to LA. For a day or two. Not a week."

Color started to return to her cheeks. "Honest? You would do that?"

"What, am I that big of monster that I wouldn't?" He was joking, but Contessina's mouth opened and closed a few times.

"No?" The word came out as a question.

Xavier filed away her reaction for later. He knew he had a reputation for…ensuring the production adhered to his vision. On the other hand, having a unique, singular vision for his films and a track record of executing precisely on that was what landed him the assignment to direct *The Quantum Wraith* the first place. "I'll do my best."

"Thank you." Moisture started to well in her eyes and

she rapidly blinked. "I just… I really love being Lys. I don't want to jeopardize anything."

"We're not replacing you." He checked his phone. Still nothing from Pauley. Strange. Pauley was glued to his devices. Xavier usually received instantaneous responses to his text.

He shrugged it off. They were all under more pressure than even the usual metric ton of stress and duress that came with making a multi-million-dollar movie with a crew of three hundred or so. Monument hadn't wanted them to film on location, especially not in a relatively remote corner of Arizona's Sonoran Desert. The studio was extra unhappy when Xavier insisted on hiring conservation workers familiar with the area and representatives from the local Native American nations to ensure the production treated the land with respect and didn't harm the delicate ecosystem. No doubt Pauley was on another of his marathon phone calls with the executives in California.

He turned back to Contessina. "I'm breaking you for the day. Get changed and relax, start your Friday evening. I'll call you if I can work out something regarding the schedule."

"Thank you!" She threw her arms around him. "Thank you so much!"

The exuberant hug took him by surprise. He knew the actress was a hugger. But he didn't invite physical contact, and the people in his vicinity knew not to provide it. He patted her on her shoulder…once.

She let go, her trademark bright smile back. "Talk to you soon," she said, and walked toward the trailer that housed Wardrobe.

Xavier exhaled and slowly turned to the group waiting for him under the awning. Jay had correctly interpreted the headshake and passed on the command to stop for the day. The crew was swinging into motion like the well-oiled machine they were. Lights were in the process of being taken down, the generators shut off in sequence as they were no longer needed. The big set pieces were covered with protective tarps while the smaller pieces and props were gathered to be locked up safely overnight. But there were still some people waiting to speak with Xavier directly, including—he squinted—the unit production manager? What did Luisa Solera need that couldn't wait until he was in his office?

He wasn't kept in suspense for long. Luisa barely let him confer with his first assistant director, who took over answering general questions from the crew for him, before she pounced. "We have a problem."

"And the sky is blue. What's up?"

"Have you seen or spoken to Pauley today?"

The weird nagging feeling at the back of his skull when Pauley didn't immediately respond to his text returned and intensified. "No. But—"

"We can't locate him."

"What?" He glanced around to see if anyone had overheard Luisa, but everyone seemed deep in focus on their own tasks. He pulled her deeper into video village and away from prying ears, ensuring his walkie was still switched off and wasn't broadcasting their conversation to the crew. "What do you mean, you can't locate him?"

"He's missing." Luisa threw her arms wide. "He's not anywhere to be found. We've looked everywhere. Called his cell, called his home. I even called his brother."

"Did someone check his cabin?" The key cast and crew were staying at the Pronghorn Ranch, a former celebrity hangout during the heyday of making Westerns, but its owners had failed to keep up with the times and the property fell into obscurity. Recently renovated to be a dude ranch, the production team was able to rent the entire estate, including the acres of land on which they were now filming. Pauley had prime accommodations, a one-bedroom freestanding cabin with an uninterrupted view of the red rock mountains in the distance.

"Housekeeping went in. He wasn't there. They said it looked like his bed hadn't been slept in."

"Have you spoken to Hera?" he asked, referring to the assistant he and Pauley shared. Before Luisa could answer, he had his phone out to call Pauley's cell, foregoing texting. The line didn't ring and went straight to voice mail, which was full, so Xavier couldn't leave a message.

Luisa's mouth pressed into a thin line. "No one in the office has seen Hera, either. She's also not in her room or answering her phone. And her car is gone. But that's not out of the ordinary. She's usually off running errands and doesn't respond until she returns."

"I see why you left air-conditioning to come to set." He tried calling again although he knew his effort would be futile. This was his first film with Pauley, who had been suggested to him as a producer by Monument. They weren't friends—Xavier rarely went out for beers with anyone, much less work colleagues, after learning his lesson about getting too close when he was an adjunct professor at Los Angeles University's film school—but he thought he and Pauley worked well together. And Pauley had a good résumé. When Xavier asked around, he'd only heard good things.

Had something terrible happen to Pauley? Maybe he and Hera were involved in an accident and couldn't use their phones. Maybe they were comatose in the hospital. But as soon as the thoughts formed, Xavier discarded them. The hospital would have called. He knew that from firsthand experience.

He turned to Luisa. "I'm sure he's fine. He probably has a meeting off-site and took Hera with him. Let me know when either of them shows up."

Luisa chewed her lower lip. "There's something else."

"The intruder at Contessina's house in LA? Which reminds me, we need to beef up security at the ranch."

Luisa shook her head. "I don't know anything about an intruder. I'm talking about the caterers."

"Caterers?" Of all the things he thought Luisa might say, that was nowhere near the list.

"They said they haven't been paid since the shoot started. So, I took a look."

"And?"

"Electronic checks were distributed and deposited. But not by the caterers." Her skin took on a sickly glow. "By a company whose name I don't recognize. I'm having the accountant do an audit to see if anything else is off."

"Good." The word came out sharper than he intended. He gave Luisa what he hoped was a reassuring smile. "Maybe this was a one-off oversight."

She hugged her arms close. "Maybe. But Pauley was the one who cut the check."

Xavier wasn't often flabbergasted, but Luisa's statement floored him. "Why? We have people who do that. That's not his job."

She raised her chin. "He asked to take over payments to vendors. And he hired me, he signs my pay slips. If he tells me he wants to turn the desert blue, I don't ask why. I ask how many gallons of paint he needs."

"Right." Film sets were notoriously hierarchical. And Luisa and Pauley were tight, having worked together on three previous films. But he was starting to feel the same queasiness he saw on her face.

"Pauley said the new studio suit will be here soon. The audit is good practice in case whoever it is asks to see the numbers."

"What new suit?" The throbbing pressure in his head that made its appearance during his conversation with Contessina continued to build. If there had been a change in the studio management assigned to liaison with his film, Pauley should have told him. Immediately. The working relationship he'd thought was so smooth now appeared to have major potholes. Big ones. Derailing ones, even.

"Chester Bronson is out at Monument. It happened yesterday. Pretty unexpected." She threw him a glance. "Didn't you know?"

Xavier apparently didn't know a lot of things he should. "Did Pauley say when to expect the visit?"

"No. But he wasn't too happy someone new had been assigned. He and Chester were very tight." She pulled on her ear, a habit Xavier recognized meant she was deep in thought. "Come to think of it, I didn't see Pauley again after he got the news about Chester. He called Hera into his office and they shut the door, and then I left for the day. But I didn't think anything of it." She glanced at him. "Do you think—I mean, I don't, or rather I don't want to, but—it's strange we can't find him now."

"*Strange* is one word." Allowing Pauley to handle all the communication with the studio might have been a grave tactical error. "Let's not jump to conclusions. Keep trying his phone and Hera's."

"I will." She twisted the wedding band on her left ring finger. "I'll look in Pauley's office, maybe ask Housekeeping to let me into his cabin. See if anything is…missing."

"Good idea. I can check Hera's desk when I'm in the production office—" His phone buzzed. Xavier glanced down, and the black cloud that seemed to have gathering on the horizon lifted. Relief never felt sweeter. "Never mind. Pauley just texted."

Luisa crowded over his right shoulder to look at the screen with him. He clicked on the message.

Sorry, man. The film would have been great. You're talented, you'll get another project. Hera and I wish you all the best. You'll understand some day. It's Hollywood, Jake.

He stared at the phone, tracing the words with his eyes, trying to make them line up in ways that would make sense. But in the end, there was only one conclusion he could logically draw. Pauley and Hera had ditched the production. And they took money earmarked for the film's budget with them.

Once again, people he'd relied on chose to abandon him. Control of his own destiny was slipping away from him. And he was powerless to stop the slide, no matter how much he had meticulously planned and guarded against such a thing happening.

Luisa spoke first. "What the hell does he mean?"

Xavier dragged his gaze from the text. "He's paraphrasing a quote from the movie *Chinatown*."

"No, I got the last line. What does he mean, 'the film would have been great'?"

"It means we don't need to worry if something bad happened to them. They're alive and well." Xavier turned his phone screen off. "Right. No one is to know about this for now. We'll tell everyone Pauley had to go to Los Angeles and Hera went with him. And I want the results of the accountant's audit as soon as you have them."

Luisa's face was green. He softened his tone. "Hey. This could all just be an elaborate prank by Pauley."

"You think so?" She sounded skeptical, but something like hope blossomed in her gaze.

"Sure." No, he did not. But if he'd learned anything from his previous directorial experiences, keeping morale high on the set was a must. "And whatever happens, do not tell Chester's replacement anything until we have a better handle on what's going on. We're a happy family in front of the studio."

"Got it. Don't tell the new suit."

A sound like a throat clearing came from behind his left shoulder. "Don't tell the new suit what?"

Xavier wheeled around. And his heart stopped.

Sutton Spencer stood before him. For a second, Xavier wondered if his memory had conjured her, because what else did this day need but a reminder of the first time his life had been forcibly turned inside out. And why relationships were doomed to futility in this business.

He blinked, but Sutton was still there, solid, three dimensional. So, not a mirage. The ten years since he'd seen her last had not been good to her—they'd been sensational. At age twenty-one, Sutton had been pretty. Wide gray-green eyes and round cheeks that flushed with emotion as she discussed her favorite films and an expansive halo of red-gold curls that flew about her head as she nodded or shook her head in response to other people's opinions. Smart. Convinced of her own convictions, as only a newly minted college graduate could be. But also hopeful and idealistic, as only a new graduate would be.

Charming. Challenging. And utterly desirable.

The curls were gone, replaced by controlled waves that fell to her shoulder. Her face was thinner, more angular. He assumed her eyes were the same, but they were hidden under sunglasses. Even so, he could feel the assessing stare she gave him before she turned to Luisa, holding out her right hand for a handshake.

"Hi. I'm Sutton. I'm the new suit."

Two

"I'm the nasty surprise your parents didn't warn you about but should have."

Lys Amarga, *The Quantum Wraith*

Sutton Spencer could live to be 373 years old, and she would still never tire of taking the first step onto a film set. There was something magical that occurred, a crossing of the boundary between real and make believe, like something out of her favorite childhood stories. Sure, Wonderland had a rabbit hole, Oz a tornado, and Narnia a wardrobe while she arrived in a much more prosaic manner. Her Prius had a suspension system that suggested the previous renters had taken it climbing in the surrounding jagged hills. But she knew exactly how Alice, Dorothy, and the Pevensie siblings must have felt: stomach churning, palms sweating, heart knocking against ribs upon finding themselves in an unfamiliar world. But unlike her fictional counterparts, Sutton was aware her magic world was real, the result of hard work by talented professionals.

She had wanted to work in the film industry as long as she could remember. To tell stories. After all, stories had always nurtured her. When she started a new school in the middle of fourth grade, *Anne of Green Gables* was her friend when she didn't find an immediate welcome at various lunch tables. When her parents, who always seemed to be on constant business trips, left her with a variety of paid caregivers who could care less about advising her on urgent life dilemmas, the teenagers on the Disney Channel and Nickelodeon series helped her cope and showed her different paths forward. When her first boyfriend abruptly broke things off, she lost herself in old rom-com films and romance novels, which provided promises of love after heartbreak. The first time she ever outright defied her parents was when she chose to study film at Los Angeles University in the hopes of telling her own stories, although she dual majored in business which took some of the edge off the familial frosty disapproval. She loved knowing she played a part in bringing new stories to life, to provide the same illumination and hope to others.

But many movie lovers would say her contribution to making films was a minor one, including her. Her job wasn't creative per se, at least not how the entertainment industry defined *creative*. She wasn't a craftsman or a designer, wasn't an actor or a director or a screenwriter… Her mind skittered away from ancient dreams and charred hopes. She sat behind a desk in a blocky office building instead of being a hands-on member of the film crew. Her tools as a production executive were spreadsheets and budget reports and a massive wall calendar with multicolor sticky notes and flags tracking various schedules. But she was damn good at her job. She just had to remind herself of that fact.

Especially after seeing Xavier again. Maybe her thumping heart wasn't only due to walking onto a set.

Her gaze traced his figure in the distance. She still hadn't had a chance to talk to him after she announced her presence. He'd barely shaken her hand before the first AD needed his immediate attention. She had no idea if the flash in his eyes had been one of recognition or merely an "oh shit" reaction to having been overheard by the new studio suit.

Her tote bag vibrated against her leg. She fished out her phone, smiling as she saw her best friend's name on the screen. "Hey," she answered. "Sorry I had to bail on going to the networking event tonight, but duty called. I'll be back tomorrow if you want to grab drinks."

"The crowd will be same old usual suspects, so you're not missing anything," Nikki Rosales said. Sutton could picture her leaning back in her chair in the corner office she'd earned as a vice president of finance at Monument Studios, twirling a pen as she spoke. "Your text was very cryptic. Where are you?"

"Near Tucson."

Nikki was silent for a moment. "Tucson… Wait. Did they send you to *The Quantum Wraith* set?"

"Got it in one."

"Wow, you drew the short straw. In so many ways."

"In other news, water is wet."

"I'm torn between demanding you tell me everything immediately or asking if you need to get off the phone."

"Filming has broken for the day. I can talk for now." Sutton's gaze returned to Xavier. He still hadn't glanced in her direction. Which was probably for the best as far as her equilibrium went.

Working for a Hollywood studio and living in Los Angeles, Sutton was accustomed to seeing some of the world's most acclaimed beautiful people on a near daily basis. This year's *People* magazine's Sexiest Man Alive played noisy games of pick-up basketball outside her office, which was less glamorous than it sounded when she was trying to concentrate on a complicated budget. She and Nikki had long ago considered themselves immune by exposure to falling for people based only on good looks.

But one glance at Xavier and she was in danger of plunging into a deep swoon with him. Again.

And that was the one thing she could not, would not do.

"Good, so I can ask the important questions. Like, are you okay?" Nikki's tone softened.

"Of course. Why wouldn't I be?"

"Sutton. C'mon. Even without why Monument sent you there, I know who the director of *The Quantum Wraith* is. Did the earth move as he begged your forgiveness? Or did your glare incinerate him on the spot? Either are equally possible."

Sutton sighed and turned her back on the vision that was Xavier. "Sorry to disappoint. He barely blinked when I introduced myself, and then he was called away. I'm not sure he remembers me."

"Ouch. You positive you're okay?"

If only she knew the answer to Nikki's question. "You

know what? It's been a decade since Xavier and I last saw each other—and under vastly different circumstances. Of course he wouldn't remember me. Why would he? I was just a student in his seminar. A naive, silly college senior. He probably had a good laugh and then forget all about me. Which is what I should've done about him."

"You weren't just a student. And he might have been teaching the seminar, but he was barely out of school himself. You were—what?—twenty-one and he was twenty-seven at the time?"

"I had this enormous crush on him and didn't know how to handle it. So, I kept throwing myself at him. He gets credit for not acting on my very open invitation until the night of graduation when I was technically no longer enrolled in his seminar." She groaned. "I was such a fool."

"Oh, c'mon. It's not like you slept together."

"Clothes came off." Searing mortification threatened to turn her into a pile of ash. "No wonder he walked away and forgot me."

"Enough about the past. Discerning minds want to know: is he still hot?"

Against her better judgment, Sutton's gaze sought out Xavier again. Ten years ago, he had been the most attractive human she'd seen in her admittedly short adult life. He'd returned to Los Angeles University as the filmmaker in residence to teach how to maneuver a career in the entertainment industry while using the student crew members to make his next movie. When she was one of fifteen seniors chosen for his honors screenwriting seminar, she could scarcely believe her luck. And also worried she would be too busy noting every detail about him to pay attention to his lectures.

But Xavier now...

Damn. The passage of time looked good on him. So good. He'd filled out, added some needed bulk to what an almost too-wiry frame had been. Back then, he kept his black hair cropped short and his cheeks clean-shaven. Now, his longer, unruly waves were perfect for running her fingers through. And the dark, neatly trimmed beard that accentuated his strong jawline...yeah, she could envision situations where the stubble would be entirely delightful.

But his confidence and quiet authority struck her the hardest of all, a punch to her gut. This was a Xavier who knew what he wanted and how to command others to get it. And that, more than anything else about him, made her stomach squeeze while her knees had the structural integrity of a Popsicle in the desert heat.

"He wouldn't harm your eyes," she finally said.

"Oh, babe, you still have it bad," her friend said. "That was a hell of a pause."

"It was not," Sutton protested, laughing. "And there's nothing to still have. At best, I had a childish crush. I've had far more meaningful relationships since then."

"Eh." Nikki sounded less than impressed. "I wouldn't call Piano Guy and Sunglass Stud meaningful."

"Van is a talented composer, and you know it—"

"Shame the only thing his fingers were good at stroking were piano keys—"

"And Derrick's family owned the chain of sunglasses shops, not him—"

"Yet his only topic of conversation was polarization vs. UV blocking."

"That's not fair." But not that wrong. Derrick had been a bit of a bore, chat wise. And Van… She sighed.

"Y'know, for someone who is a devoted fan of swoony happy Hollywood endings, you always choose the most boring romantic options."

"Xavier wasn't boring."

Nikki's tone turned from joking to contrite. "I'm sorry. I know you were hurt. Forgive me."

"It was a long time ago," Sutton repeated automatically. "And after I do what I came here to do, I doubt the atmosphere will be warm no matter what the thermostat says." She glanced up and noticed the unit production manager—Luisa, if she recalled correctly—was hovering just out of voice range, obviously hoping to politely catch her attention. "I better go. I'll call you later."

"Break a femur," Nikki said.

"Doesn't that apply only to actors? But I'll take all the luck I can get." She said goodbye and then turned to the waiting woman. "Hi. Do you need me?"

Luisa smiled, but the smile didn't reach her eyes. "You must be tired after your trip. Xavier suggested that you might be more comfortable in his air-conditioned office instead of standing out here."

"I'm fine. I like being on set." Besides, this gave her the opportunity to observe the crew.

Everyone appeared to be relaxed, working well and efficiently together—well, as relaxed as one could be on a production where every minute cost thousands of dollars. Which was odd, because she had been informed this film was veering wildly off the rails with expenses out of control. In her experience, a well-run set didn't often correlate to spiraling budgets. The opposite, in fact.

Which only made the mission she was on harder.

Luisa's smile tightened. "Xavier doesn't know how long he will be and we're about to break down video village. You'll be much more comfortable inside."

Sutton recognized when she was being politely told to leave. She understood. Sets were their own communities with their own rules and hierarchies, and outsiders—no matter how benign their presence—tended to be looked on with suspicion. And as a representative of the studio, her presence would arouse a metric ton of suspicion.

Of course, that meant her gaze could no longer linger on Xavier. Which was probably for the best. She nodded at Luisa. "Sure. Can a PA show me where to go? I should introduce myself to Pauley."

Luisa's smile tightened. "I'll take you. And, um, Pauley is away at the moment."

"That's odd. He knew I was coming."

The other woman shrugged. "Something urgent must have come up."

"More urgent than meeting with me?" She began to revise her assessment of how well the production functioned.

Luisa held her hands out, palms up. "Who's to say?"

Sutton opened her mouth to respond, and then thought better of it. Pauley's presence made no difference to the eventual outcome of her visit. Perhaps he knew why she was there and had decided to avoid any confrontation. "Certainly not me. I'm ready to go when you are."

Two hours later, Sutton continued to sit alone, waiting for Xavier and Pauley to appear. Luisa had driven her back to the Pronghorn Ranch and then deposited her in a meeting room in the main building that had been turned into an office for the duration of the shooting. But despite the open door and the constant whirr of the window air conditioner, the atmosphere was claustrophobic and suffocating. Or maybe the room only felt that way because seeing Xavier caused the butterflies wreaking havoc on her nervous system flutter and careen freely.

For the first time since she started her career, beginning as a production assistant and rising quickly to becoming a line producer on made-for-streaming movies and then to her current executive role, Sutton questioned her life choices. Perhaps she should go back to school and become, for example, a paleontologist. Someone who no longer had to hear the name Xavier Duval, much less meet with him.

She'd looked at her emails and made a half-hearted attempt at reading the latest script acquired by Monument before admitting she currently lacked the ability to focus. Her gaze fell on the desk in the center of the room, a sleek modern set up with a whiteboard for a desktop. Xavier's distinctive scrawl in several different colors covered the surface.

Her pulse began to pound, a low drum beat reverberating in her chest. Since this was his office, then certainly he would have personal items around, photos, or mementos. Memorabilia that would tell her what was now important to him.

Who, if anyone, was important to him?

She shouldn't snoop. But—and in her imagination a cartoon devil popped onto her right shoulder—she was the studio executive in charge of production. Technically, wasn't everything related to the film her business?

Her gaze fell on the wall behind the desk. Storyboard sketches covered the surface, the graphic illustrations demonstrating how Xavier intended to tell the story, edit by edit. Looking at storyboards was exactly within her remit.

She started with the storyboard on the far left. She'd been given the script in preparation for her trip, but she couldn't get past the sight of Xavier's name on the front page and the file stayed unopened in her email inbox. The storyboards were her first real introduction to the story.

It didn't take long for her to be swept away by Lys's journey, from escaping from the Maro Empyreal's detention hold to crashing her ship on a hostile desert planet to her rescue by the local Filloli. They were a band of hardened warriors who kept her alive only to exploit her knowledge of tech, not knowing the Empyreal would pay a hearty ransom to have her in their clutches.

She breathlessly went from one storyboard to the next. There was nothing in the world she loved more than a good story. While her dream of being a scriptwriter had been long revealed as an impractical notion, she still got goose bumps whenever she came across an engaging, exciting tale.

And the skin-raising sharp tingle was back.

She was familiar with *The Quantum Wraith* comic book, having read it as a child. But Xavier, who wrote the screenplay in addition to directing the film, had taken the beats of the story and twisted them into something new. He maintained the core themes, but his adaptation made the emotional connections deeper, drew resonant parallels to real-life situations and current issues. She flew through the illustrations, eager to discover how Xavier would approach Lys's choice between making an ally of the Fillolis' fiercest rival or betraying them to the local Empyreal garrison—

A knock came from the door, and then it was pushed open before Sutton could answer. "Xavier? Sorry to bother you, but I was wondering if you'd had a chance to talk to Pauley—oh!"

Contessina Sato stood in the doorway. Sutton recognized her right away even though it had been a few years since she'd seen *Keiko Stowe, CEO*, the sitcom that first brought Contessina to prominence as a teenaged toy company tycoon. The actress smiled, and the room became less oppressive. "My abject apologies! I thought Xavier was here. Usually when the door is closed, it's because he's holed up inside."

"I think he's still on the set. I'm waiting for him myself."

"Can I wait with you? I'm Contessina." She held out her right hand, which Sutton shook.

"I'm Sutton. It's a pleasure to meet you. I hope you don't mind if I say I really enjoyed your performance as Keiko?"

Contessina laughed. "Just don't yell, 'Oh my bulls and teddy bears,' whenever you see me, and you can say anything else you like."

"That must get old."

"You have no idea. Word of advice: choose your character's catch phrase carefully, because you're going to hear it for the next twenty years. But I wouldn't have been cast in this film without being ol' Keiko, so I'm pretty fond of her."

"I was looking at the storyboards. Lys is an amazing character."

If Sutton thought Contessina's smile chased away the room's shadows earlier, that wattage was nothing compared to how she lit up at the mention of Lys. "She's awesome. I'm so lucky to have landed the part. A kick-ass assassin turned revolutionary leader? And I get to fly a starship? And this could turn into a franchise? With my own action figure? Every dream I've had, box checked." She threw her arms open in emphasis. "But on the other hand—" she lifted her right shoulder in a half shrug "—it's scary as hell. And getting scarier."

"I bet." Sutton flicked her gaze toward the door. *C'mon, Xavier, make your appearance.* She didn't want to know more about Contessina. She absolutely didn't want to like her. That would only make the upcoming conversation that much harder.

"Oh, I don't want to sound ungrateful," Contessina said, pushing aside a haphazard stack of comic books so she could perch on the edge of the desk. "And Xavier is awesome. He's the best director I've ever worked with. I mean, he knows what he wants, and he has a firm idea of how he's going to get it. But he also gets you on board and makes you feel as if you are a valuable contributor to the creative process. The entire crew feels that way. I can tell, because believe me, *Keiko Stowe* was not a functional set. And I've been on even worse."

Sutton didn't need to be reminded of how Xavier made her believe she had talent worthy of being shared with the world. But had his encouragement been real because he'd truly believed in her, or had he been stringing her along because he enjoyed how she hung on his every word? From Contessina's description, his charisma hadn't diminished in the past decade. And if the stars in Contessina's eyes—which Sutton very much recognized, having had them in her own eyes once upon a time—when Contessina talked about Xavier were any indication of how everyone else involved in the production felt about his leadership... Sutton inwardly sighed. She'd have earned her glass of wine with a multicourse meal from room service at her airport hotel when this day was through.

"And have you seen the dailies?" Contessina continued, excitement coloring her voice. "I was there when the scenes were filmed, and I can't believe how amazing they look. Not to brag, but I'm a damn good actor. You don't make it through five seasons of *Keiko Stowe* without being able to sell a ridiculous concept. But he makes my performance... elevated somehow."

Sutton believed her. The storyboards alone demonstrated a uniquely Xavier approach to framing the story. The film did show potential. But every word of praise only reminded her why she'd been sent to Arizona. "I appreciate you sharing all this with me, but—"

Contessina spoke over her. "We're all so thrilled to be a part of this project, especially because Xavier is taking a chance on a lot of us. Raul, who plays Autarch Zear? He couldn't get an audition after his last movie bombed, but he's so good in this, he's going to blow everyone away—"

She stopped and covered her mouth with her right hand. "Oh, but I didn't let you speak. Sorry. I tend to babble when

I'm nervous. My wife says I need to stop doing that. She thinks one day I'll talk too much to the wrong person and I'll lose an opportunity or implode my career or find myself on *Page Six* or worse, in the *Daily Mail,* with my deepest secrets revealed." She laughed. "However, you're in Xavier's office and he only allows a select handful of people to enter, especially if he's not in it, so I figure you're safe. You're a friend of his, right?"

"Actually, I'm—" Sutton started.

"She's with Monument," Xavier finished from the doorway, causing Sutton to jump. Her cheeks flushed hot. "Meet the new Chester Bronson."

"Oh." Contessina slid off the desk, standing ramrod straight. Several emotions quickly flitted across her face before her features smoothed into a bland, pleasant expression. "What happened to Chester?" she asked lightly. "He was very enthusiastic about the film whenever we spoke."

"He's…pursuing other opportunities elsewhere," Sutton said, using the shorthand that appeared in entertainment trade journals whenever someone left their job, perhaps not of their own volition.

"That's rather sudden." Contessina's gaze narrowed.

"I agree. But that's all I know." The studio grapevine had gone into overdrive as soon as Chester's departure was made known. The current favorite rumor was that he was starting a new production company with money out of Silicon Valley. Others thought he had been caught in bed with the wife of the chairman of Monument's board of directors. Sutton was merely happy she no longer had to work with him. He'd had an annoying habit of taking credit for other people's ideas, especially hers.

Xavier turned to Contessina. "I assume you're here about our earlier conversation. I don't have an answer for you yet."

Disappointment briefly creased Contessina's face. "No worries. I was just checking."

"Checking what?" Sutton asked.

"Contessina, if you would excuse us, I need to talk to Ms. Spencer—" Xavier began.

"It's urgent I go to LA, but the production schedule might not permit it," Contessina explained at the same time.

Sutton let the "Ms. Spencer" slide. If he wanted to keep things formal and distant between them, she wasn't going to complain. In fact, she welcomed the distance. Even as she was annoyed at him for introducing the distance and then annoyed at herself for being annoyed.

In the meantime, she could solve the immediate problem. Contessina returning home wouldn't impact the film's future. At all. "Contessina can fly to LA."

His dark eyebrows flew up, just for a second. "Oh? You know our schedule, just like that?"

Before Sutton could answer, she was tackle-hugged by Contessina. "I can? Thank you!" Then the actress stepped back, her right hand to her mouth. "I'm so sorry, I didn't ask if you like to be hugged. My dad likes to say I got that from my Italian half, but my mom disagrees."

"It's fine. I'm not bothered at all. I like—" Sutton was suddenly mindful of Xavier's gaze on her. Flashes of her senior year, of throwing her arms around him for a spontaneous hug when she learned her first screenplay had been selected for a competitive festival, played across the screen of her inner mind. "Being thanked," she finished.

"Contessina," Xavier began, his voice a warning.

"Don't worry, I'll only be gone a day." She appeared to almost float toward the office door. "And I promise, no more flubbed lines."

"Don't make a promise I don't expect you to keep," he said before she closed the door behind her. Was that a smile threatening at the corners of his mouth? Damn it, Sutton didn't want to be reminded—again—that this was a happy set. Or how attractive Xavier was when his expression relaxed from stern controller of all he surveyed to human.

Really attractive.

And now Sutton was very aware that with Contessina's departure, she was alone with Xavier for the first time since that long-ago night.

For years, Sutton had wondered when—if—she would see Xavier again. But despite rehearsing their encounter in her head 11,738 times, she was woefully unprepared for the reality of having Xavier Duval's entire focus once more turned on her.

Suddenly she was twenty-one years old again, convinced by Xavier the world was hers for the asking. And the one thing she wanted, more than anything, was him.

It was hard to think of those days now. When she pictured her younger self, she saw a newly hatching chick, awkward and stumbling but joyous, almost free of the safe but boring walls of her college egg. Her life stretched out before her, a golden road filled with dips and curves she couldn't see, but she knew with an absolute faith she would be able to maneuver whatever was ahead of her with ease.

She'd been so trusting. So blindly confident. So naive.

Concentrate, Sutton. The shoe is on the other foot now. He's not the one who gets to determine the outcome, you are. Get this meeting over and you can be back in your hotel with a room service order and maybe read a book for fun instead of scripts for work.

Xavier's smile faded as Contessina exited, taking all traces of human emotion from his expression. But damn it, still appealing. He settled into the massive leather chair behind the desk, his gaze neutral. "Hello, Sutton. It's been—what?—several years."

"Ten," she said without thinking. Then she kicked herself for showing she had been keeping count.

"Right. Good to see you again." He smiled, tight-lipped and not reaching his eyes.

Good to see her? Was he kidding? Did he not remember what happened the last time they were alone together—and that they hadn't spoken since? That he left her breathless, weak with desire, but oh so hopeful and excited—in so many ways—only to go radio silent forever? Or at least, until now.

She wasn't going to touch the final betrayal, the "C" she received as her grade in the seminar. Not that she had expected him to play favorites. He'd made that clear. Still, seeing what he truly thought of her been the ultimate, conclusive slap in the face.

If he wanted to pretend that they were nothing but long-lost former acquaintances, so be it. "Thank you for meeting with me on short notice. Luisa said Pauley didn't inform you I was arriving. Where is your producer, by the way?"

"No problem. How can we help you?" His shuttered gaze gave nothing away, although she noticed he didn't answer her question about Pauley. "I assume you're not here to observe filming, because you just sent the primary actor home. I also assume Monument is signing off on the extra days that need to be added to the schedule by allowing Contessina to go to LA."

Sutton licked her dry lips, her heart rate accelerating. When she was told to take over for Chester on *The Quantum Wraith*, having the upper hand over Xavier held much appeal. Finally, the universe delivered some karmic retribution. But now that the moment had arrived, delivering bad news to him, without a buffer, alone in his office, was almost more than her tolerance allowed. "We should wait for Pauley to join us."

A shadow flickered across Xavier's expression. "He's otherwise occupied."

"He needs to stop occupying himself. This is important."

"He can't. He's…indisposed."

She scoffed. She'd heard that one before. "I made it clear in my email to him that he needed to be present for this meeting. If he's upset because a woman replaced Chester, too bad."

Xavier raised an eyebrow. "That's quite the accusation."

"Not in my experience. This isn't my first film."

"I know."

He kept tabs on her career? That shouldn't make her heart jump, but it did.

"I receive the LAU alumni newsletter," he continued. "You're featured often in the class announcements."

"Are you accusing me of bragging?" Because he would be right. After that disastrous night, she'd sleepwalked through graduation and into the first several months of postcollege life. Many had questioned out loud if she had what it took to succeed in a cutthroat industry, the loudest being her parents, who made their opinion clear she would wash out eventually and she must join the family real estate business before she failed. So she jumped at every opportunity to let the people in her world know she was thriving.

And maybe—okay, definitely—she'd hoped that Xavier would see her name, see how well she was doing despite… well, just despite.

Xavier regarded her. "No. I'm congratulating you. It's good to see a former student succeed."

Oh. The winds of indignation started to die down, only for irritation to set in at "former student." Which technically was true, but still. "Thank you."

He began to shuffle through papers on his desk. "As much fun as catching up is, I'm busy and I assume you are, too. To what do I owe the honor of this visit, Sutton?"

She'd always loved how he said her name. In her opinion, Sutton was a collection of harsh sounds, starting with a sibilant "S" and then the hard "T" and "N." But on his lips, her name was the romantic song of poets.

She shook her head to clear the nonsense out of her brain. She couldn't lose her focus. Not now. "You've seen the latest news about Monument Studios, I'm sure."

"What news? Again, busy here."

She inhaled, weighing her words. In a perfect world, Xavier would start putting two and two together on his own but apparently that wasn't happening. Oh well, she already knew she would be shot as the messenger, might as well earn the anger.

"Monument's investors are demanding a change in how the studio does business." She stopped. "This meeting requires Pauley. I'll be able to answer your questions in one sitting."

Xavier's gaze searched hers with an intensity she remembered all too well. Icy hot sparks traced her spine, her nervous system fizzing with pleasure-pain. He appeared to find what he was looking for as he nodded, a quick, almost angry movement. "Pauley isn't here. He's gone."

"Gone? What do you mean, gone?"

"That's what I said when I was told. He disappeared sometime between last night and this morning, along with his—our—assistant. This is the text he sent just before you arrived." He handed his phone to Sutton. Her fingers brushed against his and she couldn't suppress her shiver. He frowned. "Cold? I can turn down the AC."

She chose not to answer, concentrating on the message on his phone screen. "'It's Hollywood, Jake'? How utterly pretentious."

"Who doesn't appreciate a reference to a sixty-year-old film?"

"It could be worse. He could have said, 'Here's looking at you, man.'"

"We'll always have Tucson."

"Round up the usual on-set suspects," she countered, for a second losing herself in the game of Top This Film Reference they used to play, the fun and the laughter of that semester flooding back. Then she snapped out of it. She wasn't here to skip down memory lane.

She handed the phone back. "This was his goodbye note?"

"That and…missing payments to vendors." His lips pressed together in a firm line.

Sutton blinked. "I see."

"And you also see why Pauley won't be coming to this meeting."

She finally sat in the chair he indicated earlier, her mind churning with Pauley's defection from the crew. But she was on the clock. She didn't have time to puzzle through the implications. At least, not right now. "I'm here because *The Quantum Wraith* is thirty million dollars over its allotted spend."

Xavier became very still, the slight flare of his nostrils the only sign of movement. "That's impossible."

"It's not." She folded her arms across her chest. "I ran the numbers last night, when I was asked to take over for Chester."

Xavier's gaze searched hers as if trying to determine whether she was bluffing or not. But she wasn't. The numbers were all too real. And he had to know that. That much money didn't evaporate into nothingness.

"Earlier today, I was told the caterers weren't paid and the funds meant for them had disappeared," he said. "But that doesn't account for—I'm sorry. Did you say thirty million?"

His expression couldn't be more shocked if an earthquake had just opened a fissure in the ground beneath him.

But she wouldn't feel for him. Couldn't feel for him. This was her job, she repeated to herself. "Yes. Thirty million."

"That's impossible—" he started to say.

She cut him off with a curt wave of her hand. No need to prolong the back and forth. "The exact amount doesn't matter. The issue is Monument is currently under increased scrutiny from Wall Street. Their recent acquisition of Vestar Pictures put a strain on the company's debt load and the P/E ratio is causing concern among investors—"

He shook his head. "I don't speak jargon."

She inhaled deeply, but her lungs still screamed for oxygen. *Just to stick to the script, Sutton.* "As a result of the increased scrutiny, Monument is reassessing its priorities and making some tough but necessary decisions in response to the changing and evolving marketplace and the current needs of the cinema-going audience—"

"Still jargon."

"Fine." She folded her arms, hugged them close to her chest. An extra layer of protection for her heart, to guard against the horror she could see dawning in his eyes as he parsed her meaning, but also the hope he interpreted her words wrong.

He hadn't.

"The production budget has spiraled out of control and Monument is under increasing pressure to cut costs, which has led to a difficult but necessary decision for the financial future of the studio."

Xavier's gaze bore into hers. "You're weaseling. Spit it out."

She kept her chin up, but her gaze slipped to land, unfocused, on a spot somewhere vaguely over his left shoulder. "Monument is pulling the plug. *The Quantum Wraith* is being shut down. Immediately."

Three

"The sky is always darkest just before the planet rotates to face the sun."
"That's a black hole."
Con Sulley and Lys Amarga, *The Quantum Wraith*

Xavier must have heard Sutton wrong. *The Quantum Wraith* couldn't be shut down. They were midway through the first unit schedule. The actors' performances were impeccable. The daily footage, even in a rough stage without being color corrected and put through the postproduction process, looked amazing, if he did say so himself, but also mostly thanks to Jay's cinematography.

The mere idea of everyone's hard work, the soul and sweat they had invested for weeks if not months in many cases, thrown away just for a tax credit was… His heart pulsed like the wings of a wild bird suddenly trapped in an iron cage. "I'm sorry. Repeat that."

Sutton stood, her arms continuing to be tightly crossed

like a schoolteacher impatient with a willfully misunderstanding student. "You should speak to your representation about any contractual obligations you feel are owed you, and Monument will be in touch with the various guilds about compensating the cast and crew, as well as with their representation as warranted. I'm sure you'll have lots of questions once you've had time to digest the news and starting Monday, Monument is prepared to devote as many resources as necessary to answer them and ensure production is properly wrapped up."

Her gaze was blank, her delivery almost robotic as if reciting memorized lines. Which no doubt was exactly what her speech was. Her lack of emotion was more of gut punch than her actual words.

This couldn't be happening. He couldn't lose *The Quantum Wraith*. All he had dreamed, all the plans he had not just for himself but for those closest to him.

He'd suffered catastrophic loss before. But the loss had been taken out of his hands, the outcome something he was powerless to affect. This was different. As long as he was still the director of the film, he would not give up. He would fight. His colleagues, his family, the people who mattered most to him deserved nothing less.

She was almost to the door before he could recover his power of speech. "Sutton?"

"Yes?" She slowly turned to face him.

"We didn't go over budget. Strike that, *I* didn't go over budget. If that's the studio's objection—"

"Monument is reassessing their entire slate, your film is

not being singled out. I assure you this isn't personal, it's just business—"

"Is it? Really?" He tried to search her gaze, but she refused to meet his.

"I didn't make the decision, Xavier." She raised her head, but her eyes focused on a point over his shoulder.

"But you came to deliver the message."

Her gaze flashed. But why, he wasn't sure. "I'm doing my job."

He could admit it now. He had been in over his head when he spent that semester at LAU. At the time, the offer to be the filmmaker in residence arrived like the answer to all his needs. His first feature-length film had been financed by a bequest left to him by his grandmother. But while the film performed well, winning an audience award at Sundance and securing a distribution deal, the financing for his next project was harder to come by. LAU offered him the school's equipment and resources in return for employing student crew members and teaching a seminar, and he leaped at the opportunity, seeing only the ability to have complete control over his vision.

He never anticipated Sutton Spencer would sit in his classroom, upend his emotional world, and then disappear from his life. Only to show up now out of the blue and upend his professional world.

"Yes, I heard the corporate double speak," he said. "But we haven't gone over budget. There are missing payments meant for vendors, and I've asked Luisa to do an audit to see if more money is missing. If you could wait until she—"

Her headshake cut him off. "I told you. I've already examined the accounts. You're going through money faster than Lys's star fighter at warp speed." Sutton took a laptop computer out of her bag and opened the device. After typing a few keys, she passed the machine to him. "Here." A spreadsheet was on the screen. "This is the current status of your spending."

Xavier ran his gaze over the numbers. One entry after another leaped out at him, each more nonsensical than the last. The vat of acid formed in his stomach upon learning of Pauley's defection expanded into a vast, bubbling ocean.

He hoped Pauley and Hera were enjoying wherever they were holed up, because if they ever showed their faces around Hollywood again, he would make sure they were both banned from ever setting foot on a film set. He handed the computer back to Sutton and picked up his phone. "Luisa? I need you in my office. Now."

"I appreciate you bringing in Luisa. She'll be helpful in helping you craft a plan to wind down—

"We're not doing that." He opened a file on his computer and began to document everything he knew about Pauley and the missing money, creating a timeline.

Sutton sighed. "You have no choice. This was a decision made far above both our heads." Her gaze remained distant, aloof. Impersonal. And then she shrugged, as if destroying the project on which so much depended—his big gamble on his future, the paychecks for the cast and crew—was nothing but an inconsequential minor inconvenience for her.

Was this who Sutton had been along? If so, ten years ago, she'd been a better actor than any of the award winners he'd worked with.

"I always wondered why you didn't pursue a more creative career. You were one of the most promising screenwriters I'd ever met. I was shocked when you didn't continue that. But now I understand."

Her eyes widened, her gaze flying to his. Finally, some reaction out of the stone statue that Sutton Spencer had become. "What is that supposed to mean?"

"You measure art by nothing but dollars and cents."

"First, you don't know me."

"Obviously, I don't. Apparently, I never did."

"And whose fault—" Her lips slanted into a thin line. "Regardless. This isn't show art. It's show *business*. The entertainment *industry*." She stressed the words. "Monument has investors who provide the studio with money, and in return, Monument gives you the budget to create a product that will hopefully make even more money for everyone. I know this is your first major studio film, but even you can't be this ignorant of how the game is played."

He rose from his chair, his hands flat on his desk. "I was hired because of my *artistic* experience."

"To make a commercial product."

"To make a *film*."

She matched his stance on the other side of the desk, meeting his gaze head on. "A piece of intellectual property that belongs to Monument."

He leaned farther into her space, his anger growing. "Property? Film is an *art*."

She closed half the distance between them, her eyes burning bright. "Art doesn't matter if it doesn't put paying butts in chairs at cinemas."

He pulled back, suddenly aware of her closeness. Of her lips just scant inches from his. "What happened to you, Sutton?"

Her gaze sparked, half fury, half hurt as she pressed her lips together, her chest visibly rising and falling. Finally, she spoke. "I grew up."

The sound of a consistent knock at the door broke through the tension. Whoever was trying to gain admittance had been there for some time, judging by the increasingly rapid percussion. "Come in," he said.

Luisa appeared, looking as devastated as seeing Sutton's spreadsheet had made him. "Let me guess," he said before Luisa could speak. "You found more missing monies."

"Pauley signed off on—I didn't know—the accountant didn't—there's a separate book." She wrung her hands. "The numbers are bad. Really bad. I should have paid more attention. I take full responsibility."

"The only person responsible is Pauley." Xavier turned to Sutton, barely keeping the hurricane of frustration swirling around his head out of his voice. "Pauley was Monument's condition for hiring me. They wanted an experienced producer on the film."

Sutton glanced between him and Luisa. "I'll let you two confer. Xavier, the studio will be in touch on Monday to go over the next steps."

"Dinner is an hour in the dining room in the ranch's main building. You can't miss it. Look for the green-and-white striped awning." Luisa blinked. "Oh, I didn't even ask. My apologies. Are you staying the night? I can arrange a room for you."

"I have a flight back to Los Angeles." Sutton gathered up her laptop. "I should go now."

"Sutton."

She slowly wheeled to face him.

"You can't leave."

She raised her eyebrows. "I most certainly can."

"No. You cannot drop a bombshell and run."

"I'm not running. I came here to deliver a message. Teams from Monument will take over starting tomorrow and they will help you through the next few weeks. You're not being abandoned."

His stomach roiled. "The studio is abandoning this film. This crew. And you're about to get on a plane without a backward look."

Her face paled, then two spots of red appeared high on her cheekbones. "You think I'm abandoning you? Well, now you'll know how it feels—" She snapped her lips shut. "This wasn't my decision."

"But you're the Monument production executive. You can stay here. Investigate. See we didn't knowingly spend all that money. Right, Luisa?"

The older woman still wore a shocked expression. "Swear to heaven, as far as my people knew, the film was on budget."

Sutton glanced at Luisa. "There's a second set of books?"

Luisa nodded. "I guess Pauley thought the jig was up and didn't take them with him."

Sutton's lips pressed together. He'd forgotten how full they were, how sharp and precise the curves of the Cupid's bow. "If money was embezzled, that does fall under my remit," she murmured, as if to herself.

He saw an opening. A chance to keep control of his project and ensure he could keep the promises he made to his nearest and dearest. "Stay at the ranch," he said. "Have dinner. There are plenty of flights to Los Angeles."

Her head rose. "I'm not sure that's a good idea."

"Why? Don't you want to eat with the crew? Get to know the individual people behind the piece of intellectual property?"

Her narrowed gaze was not amused.

But before she could respond, Luisa jumped in. "It's getting dark and the roads around here aren't lit, and they aren't all that well marked. If you're not a local, we don't recommend driving at night. Too easy to find yourself lost. Why don't you stay the night, and we can go over the books in the morning, if you don't mind working on a Saturday. The room we usually gave to Chester is available, you're welcome to it."

Sutton's forehead creased, a sign he remembered meant she was wavering. "That's kind of you to offer but—"

He pressed his advantage. "We don't want to lose another production executive. There's a shop in the main building. You can buy what you need to spend the night there."

"I still don't think—"

"If Monument is so concerned about costs, then staying here to investigate the missing funds instead of flying back to LA and then flying back out would save time. Since time is money and money is all that matters. Right?"

Her mouth twisted at his echo of her earlier words. "I don't want to put anyone out. I can stay at a hotel."

"Your hotel room will be charged back to this production, adding to the budget overrun, while the ranch is already paid for. I didn't think I needed to remind you how the game is played." Throwing her words back at her felt surprisingly cathartic, considering his other option was to engage in a long, loud primal scream.

"I really would like you to look at the books," Luisa offered. "Get a fresh set of eyes. I can't..." Her voice shook. "I can't believe mine."

Sutton's shoulders fell. "Let me make some phone calls. If there are irregularities, I should look at them and report back to Monument."

Luisa's smile could light a soundstage. "Talk to the front desk. Tell them you're in Chester's suite. They'll know what to do."

"Thank you. You said dinner was in the main building?"

"Do you need an escort? I can arrange for one."

Sutton shook her head. "No, no, I'll find it." Her gaze met Xavier's. Perhaps that was the thing about Sutton that had changed the least. Her eyes were still moss green, the color changing from brassy gold to deep verdant depending on the light. Or her emotions. Right now, they were opaque shade of olive. "I'm going to make those phone calls now."

"You can use my office," Luisa offered. "Turn right out the door, then second room on the left."

"Thanks." Sutton left with her head held high. Xavier couldn't help noticing her hips were rounder, wider, her stride as graceful and her movements as arousing as ever.

"I hope I did the right thing convincing her to stay." Color began to return to Luisa's face.

Xavier's anger at Pauley resurfaced all over again. How

could Pauley betray Luisa like this? Her name was tied to his. She had a family, including elderly parents, for whom she was the main provider. Pauley torpedoed her career apparently without a care.

And what about all the other crew members? Especially the local crew for whom studio productions like this didn't come around all that often? Pauley might have destroyed all their work as well.

Damn it. He would not let the studio steal this much-needed opportunity from him. From all of them. The people on his crew were talented, creative and worked their asses off in an industry that rarely appreciated them. They didn't deserve to have Monument dismiss their hopes and dreams. He owed them that much.

And what about his hopes and dreams? He owed the people in his life even more. "Thank you for that. You did the right thing."

Luisa threw him a crooked grin. "So much for playing happy families in front of the suit."

"Or any kind of family. Monument wants to shut us down."

"What?" Luisa's queasy expression was back.

"Monument thinks we're over by thirty million. We need to show Sutton we're not responsible for the overages. If we can do that, maybe we can save the production." Maybe. But the effort was worth the try.

Luisa searched his gaze and then nodded. "I'll call everyone in Accounts and let them know it's an all-hands-on-deck-all-night situation."

"Good. Oh, and Luisa? Tell them to bring their coffee maker with them. We'll require the extra machine."

Stumbling, Sutton exited Xavier's office. But instead of taking Luisa up on her offer, she left the building. She needed air, lots of air, and she took deep gulps once outside. The heat seared her lungs and woke her up from her stupor. "Go to Arizona, it's a dry heat, they said," she muttered under her breath. "No, the San Fernando Valley is a dry heat. This place could burn water to a crisp."

But she had to admit her surroundings were beautiful in an austere way. The pathways that wound around and connected the various one- and two-story buildings and cabins that made up the Pronghorn consisted of large terra-cotta paving stones, interspersed with white gravel. The grounds were absent of grass, but succulents and cacti were laid out in geometric patterns that emphasized the whitewashed adobe buildings with red Spanish-style tile roofs and arched windows and doorways. The ranch vaguely reminded her of childhood visits to the missions built by Spanish priests up and down the California coast in the eighteenth century, but with less religious symbols and more sun-bleached cow skulls and iron horseshoes for decoration.

Her stomach growled, reminding her the last thing she'd had to eat was a packet of pretzels handed to her by a flight attendant hours ago. But—damn him for knowing exactly where to hit—Xavier was right. She didn't want to go to dinner and make small talk with the crew members she was putting out of work.

Where was the catharsis, the cascading relief from the

twisted knots that had taken up permanent residence in her gut? She'd faced Xavier. She'd looked him in the eye—well, mostly. She'd shown him she had attained success despite his obvious low opinion, to the point of being the one with the power to pull his projects.

So why didn't she feel more victorious? Or at least vindicated? Shouldn't she be thrilled she turned the tables so definitively on him?

Because he doesn't deserve to have the film shut down, a small voice inside whispered. He didn't know anything about the budget overruns. They weren't his fault. Xavier was a brilliant director, but his acting skills weren't nearly on par. No one could have faked that much surprise or dread.

She found a stone bench under a mesquite tree and called Nikki back. If anyone could help her puzzle out what was going on with *The Quantum Wraith*, it would be her. Her friend was talented at many things, but her ability to plug herself into the various gossip grapevines was truly unparalleled.

"Hey!" Nikki answered Sutton's FaceTime call on the first ring. "How did it go?"

"It went," Sutton said.

"You don't look too happy. You still okay?"

Sutton traced the worn stone of the bench with her index finger. "I don't think Xavier knew the film was in trouble. He seemed sincerely shocked."

On Sutton's phone screen, Nikki frowned. "How could he not know? I looked at the spreadsheets you showed me. The sign-off on those requisitions had to come from the director."

"Or the producer," Sutton said slowly. "What do you

know about Pauley Robbins? He's producing *The Quantum Wraith*. Or he was."

"Was?"

"He quit the crew today. And apparently, he took some of the production's funds with him. Not sure how much yet."

"Seriously? He stole money?" Nikki glanced down and Sutton could hear computer keys clacking, followed by Nikki frowning as she read whatever was on her screen.

"What are you looking at?"

"The last films Pauley Robbins worked on… Hold on a minute. I want to confirm a theory that popped into my head." Nikki clicked her tongue. "Yep, Pauley worked on *Heaven Is a Place Next Door*, *Chasing Lightspeed*, and *Destiny's Dragons*."

"Those are Monument films," Sutton said.

"Even more of interest, they were Chester's films." Nikki held up a finger. "I'll be right back."

"Where are you going—"

But Nikki returned to her chair before Sutton could finish speaking.

"I closed my door and made sure it's locked," Nikki said. "This is Code Silence, okay?"

Code Silence was their signal that whatever one had to say, the other would take the words to the grave. "Of course," Sutton answered.

"Chester didn't quit. He was fired."

"What? But that makes no sense. He was doing well. He was rumored to be the next president of production someday."

"Apparently, he was doing a bit too well. The story I heard

is Zeke Fountaine got suspicious when he saw Chester driving a Maybach. There was no way Chester could afford a car like that on his salary, and he didn't come from money. Zeke took it to Kellen and triggered a hush-hush investigation. But this is all rumor, mind you. No one is confirming anything due to legalities."

Sutton wasn't sorry Chester had left Monument. But she didn't like the idea of being accused of malfeasance simply for driving a car. "Maybe Chester rented the Maybach. Or borrowed it. Or took out a massive loan. What business is that of Zeke's?"

"As it turned out, others had noticed additional examples of Chester living above his means, but Zeke was the first to put the suspicions into words. I agree Zeke likes to cause trouble, but every once in a while, even a shit stirrer strikes gold."

"We have to work on your metaphors," Sutton said. "So, Chester…?"

"I'm still getting details. Everyone is understandably freaked out, what with all the stories about Monument's board of directors cracking down on spending and potential layoffs."

"You don't have to tell me," Sutton said. "I'm being desiccated in the desert because of that anxiety."

"Word on the street is some of the panic is thanks to Chester. He was a naughty boy, and not in the fun red room of pain kind of way. I'm hearing he skimmed money off his productions. A lot of money."

"How is that even possible?" Sutton knew firsthand how many eyes were on film budgets.

"The best I can put together is he created several dummy corporations and sent invoices from those corporations to his productions to be paid out of the films' budget."

"But…" Sutton stared at Nikki's face on the screen. "How did he think he would get away with that? There are armies of accountants watching the money. And if the movie had any profit participants, their people might comb the books as well."

"Sutton. Honey. Dear sweet summer child. It's Hollywood." Nikki shrugged. "You know how tangled the accounting can get, between all the partners and the investors and the participants and the various windows and the—"

"You're right." Sutton rubbed her forehead. "I just…it's inconceivable to me, to even think of such a thing. That's fraud. Major fraud."

"From what Fatima in Accounting told me, Chester started out small, using the dummy corporations almost as a way to make loans to himself because he would put the money back in by creating a refund—"

Sutton shook her head. "You know what my problem is? I'm not smart enough to come up with a scheme like this."

"You're not criminal enough. And your parents made you so afraid of setting a foot wrong and jeopardizing your salary, you would die on the spot if you did think of such a thing."

"I have ethics, you mean."

"I'm not saying that's a negative, at least not about work, although you could be less uptight about dating—"

"No. I am not calling back that guy who said he works for Beyoncé. You want concert tickets so bad, you call him."

"Anyway," Nikki said, drawing out the word, "I caught

Tam Shankar from Business Affairs this afternoon on a smoke break—"

"You don't smoke."

"No, but Tam does. Keep up. My best guess is Chester got overconfident, because according to Tam they just discovered several films have tens of millions outstanding in unreconciled accounts."

"Tam told you this? Mr. 'Act at all times as if I'm under an NDA.' That Tam? Damn, you're good."

"I know." Nikki made a fist with her right hand, blew on her knuckles and then pretended to shine them on her blouse. "And Tiago in Corporate Communications said Monument is scared because there is a potential internal scandal brewing that they're trying to stop from going public because of the investors' cold feet, so I'm betting that's also about Chester. Do you have a list of the vendors used by *The Quantum Wraith*?"

"I can ask. I'm meeting with the unit production manager tomorrow."

"My bet is some of them are Chester's dummy companies."

Sutton pinched the bridge of her nose. "And since Pauley Robbins conveniently walked off just as Chester 'left'…"

Nikki nodded. "That's what I'm thinking. The two of them were probably working together. It's even easier to get your fake invoices paid if you have someone inside the crew rubber-stamping them without question."

"Xavier said hiring Pauley was a condition of Monument. I bet that means Pauley was Chester's condition." Sutton chewed her bottom lip. "Coincidence isn't causation, but this doesn't feel like coincidence."

"I concur. Which is good news. Your man Xavier might be in the clear since Pauley is the link to Chester."

"Not my man."

"Uh-huh. Sure."

"Regardless," Sutton said, enunciating each syllable, "I honestly think he isn't responsible for the overruns."

"As long as you're thinking with your head and not other parts of your anatomy. Listen, I'm not just spilling tea—"

"Except you are."

"Except I am," Nikki agreed. "However. I think we both agree that if Chester was defrauding Monument, it's a good thing he was caught. But the way he was caught..." She shook her head. "Just be careful around Zeke Fountaine."

"C'mon, we're women who work in the entertainment industry. We're tough. I'm not scared of Zeke." With that, Sutton said goodbye and ended the FaceTime call.

The sun was now below the horizon, and some of the day's heat had started to dissipate. The shadows had taken over and without the glow of her phone, her surroundings were still and dark with only nearby lit windows to remind her she was still somewhere resembling civilization. Luisa had been right. Sutton was glad she wasn't trying to negotiate the long empty road she took to get to the ranch with only the headlights of her rented Prius.

A burst of laughter from afar splintered the silence. Sutton followed the sound to a row of open windows. She peeked through as she passed by, spotting a large room filled with long communal tables packed with a diverse array of people.

The atmosphere was relaxed and cheery, with smiles and animated conversations in abundance everywhere she glanced. Contessina sat at a table in the middle, her face glowing and her fork waving as she spoke to the person on her left.

They looked so happy. Like a team who liked each other. Sutton was sure there must be disagreements and arguments among crew members. Making a film was a long, arduous and often tedious process interspersed with moments of sheer tension and often panic. But she'd been on enough sets to tell that this group was comfortable and confident, just as Contessina has said.

And she was breaking up the team. Correction: she was breaking up Xavier's team, through no fault of his own. What good was besting him if the victory came on a technicality?

No matter her feelings about Xavier—and she didn't have time to untangle that hopelessly convoluted mess right now—the film didn't deserve to be canceled from underneath him. Looking at the storyboards, hearing the zeal in his voice and witnessing the excitement in Contessina's gaze… Sutton's job might require her to act like a jaded studio executive, but she saw the potential. Artistic vision, innovation and passion were being poured into *The Quantum Wraith*, and she was convinced audiences would respond well. Shutting production down was perhaps more of a risk to Monument's future financial success than taking a tax write-off would be.

She went to the front desk to get her key card and directions to her assigned suite and then asked if a plate of food could be brought to her. She had several more phone calls to make before she could call it a night.

Four

"Defeat is just an opportunity to get up and kick even more ass next time."

Lys Amarga, *The Quantum Wraith*

Damn, the sun came up early—and far too bright—when one stayed up all night staring at a computer screen.

Xavier blinked and raised his head from where he had put it on his desk, only for a second, he'd sworn. The brilliant light caused him to squint, but his eyes were so dry and scratchy,

The momentary pressure of his eyelids was painful. He turned to Luisa, sitting in the guest chair opposite him. She looked as tired as he felt. "Coffee me."

"We're out. We need to go to the dining room in the other building," she said, her tone as dire as if she'd said, "The building is on fire and there's little chance of escape."

"How do the numbers look now?" He, Luisa and her team had combed through the budget, looking for cuts while ensuring Xavier could still make the film he had in mind. They took a big swing for the fences and put together a new proposal. The question was whether Sutton would listen.

He still couldn't reconcile the poised, polished woman who calmly told him with dead eyes that she was killing his film with the Sutton of his memory. The warm, caring woman with audacious creativity and even bolder dreams, whose shining presence in his classroom challenged him in all the best ways—while torturing his nights knowing she was off-limits. Until graduation…

The sharp pain in his chest reminded him that was a path he never, ever revisited. He let her know where he stood, what he wanted. And then he left the ball in her court, letting her know what happened next was entirely up to her.

She never tossed the ball back over the net to him. Nothing but radio silence, until she walked onto his set.

"I think this is about the best shape we're going to get the budget into without knowing the full extent of what Pauley siphoned off," Luisa said, thankfully snapping Xavier out of memories better left unvisited, gathering dust and cobwebs. "Do you think it's enough?"

"We'll see." He had no idea. He couldn't read the current Sutton. The only impression he got from her was their history was a debit on her personal ledger.

He'd been so blind. Or rather, if he was being honest with himself, he so needed his first studio film to succeed so his life could attain some stability that he threw out the instincts that had served him so well on his smaller independent productions. Everything was so much bigger on a studio film—bigger sets, bigger explosions, bigger budgets—and he let his head be turned by Pauley's air of supreme confidence, of his reassurances that he had all the financial details in hand and all Xavier need to do was concentrate on making the film.

Pauley played him more expertly than a concert pianist on a Steinway at Carnegie Hall.

After Sutton bounced out of his office last night, he called his agent, who confirmed they'd received a call from Monument, and the studio was, indeed, pulling the plug on production. No, his agent didn't know if he would be able to secure another directorial assignment for Xavier anytime soon.

His dreams of having his pick of his next project—much less his ability to take care of others in his life and give them the stability they deserve—were all in danger of being extinguished. And Sutton Spencer, of all people, was the angel of death come to punish him for not paying enough attention for letting a slick producer run away with the production. Literally.

Luisa handed him a stack of papers. "I've printed out the new budget and the new schedule. My eyes are too tired to look at a screen."

"Same." He ensured the documents were neatly aligned, not a corner out of place, before asking in what he hoped was a casual manner, "Has anyone heard from Ms. Spencer this morning?"

"The suit?" Luisa shook her head. "Not yet, but it's pretty early."

"If you see her, ask if she's available for a meeting this afternoon. I'm going for a walk." He should return to the residence that was assigned to him for the duration of the location shoot, check in to make sure all was running smoothly on the home front. But the household was probably still sleeping. He'd catch up with them later.

"Walking is too ambitious for me. But if you can bring some fresh air back, that would be appreciated." Luisa waved as he exited.

The morning temperature was still temperate, but the sun was even more annoying without windows or curtains to diffuse its glow. Xavier reached for his sunglasses but realized he was so tired he'd left them in his office. He turned to retrace his steps and then stopped.

Sutton was on the same path, mere feet behind him, her gaze focused on the ground in front of her.

The tightly wound professional who upended his world yesterday was less in evidence, replaced by a Sutton who more matched the woman in his memory. Her hair no longer fell in controlled waves to her shoulders but was worn in a ponytail, escaped red-gold strands waving and curling around her face. She was dressed more casually, too, wearing an oversized T-shirt that said "Meet Me at the Pronghorn Ranch" and black yoga pants that clung to her thighs. But what caused a sudden sharp jab in his heart was how tired she appeared. Apparently she, too, didn't have a restful night.

He raised a hand in greeting. "Hi."

She looked up, her eyes wide with surprise. "Hey."

"Out for a walk?" He had too much to say and couldn't choose where to start. He settled on the smallest of small talk.

She rubbed her neck. "Rough night. I thought exercise might help."

"Same."

Silence built between them. Sutton shifted from foot to foot. Xavier still couldn't decide how to best open a conversation, his mind churning with options but no actual words. Finally, he stepped aside to let her pass. "After you."

She moved in his direction, but instead of brushing by, she stopped just short of his position. Her gaze glowed a soft grassy green in the clear morning light. "I don't want to interrupt anything you're doing, but can we talk?"

He looked at her shoes. Sneakers, perfectly fine for what he was going to suggest. He'd have to forego his sunglasses, but whatever had annoyed him earlier about the day now didn't seem to matter. "I was going to take a quick hike. Want to join me?"

"Sure." She fell in beside him and they started down the path, eventually reaching the dirt trail that led into the nearby hills. Despite Sutton asking if they could talk, they continued in silence, but a much more companionable one than earlier. She kept up with his pace regardless of the incline, and in fifteen or so minutes they reached his favorite spot, a flat area carved into a small canyon that overlooked the surrounding area.

"Wow," she finally said, taking in the vista before them. The desert spread out below them, the landscape a mixture of ochres and oranges and yellows with greenish-brown sagebrush and mesquite adding punctuation. Tall saguaro cacti stuck their arms far into the sky, which was turning from the light blue of early morning into a deep aquamarine. Hidden birds sang while wind rustled through the nearby rocks. And in the near distance, the white trucks and trailers that marked the set easily stood out, as did the crashed starship wrapped in its protective tarps.

He glanced at Sutton. Rosy color filled her formerly pale cheeks. Her eyes sparkled as her gaze darted from one view to another.

"Wow," he echoed, then tore his gaze away.

"So," she said.

"So," he replied.

She turned to face him. "About yesterday. I have a plan for the best road forward."

There went all the relaxation the hike might have brought him. His shoulders tensed, the knots tighter than the night before. "We also have a plan. Why don't we meet in my office in an hour—"

Her head began to shake as soon as he started talking. "Xavier, a meeting isn't necessary."

"The least you could do is hear us out."

"I don't want to waste everyone's time."

"Let me finish." His words echoed off the canyon walls.

Sutton blinked at him. "Okay. Finish."

"Luisa and her team worked very hard to account for the stolen money and readjust the budget. You can't make a final decision without looking at the result."

She waved off his words. "I appreciate their dedication, but after several phone calls and more emails, it's become clear to me and my bosses at Monument—"

The Quantum Wraith was slipping through his fingers. And nothing he said was getting through to her. A hopeless panic he hadn't felt in years started to swamp his system. "Damn it, Sutton! Stop being a suit and be a human for once."

"I am!" She met him halfway, her cutting gaze emerald bright. "That's what I'm trying to tell you. I made a lot of phone calls last night and—"

"I'm not giving up," he gritted through his teeth, taking another half step forward. "I'm not letting you or anyone at Monument stop production of *The Quantum Wraith* without a fair fight."

"You don't have to fight!" She invaded his space, her chin high, her fists balled on her hips. "You won't let *me* finish. I can persuade the studio to keep the film in production."

They stood toe to toe, gaze battling gaze. With a start, he realized barely a handbreadth separated them, standing so close he could see the freckles beneath the angry flush coloring her skin. Her gaze dropped first, and he watched with intense interest as the pink tip of her tongue came out to wet her lips before he caught himself and stepped back to give her room.

"Okay," he said.

"Okay," she echoed, and she took her own step back. "So. I was up all night—"

"That makes two of us. More if you count Luisa and her team."

"You do look a little worse for wear," she said, a small smile appearing and disappearing.

He had no doubt he did. But while he could see faint purplish shadow below her eyes, testifying to her lack of sleep, he would be hard-pressed to call her looking worse for anything. "Go on."

She pushed an escaped tendril of hair behind her left ear. "My phone has been on fire all night. The studio is now certain Pauley and Chester were running a scheme to defraud Monument by cutting checks to dummy companies that were owned by them. *The Quantum Wraith* is not the only film that was affected, but it is the production where they stole the most money."

Oof. Pauley's betrayal slammed him square in the solar plexus, all over again. "Luisa and her team found dozens of payments to vendors we've never dealt with."

"That would be helpful evidence."

"So, you'll take a look at their work?" He couldn't help a small grin.

She huffed, but there was no animosity in her expression. "I was only trying to save time. But I should have heard you out."

"And I apologize for talking over you. I'm not at my best when I haven't slept."

"Oh, I don't know, I remember—" She stopped, and then shook her head. "Never mind. Look, here's the deal. Monument still believes in the film. In fact, because of the new information about Chester and Pauley, they're giving you a week of stay—"

That sounded like good news. But he wasn't taking anything at face value. "What does that mean?"

"They're not stopping production until after next week. They want time to investigate how much of the budget overruns are due to Pauley and Chester."

"But only a week." His stomach, already sour from too much coffee and not enough solid food, threatened to erupt.

"Monument thinks the Empyreal Chronicles could be the next Star Wars. But because the film was bleeding money and no one noticed, they're still thinking of shutting down and removing you as the director. They're wondering if you're too inexperienced and don't have the gravitas to handle a project of this magnitude." She gave him an apologetic half shrug.

"If that's the consensus and word gets out around town, I might not get another job." His skin prickled with cold despite the rising heat of the day.

"You might not get another assignment from a studio, no. Well, not until your next indie success and people have enough time to forget you were fired off this film." Her gaze skittered away from his. "But that's not my concern."

Ah, he wondered when the suit version of her would make another appearance. "Of course not."

"What is my concern is Monument's well-being," she continued.

"Dollars and cents. You've made that clear." He folded his arms and gazed at the set in the distance. His chest constricted at the thought of watching everyone's blood, sweat and tears be torn down like so much abandoned refuse.

"Scoff all you like. But it's the overall financial argument will keep production going."

Xavier narrowed his eyes. He wouldn't allow himself to feel hope. Not yet. "Explain."

She stifled a yawn. She still covered her mouth with the back of her hand instead of her palm, her nose scrunched as if she were about to sneeze. Odd how the images came flooding back, of early morning meetings over coffee, Sutton's cheeks still creased from sleep but her brain working a mile a minute. "Yesterday, I watched you direct the scene of the ship exploding."

"Not seeing how that changes the decision that was previously out of your hands."

"I saw how you managed the set. Then I examined the storyboards in your office when you decided you needed to warehouse me for a while—"

"We weren't expecting you. There were more urgent matters—"

She raised a hand. "It's fine. I didn't really know much about the movie before I got on the plane, so going through the storyboards was helpful. Then last night I read your script, which led to staying up all night to watch dailies on my laptop. And…"

His brow furrowed. "And?"

"Not that your ego needs this—"

"My ego?" He didn't have an ego.

"But—" her gaze finally met his again "this is going to be an amazing film. Perhaps a spectacular one. I don't know for sure, because my script was missing the final act."

Maybe he had an ego after all, as hearing her praise made his chest swell. "The ending is under lock and key. To avoid spoilers getting out to the public."

"But I'm the production executive— Y'know, I'm too tired to argue this." She started pacing around the flat area, making a figure eight with her steps that brought her tantalizing close to him, then veered away. Xavier watched her, still unsure where she was going with her line of thinking. Although part of him was deeply gratified to hear her compliments. The Sutton he remembered had a discerning eye and she'd been the toughest but fairest critic in the screenwriting seminar class he taught. Not for the first time, he wondered why she took a left turn into production. She should be making her own films, not project-managing other people's.

But he had no right to question her choices. They weren't anything to each other. No matter how much he thought they had connected. No matter the passion he thought they'd shared at the end.

But she didn't contact him after that night and he could not, would not, ask why. If she had wanted a relationship, he'd made it clear how to tell him. Not that he would have been in any shape to pursue a relationship at that time, as it was. His world had turned upside down in a heartbeat soon after their last encounter.

That's all the time toppling a life took. A blink of an eye and the universe shifted on its axis.

"Pulling this film leaves a hole in Monument's release schedule for next summer." She had continued to pace while his thoughts went down paths best left forgotten. "But the studio decided the cost overruns outweighed the potential loss of box office revenue."

He opened his mouth to object, but she cut him off before he could form words. "However, because of the pressure from Wall Street, the new films being greenlit are safe, familiar, appear to be safe bets. Between us, they're boring."

"But *The Quantum Wraith* isn't." He was sure of that.

"No." She stopped pacing and turned to face him. "Reading the script, seeing the dailies—yes, the footage is still in a rough stage, but the potential is there. *The Quantum Wraith* is exciting. Fresh. The film could really break out. It's exactly the shot in the arm the studio needs." Her mouth twisted into a mock frown. "I hate to say it, but… I see your vision. It's good."

"Thanks. I think." He couldn't help the left-sided smirk. "So. All it took was exposure to my work."

She sighed. "Your work was never in question. Only your management."

That felt like another dig at him. When this matter was settled, he and Sutton needed to have a long, illuminating conversation about what exactly happened that semester. "Cut to the chase. Will Monument shut us down or not?"

She visibly took a deep breath and pushed away the strands of hair threatening to fall in her eyes. "We're positive Pauley and Chester committed fraud. But my bosses still have questions. Such as, why was Pauley allowed to get away with cutting large dummy checks on this production, and what measures will be put into place to make sure that doesn't happen again?"

Yeah. He'd been asking himself the same things over the past twenty-four hours. "You have an answer?"

"The film needs a new producer."

He nodded. "Obviously."

"And you need one now. The budget remains overstretched. We may know where the money went, but it's still gone." She rubbed her thumb over her lips. She would do that in class when deep in thought and formulating her response to a question. That gesture used to drive him to distraction. "And you need someone who understands what Monument will approve or not approve in a timely manner to avoid costly delays." She gave him a swift grin. "I can't believe you let your leading actor go to Los Angeles."

"Very funny."

"Sorry." Her half smile was rueful. "But I know a producer who satisfies both the needs of the production and Monument."

"You do? Can I speak to them today?" He tried to tamp the rising hope down. The ground could still quake under his feet.

"Oh, speaking to them won't be an issue. And they're available, as long as the studio signs off on their hiring."

"Great. What's their number? Or email?" He took out his phone, ready to take notes. "I'll reach out immediately and start the ball rolling while you speak to Monument."

"I have both of those, but you don't need them."

He looked up from his phone. "Why? Do you want to be the one to reach out?"

"Don't have to. Because I'm the solution, Xavier. I'm going to take over as producer." She lifted her chin and stared him down with the cool, disconnected gaze of the day before.

Sutton? Producing his film? A close, almost symbiotic partnership, on call for each other twenty-four hours, seven days a week?

This cold, dismissive Sutton who spoke of films made with blood and soul as nothing but commodities, pieces of property? Did he want to work so intimately with her?

Could he handle being in such close proximity to her?

Xavier learned a long time ago that work and pleasure

do not mix. His first, most painful lesson stood before him. That semester at LAU would be forever seared across his memory for multiple reasons, not the least learning when he played with fire—like falling head over heels for the brilliant, witty, challenging Sutton as soon as she set foot in his seminar—the result was his heart in ashes. And he could take the pain. But it was one thing to turn his life into a crisped wasteland when he only had to worry about himself, quite another now that he had people dependent on him.

He could take the blistering heat of a failed relationship. He was used to rejection, even expected it by now. But he refused to let his loved ones be the collateral damage. Not again.

"Why do you want to be the producer?" The wind had picked up and she didn't seem to hear him. He closed half the distance between them. "Yesterday you were dead set on shutting this production down. If you intend to come on board to find new excuses to pull the plug—"

"What? No! That's not my intent."

"Then what is?" His gaze searched hers. But those opaque shutters were still in place.

"I'm not trying to sabotage your job. I'm not trying to save it, either." She shifted her feet. "I want Monument to succeed, and I think *The Quantum Wraith* will perform well at the box office. But the production needs to be put back on the rails."

"And you're the one to do that? No offense, Sutton, but you don't have the résumé for this."

"I produced *Pinecones and Holly Berries* for Crowing Films and *The Tree in the Grand Hotel* for SnoringCat Productions—"

"Made-for-television Christmas flicks."

Sparks lit her gaze, the first sign of animated emotion he'd seen that morning. "Do you know how popular those films are? *Pinecones* was the most streamed title across all services the month of release—"

He couldn't help it. He laughed, stifling the sound at the last second. Not because of her credits, but because he'd finally glimpsed the Sutton he remembered, passionately defending her work.

She balled those hands on her hips. "Holiday movies aren't something to laugh at. People love them. The stories are fun. They provide comfort and inspiration."

"I'm aware there's a very appreciative audience—"

"You snorted."

"You're mistaken."

"You did. Like a bull with a deviated septum."

"That's an oddly specific description. I'm not knocking your experience producing *Pine Trees and Cranberries*—"

"*Pinecones and Holly Berries*."

"My bad. Obviously, that would be a vastly different movie." Her lips pressed into a dangerously thin line, and he decided to stop any further discussion of her job history. "But when it comes to *The Quantum Wraith*, the film isn't…" He chose his next words carefully. "Made for the small screen."

"Snob about television, are we?"

"Not at all. But as you reminded me earlier, the scope of this production is bigger than anything I've done before.

Or anything you've done. Would Monument agree to your plan?"

"I've worked for the studio these last three years. I know what the executive suite wants. How they think. What they are looking for. This is the path with the least risk." She shifted, and her foot rolled on a rock.

Xavier caught her upper shoulder and held her steady. Her startled gaze flew up to meet his, and for a moment he was lost in the green-gold depths before she gently pulled her arm free.

"Thanks," she breathed, then cleared her throat. "Thank you," she repeated in a firmer voice.

"You'll need shoes with a better tread than these if you want to work on this production. Those are fine for soundstages and short hikes, but conditions are more unpredictable out here."

"Does that mean you agree?" The cool, professional veneer had returned. But there was a warmth to her words that hadn't been present before.

"If that's what it takes to continue filming." He focused on the trailers and trucks of the set visible below them. In the end, only one thing mattered: *The Quantum Wraith*. "If Monument says yes—"

"They will."

He faced her. The sun was to her back, and the light turned the red-gold locks curling around her face into a fiery corona. Earlier he'd thought of her as an angel of death. But maybe together they could keep *The Quantum Wraith* alive.

He held out his right hand. After a second, she joined the

handshake. If she, too, felt the sharp spark at the glide of his skin against hers, her expression gave no indication.

He firmly pushed the sensation out of his brain. To save his film, he would survive whatever was thrown at him. Even her.

"Welcome to the crew, Sutton Spencer."

Five

"The Maro Empyreal does not make mistakes. We realign our judgments."

Autarch Raez, *The Quantum Wraith*

"In conclusion, *The Quantum Wraith* is on track to becoming the perfect four-quadrant film Monument needs and will fill an important hole in our current theatrical release strategy. I understand the decision to cease filming has already been made, but I hope you can see how extenuating circumstances may mean the decision was made without having all the information. You should have in your email a revised production book, plus an updated budget and schedule, and I want to note the location schedule has a firm stop because we don't want to push into Arizona's monsoon season. You can be assured the dates won't move further out. I've included projections that demonstrate the film will be worth far more to Monument if allowed to be completed and distributed than if work ceases now. Thank you for your time and consideration."

Sutton smiled into the camera on her laptop, keeping her gaze steady on the lens. She wanted to appear calm and dispassionate, not eager and desperate. While meeting via webcam was not her favorite, at least being behind a screen several hundred miles away meant the room of mostly older men couldn't see how she needed to continually wipe her palms on her trousers. Her heart thumped so loudly, she was surprised the microphone didn't broadcast the sound to everyone else.

She glanced at the notes on her electronic tablet. Since arriving in Arizona a week ago, she'd furiously worked to recover what she could of Pauley's files, matching them with Xavier's and Luisa's budget and pulling all the documentation into a cohesive story to persuade the executives sitting around the conference room table in Los Angeles to continue production while she stepped in as the producer. Yep, she covered everything. Now the decision was out of her hands.

Kellen Felder, the president of Monument's feature film division, leaned over to Harry Moss, Sutton's boss and the senior vice president of production, and said something in a tone too low for Sutton to hear despite wearing state-of-the-art headphones. Then he nodded at the camera in the conference room where the rest of the attendees were gathered. "Thank you, Sutton. Our team has concluded Robbins is responsible for the cost overruns, and the studio is working with law enforcement to track him and his accomplice Hera Marshall down."

Sutton smiled into her camera. "I've sent all the evidence

of Pauley's malfeasance we could find to the attorneys. The film is otherwise in excellent shape."

"But," Kellen said, raising an imperial hand, "we're under pressure to cut costs, not create more. The company can take a tax write-off if we shut down now. We don't need to buy into a sunk-cost fallacy." He looked into the camera. "You've done good work here, Sutton. When we next put *The Quantum Wraith* into production, I want you as the exec in charge."

"Thank you," she said, her face hurting with the effort to keep her smile wide. This was the downside of video meetings. She had to stay focused and present when she wanted to leave her desk and rage against the shortsightedness of her bosses. There were no sure things in moviemaking, but she was positive this film qualified as a safe risk.

"Y'know—" Zeke Fountaine leaned into the camera frame "—Sutton obviously understands the production and its needs. And not having a summer tentpole will probably be more costly in the long run. So why not have her step in as the producer?"

What? Why would Zeke, of all people, help her? She didn't realize she was frowning until she caught Harry's eye, who mimed putting on a smile. Right. Her lips were so stretched and dry, she was going to need an ocean of balm.

"If I may." Zeke took control of the meeting's audiovisual controls without waiting for permission and put Sutton's revised budget on the screen. "If the production sticks to forty-five days, the film will be brought in around the original estimated cost. Minus, of course, the monies stolen, but that's where the studio can take the write-off, correct?"

Kellen leaned forward as if taking a closer look at the spreadsheet. Sutton resisted the urge to turn her camera off so she could indulge in the biggest eye roll of her life. She'd sent the presentation to Kellen hours ago. Was he just now looking at her documents because Zeke freaking Fountaine asked him to?

"Yes," he said slowly. "The numbers work. If they're accurate."

Harry spoke up for the first time in the meeting. "I went over them with Sutton. They're solid."

"If the movie comes in on time and on budget, it will be a win, and if it isn't delivered, you still get your write-off," Zeke pointed out. "What do you say, Kell?"

Kell? Zeke was on a nickname basis with the president of the film division? But before she could ponder on what that might signify, Kellen called the meeting to a close.

"All right. Zeke makes a good point. We'll continue with *The Quantum Wraith*, based on these numbers and the revised projections. Sutton, sorry to stick you in Arizona, but you're there until we find a replacement for Robbins."

A replacement? She started to ask what Kellen meant, but a brief headshake from Harry warned her to stay quiet.

"I'll work with Sutton from this end," Harry stated.

"Good." Kellen turned to Zeke. "In Sutton's absence and with Chester…no longer with us, you'll take over her existing projects and report to Harry."

What? No. No no no no no. Zeke couldn't take her projects. She'd shepherded those films from the start. She knew, with the sharpness of an arrow to her heart, she would never get them back. "I can handle my usual workload alongside this production," she began, but Kellen spoke over her.

"Everybody clear? Great. Let's get some work done before the weekend starts." Sutton's view of the conference room disappeared, replaced by white text box that read, This meeting has been concluded by the host.

"Oh, c'mon." She called Harry's cell phone but got his voice mail instead. Why did she feel like she won the battle to keep *The Quantum Wraith* afloat, but she may have lost a war she wasn't aware she was fighting? Her hands shook, and she wasn't sure to attribute that to anger or to the dozens of energy drinks that had kept her going over the weekend as she prepared her presentation.

Focus on the positives, she admonished herself. She'd achieved her goal. Filming would continue. She thought about going to the set to tell Xavier in person the good news, but word had come over her radio handset that they were setting up for the martini, aka the last shot of the day. By the time she traveled to the location, they might be mostly wrapped. She'd wait for him to return to the production office.

At least she would have plenty of opportunities to observe Xavier over the next several weeks. More opportunities to marvel at his command of his craft, the way his eyes lit with excitement when the camera captured a moment the way he intended, his long fingers tightening on the arms of his chair when he was excited—

Was the AC out? Her cheeks were burning. She rose from her desk to check the thermostat, which hadn't budged from its usual setting.

Yes, Xavier was talented. And that talent was seductive. She had always been susceptible to people who were passionate about their art. Once she even believed she could join their ranks, change the world with her creative vision, but that had long been revealed to be a childish dream.

She stayed with Van long after their relationship had reached a natural expiration date because she truly did enjoy listening to him speak about his music. And Xavier… Xavier had been her deepest, most intense crush on someone's creativity. His first indie film, made when he has been a student at LAU, had been one of the most audaciously original films she'd seen at the time. And to have someone she so admired seem to think she was talented…

At the time, she'd thought their connection had been more, meant more. That all his flattering words about her screenwriting had been based on the potential he saw.

Then he ghosted her after what to her had been a mind-blowing night of heart and soul union, but for him had been apparently a forgettable yawn. What a gullible, easily seduced fan girl he must have thought her to be.

Ugh.

Pull your head out of the past. She was a Monument production executive. A big-budget film was hers to produce. She had nothing to prove. Not to her parents, who continued to disapprove of her career in the entertainment industry and warned her she was about to find herself in the unemployment line and unable to pay her expenses at any minute. And certainly not to Xavier.

Her phone rang. Harry was calling her pack. She punched the speaker button, which would allow her to scroll through the files on her computer should she need to locate a piece of information quickly. "Hi, Harry."

"Congratulations on Kellen's approval." Harry's gravelly tones rumbled in the air.

"Thanks." She decided not to mention Zeke accomplished that, not her. Appearing paranoid would only harm her. Even if she suspected the paranoia was justified. "Although getting his greenlight felt precarious for a while."

"Money talks. But I want you to know what you're taking on. If the film is a hit, everyone in that room will take credit. Failure—that's just going to be on you. All of it. By yourself."

"Is that why I'm only on the film until a replacement for Pauley can be found?" She tried to broach the subject as delicately as she could without appearing too defensive.

"In part. Look, I have your back, but only for now."

The acid that never fully retreated from her stomach started to swirl again. "What does that mean?"

"Am I on speaker? Take me off."

Now her stomach was a bubbling volcano, flows of fear flooding her other organs. She picked up the phone. "You're off speaker."

"Kellen wants to fill Chester's VP role from within the ranks. The search period will be short."

"Makes sense. Does he have someone in mind?"

"You. If you play your cards correctly."

In a week of shocks, each one more ground-dissolving than the other, this one ranked up there. Right next to realizing she still found Xavier supremely attractive. She coughed. "I don't think I heard you correctly. Did you say I was replacing Chester?"

"If you play your cards correctly," Harry repeated. "But it's not set in stone. Zeke Fountaine is also in contention."

"Zeke? But he just started on this team." Her tone was light, but her fingers dug into the armrests of her chair.

"His father is the managing director of Whitefield Capital," Harry said. "Whitefield papered the deal for Monument's acquisition of Vestar Pictures last year. His family has known Kellen's for ages."

That figures. "Zeke did seem close to 'Kell' in the meeting today."

"You know the drill. It's not just what you do but who you know. Therefore, you can't do a good job with *The Quantum Wraith*. You must do an excellent one."

"I understand. I will." Half of her wanted to jump with exaltation. The promotion would put her among the youngest VPs at Monument. The other half—well, she'd just have to ensure the intense pressure turned her into a diamond, not a pancake.

"And most of all, you have to want the position."

"I do." Excitement started to win her internal war, bubbling in her veins. Dare she truly hope? This was the goal she had worked toward since she first set foot on Monument Studio's lot. "More than anything."

"Good. All eyes are going to be on you, Sutton. Act accordingly."

"You don't have to worry about me."

"I'm not worried. But I am going to give you advice."

"I'm listening."

"This is the most passionate I've seen you about a project. But get out if the film starts to go south again. You don't owe loyalty to anyone on the production. Not with a promotion on the line. Don't screw up your future."

"I won't." She and Harry continued to talk about the projects Sutton was handing over to Zeke, and then they hung up as Harry was eager to start his weekend.

Sutton remained in her chair, staring at her computer screen, but not seeing the words and numbers in front of her. The stakes of her situation confronted her hard, like an ocean swimmer out for a dip in a calm sea who didn't notice the giant wave until after she was pulled underwater and tossed around.

Take a deep breath. You're in line for a promotion. Your parents will be thrilled. They might even finally acknowledge you can succeed on your own and stop hounding you to join the family business, where they can look after you and ensure you won't fail.

She rested her elbows on the desk and let her head fall forward into her cupped hands. Just for a minute, she told herself. Just to think. Or maybe even grab a catnap, a very brief one. Sleep had eluded her almost since the moment she set foot on Arizona soil. She was running on nothing but coffee, energy drinks, and adrenaline. Now that the meeting was over, the adrenaline had fled, and the injections of caffeine were wearing off. Maybe if she put her head down and shut her eyes, the room would stop spinning...

"Sutton? You okay?" Even when trying to block out the world, she still heard Xavier's voice—wait.

She snapped her head up. Xavier stood before her desk, a frown creasing his brow. His blue shirt was open at the neck, revealing skin bronzed by the sun and a smattering of dark, curling hair. As a student in his seminar, she had been obsessed with that triangle, wondering if his chest was heavily furred or only lightly dusted. Her daydreams about exploring what was under his shirt caused her to miss at least one lecture, if not more.

She blinked, coming fully awake. These ridiculous vivid flashbacks would eventually subside, return to being buried below work and daily errands and reside with the other inconsequential memories, like the time she dyed her hair magenta, but two weeks later the color was a weird, carroty orange. Xavier was a professional colleague, nothing more.

"I'm fine," she said, shutting down the computer on her desk. "Just giving my eyes a break."

"So, a brief rest? Not wallowing in despair?"

"Why would I wallow…? Oh! The meeting. You want to know how it went?"

"As much as I enjoy being Schrödinger's cat, yes, I'd like to know if my directing career is alive or dead."

She tried to keep a straight face but failed. "The box is open and the cat lives to film another day. Congratulations. Kellen agreed to the new budget and schedule."

A grin lit his face, the past decade of wear disappearing from his expression. "Sutton! That's great!"

"It is, isn't it?" His smile was infectious, and she finally allowed herself to feel the joy and relief of knowing production would continue. She hopped up from her chair, her arms outstretched victory. "We did it."

"No, you did—" Xavier reached out his right hand as if to touch her on the shoulder, maybe even draw her in for a hug, but then his hand changed direction and smoothed his unruly dark hair off his forehead instead. Much to her unbidden disappointment. "Thank you," he finished. "An inadequate pair of words for all I owe you. For all the production owes you."

He was looking at her as if she had done something amazing. As if she were amazing. She wanted to bask in his appreciation, but she had fallen for that look once before, hadn't she? And look where that left her. She let her arms fall. "Team effort. Luisa's revised budgets deserve a lot of the credit, as did promising we won't push past our dates because we don't want to gamble on filming during monsoon season. And Monument had a hole in their release schedule. Overall, the risk was minimal."

His gaze narrowed slightly, but his smile remained. Gods, he was attractive when he smiled like that, as if the two of them had won a tremendous prize. "Whatever works. C'mon, let's go celebrate with a drink."

Drinks with Xavier? Just the two of them? Her heart skipped a beat. The offer was tempting, especially with his gaze warm on hers. But she wasn't certain she could handle a night with a relaxed, happy Xavier who looked at her as if she had just hung the moon and a few added constellations in the sky. Not when the production had over a month to go. Not when a potential promotion rode on her professional behavior. Not when she knew his attention, no matter how intense, could vanish like a mirage. And considering they were currently in the desert…

"Thanks, but I need to unpack. I'll see you on Monday." Nikki had gone to Sutton's apartment and put together several care packages of toiletries and clothes for Sutton's extended stay in Arizona, which had just arrived.

"Let me rephrase. I'm not asking you to come to drinks. I'm telling you."

She just saved his film, and he thought that meant he tell her what to do, even on her own time? She took back everything she thought about his attractiveness. Even if the stern crease between his brows was perhaps more appealing than his relaxed grin, if she were being honest. "Did you order Pauley around this way? Or is this behavior you save just for me?"

She moved toward the door, but Xavier was faster. His broad frame filled the doorway, blocking her exit as she was about to leave. From this close, he smelled like warm sun on freshly washed clothes. "I didn't need to tell Pauley he should be at crew drinks. He knew."

"Oh. Crew drinks. Of course. It's Friday." A tiny corner of her mind than was less tired than the rest of her brain lit up. The invitation wasn't about spending one-on-one time, just the two of them. That was merely her wishful subconscious.

It was going to be a long forty-five days.

"Drinks and dinner on the lawn of the big house," he continued. "Contessina flew in her favorite mixologist from Los Angeles. If you don't want alcohol, they're preparing something called an 'antioxidant shooter.' Whatever that is."

She laughed at his perturbed expression. "Careful, or they might not allow you back into LA if you make fun of our healthy mocktails."

"A good beer is all anyone needs."

"I remember your unadventurous taste buds," she said

lightly. Then she froze, her heart thudding. She was coming perilously close to touching the third rail of ten years ago. She swallowed, her throat scratchy, and forced herself to laugh. "Didn't you always have a packet of plain potato chips stashed somewhere in your office? Or was that that the professor who taught History of European Cinema? All my memories of college run together into one big blur."

"No. No potato chips." He stepped aside, allowing her to exit. "Must have me confused with someone else."

"Yes, I must," she agreed, keeping her gaze down and focused on the worn carpeting on the hallway. No, she definitely remembered everything. And when it came to kissing her, he was anything but unadventurous.

Six

"Do I detect the scent of love in the air?"
"That's the bio station. You need to change your atmosphere filters."
>   Con Sulley and Lys Amarga, *The Quantum Wraith*

As Sutton was slowly learning, the Pronghorn Ranch consisted of a large variety of buildings and residences. There was the main building, which housed the reception, dining room and about fifty hotel rooms—most of them occupied by crew members. Then there were about twenty standalone cabins, from studios to one- and two-bedrooms, which were reserved for heads of departments and the talent. Last, there was the two-story adobe Spanish-style casita built for the original owners of the Pronghorn but called "the big house" by everyone on the crew and occupied by Xavier.

Normally Friday crew drinks were casual ad hoc events funded by selling raffle tickets to the team members, with the winners usually opting to spend some or all of their winnings on buying a round of beer for their colleagues. Tonight, however, Contessina stayed true to her word before she left for Los Angeles and sprung for drinks—and dinner—with Xavier offering up the lawn in front of the big house as a venue big enough to hold everyone. The set decorators went to town, hanging strings of lights that crisscrossed the area and setting up long picnic benches covered with white tablecloths and decorated with rustic lanterns and potted succulents. Somewhere, someone found a long mahogany bar, complete with barstools, and set it up on one side of the lawn. A portable barbecue pit occupied the other side. The fragrant smoke caused her stomach to rumble.

Then the noise hit her, people laughing and conversing. These were not the polite, stilted murmurs she was used to at work events, but rather the exuberant shouts and laughs of a crew who had survived a tough, exacting week of work and could now blow off steam, for a few days at least. Some had gone to their accommodations to change and wash up, but many more still had red dust from the desert clinging to their jeans and shirts. The good mood was infectious.

Xavier left her side to be swallowed almost immediately by the crowd. The stream of people coming and going as they shook hands with him and exchanged backslaps was never-ending, but a small core group formed tightly around him. The tall Black man she recognized as Jay Watkins, the cinematographer. She'd met Jay before, once, during that semester when he guest-lectured on photography for the seminar students. He and Xavier had worked together on Xavier's first film, and she wasn't surprised to see they were still close. The others, she didn't recognize. Yet.

Mingling with people she didn't know well was part of Sutton's job—and the only way to stay viable in Hollywood, she'd absorbed, was by incessantly networking—but she found this crowd daunting. They were obviously a close unit, and judging by the sideways glances that always darted away whenever Sutton tried to catch someone's gaze, she was the subject of not a little gossip and supposition. That was to be expected, given Pauley's abrupt departure followed by her quick arrival, but not something she had accounted for until now. Judging by the apologetic look Xavier threw her, he also realized the situation needed to be addressed. He made a gesture she interpreted as "later," and she nodded her assent.

She was still deep in thought, wondering how and to whom to introduce herself, when a strong pair of arms tackle-hugged her from behind. "Sutton! You're still here!"

Sutton turned to find a beaming Contessina. "Hi! Good to see you again. Did you have a good trip?"

"*So* good," Contessina said, stressing the first word. "I can't thank you enough for allowing me to go."

"I spoke to the studio PR team. They said the online attacks are dwindling, but they acknowledge they're still a problem. They're working hard with the various social media platforms to minimize the hate speech, but there's only so much they can do. I'm so sorry."

Contessina nodded, the light disappearing from her expression. "Being a target sucks. I'm not going to pretend otherwise. But the intruder is in custody, and the DA's office promises to throw every possible book at him. More importantly—" her sunshine-bright smile returned, making the overhead strings of Edison bulbs appear dim by comparison "—Juliana is doing great. And now so are we. We just needed time to be together."

"I'm so happy to hear it."

"As a result, I nailed all my lines today on the first take." She took a mock bow to the left and then to the right. "Thank you, thank you, yes, I rocked the scene." While Sutton laughed, Contessina grabbed Sutton's hands and gave them a close examination. "But wait! You don't appear to have a drink! We must fix that right away." Holding Sutton's right hand in hers, Contessina tugged her toward the bar, two open barstools appearing as people moved over with a smile for the actress. "Hey, Mykchail!"

One of the most stunning people Sutton had ever seen, at least six feet tall with dark brown skin that appeared lit from within, waved at Contessina from behind the bar. "You rang?"

"This is Sutton. Give her the Socorro Special." Contessina hopped onto her stool and then swiveled her seat in Sutton's direction. "You're going to love this."

"I don't… I'm not sure I'm in the mood for a drink." The hooded stares and whispers were even more evident now that she was in Contessina's company. Xavier had the wrong idea. Being at crew drinks wasn't going to ingratiate her to the team. Instead, her presence seemed to stir up anxiety-tinged gossip, if the suspicious gazes were anything to go by.

Contessina peered closer at Sutton. "Your nails are ragged, your eyes are bloodshot and—" she squinted "—there's a vein pulsing in your forehead that probably shouldn't be as prominent as it is. You're stressed."

"Maybe because someone dragged me to the bar without asking if I was thirsty."

"Yeah, yeah, I know, I have a problem with boundaries. Apologies. But, hello, we're in a desert, you have to stay hydrated." Contessina swiveled to face the bar, accepting a tall glass of what looked like radioactive neon green sludge topped with a purple orchid from the bartender. "Here. This will help. I promise. Anti-inflammatory, boosts your immune system and protects your gut. No alcohol."

"That's all it does? No curing the common cold?" Wrinkling her nose, Sutton took a tentative pull on her straw. The perfectly-tart-just-sweet-enough taste exploded in her mouth. "You didn't mention it tastes amazing."

"That went without saying. But that's okay, you'll learn to trust me." Contessina sipped her own cocktail, a rose-pink concoction with a twist of lime on the rim.

"What does your drink do?" Sutton asked. "Cleanse your liver? Lower your cholesterol?"

"It's a cosmopolitan," Contessina said. "All it does for me is lower my inhibitions." She cocked her head to the side. "Or maybe opens a time travel portal. Juliana's mom loved *Sex in the City*, so whenever we visited, we would binge episodes with her and drink cosmos. Some of the best times I've ever had, just hanging out as a family, no other agenda." She glanced at Sutton. "Do you ever do that? Order drinks because they remind you of someone? I'm not that fond of the taste, but I adore the memories."

Sutton's gaze sought out Xavier. When the brewery stopped making the IPA craft beer she'd been drinking that night, she'd been at a loss for what beverage to bring to parties for years. Even though beer was normally not her first choice, and she was only drinking it then because there was nothing better on offer. "Sometimes."

"Juliana thinks I'm silly for drinking something I don't really like. But that's why we work. She's no nonsense. Me, I'm mostly nonsense. Together we're a functional unit." She peered at Sutton from over the rim of her glass. "What about you?"

"What about me?" Sutton finished her drink. She didn't believe an elixir or tonic or whatever the concoction was called had as many health benefits as advertised, but she did feel more human. Maybe coming to crew drinks wasn't a bad idea after all.

"Are you with anyone?"

Sutton's gaze flicked to Xavier again. He hadn't moved far from where she had last seen him. While being in this crowd ratcheted up her social anxiety, he appeared more relaxed than she'd seen him since she arrived. His broad shoulders were less rigid, his jawline no longer clenched. He looked more approachable, as if he were ten years younger—

She tore her gaze away.

"Ah," Contessina said quietly. The first quiet syllable Sutton had heard her utter, although granted they had only been acquainted a short period. "Him."

"No. Not him. There's no him of any kind. Or her. Or they." Sutton held up her glass. "May I have another? And maybe mix it with something stronger, like vodka?"

The bartender conjured up a new drink, purple this time. "Try this."

Sutton took a deep swig, welcoming the burn of the alcohol. She didn't imbibe much, usually a glass of wine or two at social events, but Xavier had a way of leaving her as disoriented as a toddler on a fast-spinning merry-go-round. Under the circumstances, one or two cocktails weren't much of a risk. "Delicious again. Thank you."

"Y'know," Contessina said, leaning her elbows on the bar and steepling her fingers like a movie villain, "when someone says, 'no, not that person' and then reaches for alcohol, that's an immediate giveaway. I can't tell you how many times we used that scene in *Keiko Stowe*, only Keiko drank ginger ale whenever anyone brought up Brock Benson, high school water polo captain."

"I always wondered why Brock played water polo instead of the usual football."

"Swim trunks and no shirt," Contessina said. "You saw Josh Jameson's abs. Whenever we did appearances, we were mobbed not only by our twelve-year-old fans but their moms. It wasn't pretty. But enough about my sordid teen star past. I want to know about yours."

"That's easy. I was never a teen star." Sutton waggled her eyebrows at Contessina.

"Ha!" Contessina set aside her empty glass and picked up the water bottle at her elbow. "So, no partner?"

"No." That was simple to answer. "Single."

"Recent breakup?" Contessina guessed. "Judging by your skin. You have the 'I used to moisturize but I now rely on my tears' non-glow."

Sutton laughed. "My last relationship ended six months ago. Amicably. We both decided we worked too much, but neither of us felt the relationship was worth working less and maybe missing out on a promotion." She touched her cheeks. Her skin did feel dry. "And I guess I should switch lotions because the one I'm using obviously isn't working."

"This place has zero humidity. I'll give you some of the fancy face stuff my stylist sent me." Contessina swiveled her stool to face Sutton. "So, since you're single…" She nodded in the direction of Xavier, still standing in the center of a tight knot of crew members. "What's up with our fearless leader?"

"Who, the director? I have no idea what's up with him," Sutton answered truthfully. "None."

"I mean between you and him. You can't stop your eyes from feasting on him."

Sutton realized her gaze was, indeed, fixed on Xavier and she closed her eyes, only opening them once she had turned her stool to face Contessina, removing Xavier from her sightline. "Can eyes feast? I feel that's more of a mouth thing."

Contessina snorted. "We'll talk about what your mouth wants later."

"Or we won't. Although right now, my mouth wants another of these." She shook her empty glass, and a new drink appeared in front of her as if by magic.

"You should switch to water." Contessina waved her bottle. "The desert and alcohol do not mix. Double the dehydration."

"I have water in my room." More like a leftover case of energy drinks, but pretty much the same thing, right? "Besides, I was told I had to make an appearance. I'll have one more to appear sociable and then sneak away. I can't wait to get some sleep."

"Who would dare tell the studio exec what to do—ah. We're back to Xavier. No wonder your eyes are glued to him like a bug in a roach motel."

"Ew. Thanks for that image."

"I call 'em like I see 'em." Contessina put her bottle down. "Look, I like you. Way better than Chester, who Juliana called Breaster for the way he would talk to my boobs instead of my face."

"Ew. I'm so sorry. He was not my favorite colleague."

"But that means you need to know the lay of the land. Or rather, who not to lay. Starting with our director over there."

Sutton choked on her cocktail. "I'm not looking for anything like that. And definitely not with him."

Contessina turned a pitying gaze on her. "If this were *Keiko*, the script would call for your eyes to have animated little hearts instead of pupils. And more animated hearts would be circling your head."

"That sounds annoying. And like something a doctor should be consulted about." Sutton managed to take a normal sip. "I'm not interested in Xavier."

Contessina regarded her for a moment and then nodded. "Okay. That's great."

Don't ask don't ask don't ask... She couldn't help herself. "Why is that great?"

"Because this is a location shoot. And hookups are a feature, not a bug."

Sutton's gaze searched the crowd. "Xavier is already hooked up?"

"No, he's not," Contessina said. "You can stop wondering who it is."

Sutton sat up straight on her barstool. "Just idle curiosity. Since we work together, it's good to know if he's…um, experiencing happiness. Because his mood will affect me. And our work. Together."

"Right. His happiness. That's your concern." Contessina smirked. "Xavier doesn't do hookups. Believe me, I know plenty of people who have tried."

"He doesn't do hookups on location, or ever?" Sutton's gaze returned to Xavier. Contessina's assessment of him didn't match Sutton's experience. Because in hindsight, that night had been nothing but a casual hookup, at least on his end.

"Currently? No to both. Not sure about ever. There's rumor he was involved with an actress—Mimi Kingston—before she hit it big."

Sutton kept her expression neutral through sheer force of will. Mimi Kingston was the talented star of a prestigious streaming television series. And gorgeous.

"But no one knows his whole story, well, maybe no one other than Jay." Contessina shrugged. "The scuttlebutt is something tragic happened to Xavier a long time ago. It's why he stopped making films for a while."

Sutton frowned. After Xavier left Los Angeles University, four years passed until he released his next indie film. She'd assumed the delay was because he couldn't find financing or a backer. Her heart pinged at the thought that something devastating might have happened. Maybe she would have heard if she hadn't spent those years studiously trying to avoid all mention of him and his career… "What was the tragedy?"

"Someone close to him died? I think? There's nothing online and it's not exactly something you make small talk about on the set. 'Hey, Xavier, in this scene I think Lys should be angrier about the systemic injustices visited on this planet by the Maro Empyreal, and by the way, please tell me your sad backstory.' Anyway, giving you a heads-up because I've watched several people be the *Titanic* to Xavier's iceberg. And I'd like it if you stuck around."

Sutton swirled her glass, creating a mini purple whirlpool. "Thanks. But no need for the warning. There's nothing between me and Xavier. Now or later."

"If you say so." Contessina nodded her head. "Okay, my good deed for the day is done." Her gaze focused on a point over Sutton's shoulder and she waved. Sutton turned to see an older white man with a well-trimmed beard waving at Contessina. "You don't mind if I leave, do you?" Contessina asked. "That's Hugh, the makeup assistant. I brought him some presents from LA."

"Be my guest." Sutton appreciated Contessina's company, but she wouldn't mind some time to herself. She needed to process what she'd learned. Especially about Xavier.

"Thanks." Contessina hopped off her stool, but before leaving, she threw her arms around Sutton in a bear hug. "And thanks again for letting me go home. I'm excited to work with you." She stepped back. "Oops, sorry again. I really am working on boundaries."

Sutton smiled. "Hugs are great. You have my permission."

Contessina blew her a kiss and ventured into the throng. Sutton watched as she found Hugh, linking arms with him as they spoke. Then her gaze slid, yet again, over to Xavier. He had made his way—or more probably, the crowd around him finally allowed him to advance—to the middle of the area set aside for dining, but he was still surrounded by members of the crew two or three people deep. Those surrounding Xavier appeared to be hanging on his every word, but out of respect as colleagues. There was nothing fake about their interactions, the typical Hollywood kiss-up game that Sutton had seen played and, yes, played herself to get ahead, gain power, secure a favor.

She should force herself to mingle. The side-eyes and whispered conversations seemed to have died down. Although that could be due to the social lubricant provided by the cocktails she drank—much faster than she should have, if she were being honest—giving her confidence to approach people she didn't know.

She turned to face the bar to say goodbye to the bartender and found Contessina's recently vacated stool had been occupied. A boy, somewhere between ten to fourteen, if her experiences visiting her cousins was any indication. "Hello," she said.

"Hey," he said. He didn't look up from what appeared to be a comic book in front of him.

"Aren't you a little young to be sitting at a bar?" she asked.

The boy kept his gaze focused on his reading material. "You try finding another place to sit around here."

"The area is pretty crowded," she agreed. There was something familiar about him, but she'd met so many new people and was still putting names and positions on the crew to faces that she didn't dare guess to whom he belonged. "Do you have a parent working on the movie? Are you here for a visit?"

"Sort of." He flipped a page and resumed his head-down position.

She could take a hint. "I get it. I didn't want to talk to random adults when I was your age, either. Actually, I guess you shouldn't talk to random people you don't know, period. Carry on." She leaned down to grab her tote bag.

"You're not random. You're the new suit." He flipped another page.

She straightened up. "I was, but now I'm the new producer. Who told you that?"

He waved a hand at the crowd on the lawn. "Them."

That was helpful. But probably what she deserved for trying to pry. "As it turns out, I have a name. I'm Sutton."

She held out her right hand. The kid raised his gaze and blinked at her before giving her a surprisingly firm handshake. "Erik."

"Nice to meet you." She glanced down, her gaze landing on the comic book. "Hey, are you reading *The Fabulous Five*?"

Erik turned to her. For the first time something like interest lit his gaze. "You know *The Fabulous Five*?"

"I started reading about their adventures when I was around your age? Maybe. I was ten."

Erik gave her a withering stare. "I'm twelve. But I started reading this book when I was nine."

"I like the current run. I thought the last writer went too far off track, taking away Hamilton's A-chromosome and saying he never had one."

Erik's stare turned thoughtful. "Yeah, Ham having an

A-chromosome is an important part of who he is. He has it back now."

Sutton nodded. "I saw. And Jain and Riley have finally reunited. Which should have happened ages ago."

Erik made a face. "That was stupid, splitting them apart. It was done just for drama."

"Well, stories need drama. Or conflict, which might be more precise. But I agree. The breakup was *bad* drama. Now, killing off Br'voor—" she exchanged a conspiratorial smile with Erik "—that was satisfying."

"Definitely. Even if no one stays dead in comics."

"No one except Uncle Ben in Spider-Man, but who wants to read Spider-Man these days? Unless it's Miles Morales."

"Miles is great." Erik slid his issue of *The Fabulous Five* over to her, revealing a stack of additional comics that had been concealed underneath. "Have you seen the latest? It came out this week. I've finished the issue if you want to take it with you. All my friends are into manga, so no one else wants to read them." He grinned, his invisible braces not so invisible. "I know where to find you so you can give it back. You're in Pauley's office, right? Since he's gone now."

"I am. You're well informed." She wondered whose kid he was. Someone who worked in the production office instead of on the film crew, she bet. They would be more likely to know about Pauley's departure. "Tell you what, why you don't keep the book and—"

"Excuse me." Xavier's voice. In her right ear. She swiveled her barstool so fast her knees almost slammed into his thighs. He stepped aside in time. "I was wondering if I could borrow you?" He glanced over and did a double take when he spotted companion. "Erik. What are you doing here?"

"Reading." Erik picked the next book off the pile and opened the cover.

"Where's Ilsa?"

"Getting food." Erik waved his hand toward the barbeque pit and the thick lines of people waiting to be served.

"I see you two have met." Xavier's unreadable gaze ping-ponged between Sutton and Erik.

"Uh-huh." Erik remained laser-focused on the comic.

"You okay?" Sutton studied Xavier. His usual calm, cool manner had taken on an edge. Almost as if he were perturbed to see her. Or maybe he was perturbed to see her sitting next to Erik. But why?

"I'm fine." But Xavier's gaze lingered on Erik before his focus returned to Sutton. "We need to make an announcement to the crew about you replacing Pauley before people wander off to start their weekend."

"I was thinking the same thing." The butterflies in her stomach turned into hummingbirds. She had no problems speaking to a conference room, even one full of executives much more senior to her, as long as she had a well-rehearsed presentation with audiovisual aids. But speaking to a large crowd, most of whom appeared to highly respect Xavier and would be wondering how she measured up, both to him and to Pauley? Instant apprehension.

"Great." He signaled to the bartender, who produced a large handheld cowbell. The sound was deafening, and Sutton had to resist the urge to cover her ears. She turned to

Xavier. "Thanks for this. I want the team to know they can approach me as the producer."

He frowned. "Approach…? No, the announcement is to stop rumors about Pauley before they affect morale. Why did you think—"

The ringing abruptly stopped, leaving the area deadly silent by comparison. Sutton broke the battle with his gaze to realize everyone was staring at the two of them. She swallowed, but the lump in her throat only thickened.

He smiled, wide and confident. As he stepped forward, the throng drew back to give him space. Someone, she didn't see who, slapped a beer bottle into his hand and he raised it to the sky. "It's been a long week. Here's to your hard work and dedication. To *The Quantum Wraith*!"

The crew cheered as if one, raising their own glasses in return. He turned to Sutton, motioning for her to join him. She did, giving a half wave with her right hand. "I want to introduce everyone to Sutton Spencer. She's going to step in for Pauley Robbins as the producer—"

"What happened to Pauley?" came a shout from the crowd, with others murmuring their endorsement of the question. "Why'd he leave?" asked another voice.

Xavier silenced the growing cacophony with one raised eyebrow. "Pauley chose to depart," he said. "And that's the end of that story. We're lucky to have Sutton come on board to replace him." He turned to her. "Sutton?"

She cleared her throat. The hummingbirds were now crows, and there was a particularly large one lodged in her throat. "Kellen Felder, the president to Monument Studios, is excited to have *The Quantum Wraith* as Monument's next summer tentpole film." Well, maybe *excited* was an exaggeration. But there was enough truth to allow her to speak with conviction. "I'm thrilled to be the newest member of team. I can't wait to get to know all of you individually and learn what your roles are on the film." The more information she had, the better she could use that data to fine-tune the budget and schedule. "If you see me on the set, please say hi."

Xavier shot her a surprised, maybe even shocked glance before his features evened out. "I'm sure some here would like to chat, when and if it's appropriate. So if you are a department head and it's the very rare occasion when Luisa or I aren't available to answer your question, Sutton will be using Pauley's old office. Otherwise, team, keep on doing the amazing work you're already doing."

"My door is always open," Sutton said, her smile wide but her jaw clenched. "To everyone. You don't need a reason to come find me if you want."

A pulse beat in his neck that hadn't been there previously. "And we appreciate that. But we know how busy you will be keeping the channels open with *Monument*," and he stressed the studio's name. "We're lucky to have someone so passionate about numbers and budgets on the team."

Murmuring assent could be heard coming from the crowd. She knew what he was doing. He was reminding the crew she was a Monument employee whose responsibility was watching the studio's money. And he was preying on the natural suspicion of creative personnel toward the entity holding the purse strings. Long held conventional wisdom said the studio would always choose money over art. Which wasn't fair—plenty of artistic films had been bankrolled by studios—but wasn't false, either.

Regardless, he was drawing a line. And she'd be damned if she let him put her in a box for his convenience. She wasn't that moonstruck girl from all those years ago who worshipped the great Xavier Duval. The shoe was very much on the other foot.

"I'm here to support the entire production," she countered, her tone so sweet, honey would taste bitter by comparison. "Nothing matters more than ensuring *The Quantum Wraith* becomes the box office hit it deserves to be. And I am thrilled to make certain the film will continue its road to success without incurring obstacles that could derail or even…" she turned to Xavier, batting her eyelashes for a half-second "…cancel the film," she finished.

His gaze narrowed, his mouth firming as he silently acknowledged she scored a point. "And we are privileged to have you do just that. In the production office. Away from the distractions of the set, so you have the time and space for your very important work," he said, and then turned to the crowd before she could formulate a comeback. "Announcement over, you can return to your evening already in progress. Enjoy the food and drinks. And let's give a big round of appreciation for our leading lady, Contessina Sato, for tonight's provisions."

A cheer for Contessina went up, and then the crowd started to disperse. But Sutton saw the various reactions to his announcement: hands covering amused smiles, eyebrows raised skeptically, mouths leaning close to ears to whisper.

She turned to confront him at the same instant he wheeled on his heel to face her.

"What the hell was that?" he started, his voice pitched low but irate.

"How dare you undermine me." She balled her hands on her hips.

He scoffed, his mouth leaning toward her ear to minimize the chances of their discussion being overheard. "Undermine? I had to drag you out of the office to make you appear tonight." His breath tickled her cheek, and she shivered.

"Make me? As if you have the power to make me do anything. As soon I realized what was happening—"

"You can't have everyone on the set come to you for every little thing. You'll be overwhelmed."

She stood on her tiptoes so their gazes were level. Their mouths, too. "You made me sound like nothing but a bean counter."

"If the description fits…"

"May I remind you this film was about to go to the great tax write-off in the sky and I—"

"Hey, guys? Can you do this somewhere else?" Erik spoke at a normal volume, cutting through their hushed argument. "I'm still reading here."

Xavier's gaze tore away from Sutton's almost with an audible pop to focus on Erik. The disconnect left her reeling, so intense had been the connection. She couldn't get enough air, her lungs flailing, and the world tilted around her for a dangerous second. She grabbed the back of a barstool.

"Take this," Xavier said, pushing a bottle of water in her direction. "Drink. You might be dehydrated."

Sutton left the bottle untouched. She wasn't dehydrated. She had been Xaviered, the old sensation of her senses going haywire whenever he was near. She took a deep breath, wishing she had paid more attention in yoga class. The ability to center herself would be useful about now.

"You okay?" he asked, their argument dropped for the moment.

She nodded. "I'm fine."

Xavier turned to Erik, his expression once again unreadable. If she had to stab at a guess, *disquiet* was the closest she could get. "You should be doing homework instead of looking at comics. Why don't you go to the house while I find Ilsa?"

Erik shot him a look that could freeze the surrounding desert. "It's Friday."

Sutton glanced between the two as they continued to argue. Now that they were standing close together…

Erik's hair was fine and straight and dark blond, while Xavier's head of thick black waves refused to stay combed. Erik's chin was pointed while Xavier's was square, Erik's eyes were a light blue in contrast to Xavier's deep brown irises.

But Erik's expressions were pure Xavier. The same ferocious drawing together of eyebrows, indicating a severe storm was on the way. The same rigid set of their jaw. The same flashing warning signs in their gazes that told onlookers to get out of the way and seek shelter, now, to avoid any fallout.

Her gaze volleyed between Xavier and Erik. The more she looked, the more similarities she saw.

And Erik was twelve. That meant…he had been a toddler ten years ago. When she and Xavier…

And Xavier never said a word.

Was that why he…

"Wait…oh my…no." The words escaped her in a breathy exhale. The cocktails that had gone down so easily less than an hour previously now threatened to make a reappearance, her stomach violently awash in acidic bile. She clasped her right hand to her mouth. She had to get out of there. Now. Before she…

Too late.

Seven

"No one has ever outrun the Maro Empyreal."
"I may not be able to run, but I can hide."
                Con Sulley and Lys Amarga, *The Quantum Wraith*

Sunlight hit Sutton's eyelids, bright and insistent, warning her the day was far too advanced for her to still be sleeping. She startled awake, automatically reaching for her phone on the bedside table as her first action of the day. Her barely open eyes made out the time on the screen—11:30 a.m.? Oh no. No no no. She had things to do and places to see and…

Xavier to apologize to, for vomiting on what looked like rather pricey hiking shoes.

The memory hit her like the softball to the stomach she took in gym class, always her top-line standard for pain coupled with social embarrassment. She squeezed her eyes shut against the fresh waves of nausea, this time from envisioning the horrified look on his face just before she…wait.

Did she also pass out? Seriously?

She might not ever show her face in public again.

Slowly her brain came back online, warning her nothing was familiar. She had on an old LAU shirt, but it was not the well-worn green-and-gold T-shirt she normally wore to bed. This was a film school T-shirt, black and white, and far roomier. And then she noticed her surroundings for the first time.

This was not her room in the main building.

She was in bedroom decorated in the usual style of the Pronghorn Ranch, the Old West via Vegas in the 1950s. There was a mid-century dresser in the corner like hers, but this room was big enough to hold a sofa upholstered in brocade fabric featuring running mustangs. There was an additional window—the source of the sunlight that woke her up—and the bedding was a step up in softness from hers as well.

Her gaze whipped around the room. Her clothes were nowhere to be seen, but her purse was on the chair pulled out perpendicular to the desk. She oriented herself based on her view of the grounds outside, and her already queasy stomach took another hit. She had to be in the big house. As in Xavier's residence. As in, what the hell did she do?

Her mouth tasted of sawdust and ash. A bottle of water was on the bedside table, and she downed the contents, which barely made a dent in her thirst. She needed more liquid, food and her clothes, in that order of urgent need. Testing her legs for steadiness—and ensuring her T-shirt was long and opaque enough to provide some dignity—she ventured outside the room.

The sounds of classical music and silverware and plates

clanking together drew her down a hallway, passing a large living room and a formal dining room. The noises came from the kitchen, cozy and warm but with the latest in high-end appliances. An elegant older woman, her silver-white hair in a stylish bob, was unloading the dishwasher while humming along to Mozart's "Ein Kleine Nachtmusik" coming from a wireless speaker.

Sutton cleared her throat, wincing at the dry soreness.

Before she could find her voice, the woman turned and smiled. "Hello! You're awake. You must be hungry," she said, with a slight Eastern European accent.

"I am." Ugh. Frogs were more melodious than her. "But, um, where…what…?" Words would not appear in her brain, so she pointed at the T-shirt she wore.

"Ah! You are wondering about your things. I have laundered your clothes." The woman indicated a pile of neatly folded clothing. Sutton recognized her jeans and top and gathered them to her. "And your phone is charging, just over there. I am Ilsa Petrovych," the woman continued. "You are Sutton, no?

"Yes." So many questions crowded her head, but she was unsure how to ask them. What happened during her memory gap last night? Why was she in Xavier's house? Who was Ilsa?

Who undressed her?

As if reading the panic on Sutton's face, Ilsa gave her a reassuring smile and pulled out a stool at the high kitchen counter. "Here. Sit. I'll bring you food." She placed a glass of water in front of Sutton. "And drink this. Don't want you fainting again."

Sutton gratefully accepted the water but remained standing. "Again? So I passed out?"

"You don't remember? No, I suppose you wouldn't, you were in and out for a while. That's why Xavier put you in the guest room on the ground floor. Much closer than carrying you to your suite in the main building."

That explained the vague impressions still floating in Sutton's consciousness: Xavier's arms around her, his dark gaze staring at her, pupils wide. His breath warm on her cheek. His fingers brushing her hair off her forehead...

Ilsa put a plate of quiche and flatware in front of her. "Eat."

Sutton's stomach growled at the appetizing smell. She sat down, picking up the fork, but her right arm hurt. She pushed up the sleeve of her borrowed T-shirt to reveal a bandage.

"Ah," Ilsa said. "From the IV. Lucky for you the production medic was at the party." She nodded at the T-shirt Sutton wore. "You woke up enough for me to help you put that on."

Sutton stopped eating as a new avalanche of embarrassment threatened to bury her. "I'm sorry to have been such trouble."

Ilsa laughed. "Not at all. I've worked for Xavier, looking after Erik since he was two. Now, that's trouble. Although he is mostly a good kid, when he isn't eavesdropping," she called out.

Erik appeared in the kitchen doorway. "Hi, Sutton."

"Hey, Erik." She gave him a brief wave, memories of the night before returning in vivid Technicolor. Erik standing next to Xavier, the same stance, the same expressions... She pushed the plate of quiche away.

"I wasn't eavesdropping," Erik protested to Ilsa. "I was waiting for you to stop talking. You always say it's rude to interrupt."

Ilsa threw her hands in the air. "Of course. You were waiting. But let Sutton finish eating before you bombard her with your comic books. She just woke up."

"Now? Really?" he asked.

"Why? What time is it?" Sutton grabbed her phone and looked at the screen, also noting with a groan she had several missed messages from her parents. "It's noon? It can't be noon."

At least there was one shiny silver lining. Xavier was nowhere to be found. She'd count her small blessings. The longer she could put off that sure-to-be horribly mortifying encounter, the better.

She gathered up her laundry. "Thanks for the food and the hospitality, sorry I slept so late. I'll change in the guest room and then get out of your hair."

"But coffee is brewing," Ilsa said.

"Rain check!" Sutton exited the kitchen as fast as she could. When Ilsa and Erik were safely out of sight, her shoulders fell from what seemed like their permanent position around her ears. Then she stopped. Which way was the guest room?

She stood in the hall, unsure. Should she go left or right? She decided on right and turned on her heels—

And came face to face with Xavier.

"Oh!" She nearly dropped her clothes.

He appeared as if he had recently showered, his dark hair brushed back and damply curling at the ends. His plain black T-shirt clung to well-defined pecs and outlined broad shoulders while gray sweatpants hung low on his hips.

She'd never seen him look better. Or more appealing. The wave of warmth that had always kindled when he was near became a tsunami, the structural integrity of her knees as unreliable as ten years ago. "After you," she said.

He didn't move. "You're awake. How are you feeling?"

"Oh, you know, fine. Since embarrassment isn't an actual cause of death."

A half smile dented his left cheek. "Glad to hear it."

"I, um, want to…" She ran her free hand through her hair and then instantly regretted that choice when her fingers met snarls. There went her plan to encounter him only on her terms. Just her luck to run into him with sleep creases in her cheeks, a rat's nest on her head and wearing only an oversized T-shirt.

A T-shirt, with nothing on underneath, made clear by the bra and panties visible in her hands. And the heat rising in her belly, flooding her chest and face. Her nipples pushing against the thin material.

Neither of them had on their usual armor. And it was intoxicating.

She didn't realize she had stopped speaking until she clocked his quizzical expression. "You want to…?" he prompted.

Right. "I, um, want to thank you for everything you did for me last night. Ilsa filled me in. I promise, I didn't sleep in on purpose."

"You needed the rest," he said. "Medic's orders. Don't worry about it."

"Your shoes didn't need the damage, however. I'm incredibly sorry."

"They're just shoes." He shrugged. "I'm glad you're feeling better."

"I am, other than the whole being embarrassed thing. I only had two cocktails."

"Dehydration was the medic's diagnosis."

She frowned. "That doesn't make sense. I stocked up on liquids."

"Energy drinks are not hydrating. Housekeeping found what they called, and I quote, 'a lifetime supply of empty Fyzade cans' in your room."

She frowned. "That's an exaggeration. Maybe a case of Fyzade. Or…two."

"You're making their point for them."

"I thought the rule was whatever happened between you and housekeeping stays in your room."

"That's Vegas. And even then, I've rarely found what happens there stays there." He shrugged, his smile spreading to both cheeks. That smile, on those damnable kissable lips.

Those lips that kissed someone else as least long enough to have a child with them. A child he didn't tell her about when they discussed working together after she graduated.

And more.

The heat left her cheeks to settle in her heart, a burning knot of pain. "I suppose you're right. We can't all keep secrets tightly zipped up. Or completely forget them. Must be nice to put people out of your mind as if they never existed. Maybe for you, they never did."

And there it was. The bitterness she tried so long to tamp down, hidden and tucked away. The anger that he could see in her again and act as if they had been barely acquainted outside the classroom. As if they never shared their dreams, their hopes, their desires.

As if she didn't matter. Never mattered. And certainly not to him.

Served her right for pursuing something her heart wanted when her head told her not to take the risk.

She pushed away from the hall wall, holding her head high, not blinking so the tears threatening to make an appearance wouldn't fall. "Excuse me."

His hand, warm and strong, grasped her upper arm. "What the hell did you mean by that, Sutton?"

Xavier stared at the woman who had upended his life. Twice. He wouldn't survive a third time. So he was determined to get through the next few months, finish *The Quantum Wraith*, and walk off into the sunset with his sanity intact. He and Sutton were adults. There was no reason why they couldn't have a calm, respectful, professional working relationship. He'd learned at a very young age he couldn't make people like him, much less love him, and chasing their affection only resulted in more rejection.

But he'd had enough of walking on tiptoes around her. She blew hot and cold, turning from almost human to stone incased in ice without warning. If he knew what the triggers were, he would gladly avoid them. But there was no pattern he could discern, just random landmines to trip.

"What did you mean?" he repeated.

Sutton tugged her arm, and he immediately let go. "I need to get dressed."

"No."

Her eyes widened. "No? Of course I need to—

"No. Until now, I've let you call the shots. I've always let you call the shots, but damn it, I'm not playing that game this time. If you want to pretend when we're around other people that we met for the first time on the set, go ahead. But right now, it's just us."

"If *I* want to pretend? I'm following your lead. You're the one who looked at me as if I'm an uninvited, unwanted studio exec come to ruin your fun."

What the *hell*? "You showed up out of the blue on a day where things were going from bad to catastrophic. How was I supposed to look at you? Thankful you reappeared after a decade of silence? Grateful you reentered my life just to take my film away?"

Her mouth opened and closed a few times. Her voice, when it came, was thin and reedy. "You were the one who left. We made plans to meet, and I went to your office and the department secretary told me you had packed your things and you were gone, never coming back. And that was it. I never heard from you again. How dare you talk like I'm the one who disappeared!"

"If you spoke to Margie, then you know why I left. And *you* never contacted *me*."

She was shaking her head. "She didn't give me a reason

for your exit, just said you weren't returning to LAU and our grades would be ready the next day. She even patted my hand like she pitied me. Why would I reach out to you after that?"

No. That can't be right. "I gave Margie a letter for you. The only contact information I had was your university email, and I didn't want to risk the chance you might not check your account or lose access to it after graduation. She said she would deliver it when you came in."

Her headshaking intensified. "All I received from her was a speech about putting college behind me and starting my real life."

The day he departed LAU would be forever stored in the wiring of his brain, no matter how much he wished he'd never lived it. He could still recall the blue cardigan draped on the back of Margie's chair, her eyes crinkling with a reassuring smile as he handed the envelope with Sutton's name written in bold black letters to her. He started to speak, but Sutton cut him off with a snort.

"Maybe she knew to pity me. Was I the only one who didn't know about Erik?"

Erik? What did Erik have to do with him and Sutton if she hadn't read the letter? "I don't follow."

"Oh, please. How much amusement did I provide you, Xavier? Did your ego get a boost by having me trail after you like a puppy with a crush? When Jay came to give his lecture about cinematography, did you go out to drinks with him afterward and laugh about me?"

He was lost. So lost. Up a creek in the middle of the woods, no sun or moonlight to illuminate a path, utterly lost. "I have no idea what you mean. And I resent that you could think that of me."

"I have eyes. I'm not blind."

"Blind? What in the hell are you talking about?"

"And. You. Left." She jabbed a finger into his chest with each word. "What else am I supposed to think?"

He grabbed her right hand with both of his, sandwiched her fingers tightly between his palms. "I left because my sister died. That night we—she was killed. Car accident."

Sutton blinked at him. Her shoulders fell, all the fight in her fleeing. "That's awful. I'm so sorry." Her hand turned in his, her palm sliding to find his right hand, and she squeezed. "I had no idea."

He hadn't talked about Rosalie to anyone but Erik in a long time. No one in his professional life—well, other than Jay—knew he once had a sister. As for his parents, the less he and his parents spoke, the better. Rosalie had been the pride of their existence, their wanted child, the offspring who followed in their footsteps and devoted herself to science and research. Xavier was the afterthought child, a later in life mistake born fifteen years after his sister, who rejected their empirical, logical world to play at what they called "inconsequential, ephemeral fantasy." His parents didn't understand him, didn't want to understand him.

But Rosalie did. Everything Xavier knew about kindness and treating others with respect, he learned from his older sister. She took on the role of caregiver for him far more easily and readily than his biological parents, who paid much more attention to their lab specimens and computers than to him. And she encouraged his imagination when his parents would stifle his stories and drawings.

It was Rosalie, who became an ER doctor, who helped him pay for film school when their parents refused to support his "frivolous" education and cut him off from their financial resources.

"She was coming out to California," he said, finding the words one by one. "She needed a break, and we were going to drive up the coast after my seminar finished. She was running errands, picking up last-minute things before her flight, when she witnessed a traffic accident and got out of her car to help. That was the physician in her. But it was a busy street, and dark, and…"

"Oh, Xavier," Sutton whispered, her hand tightening on his.

"We don't think she saw the SUV coming. Doctors said she would have died instantly, so hopefully she didn't feel any pain." He may not talk about Rosalie much, but he didn't forget. Recalling her death freshly pierced his heart anew each time.

He rubbed his free hand over his eyes. "Leaving LA, going to Connecticut—it's all a blur now. But I know I gave Margie the letter for you."

Sutton nodded, her fingers still tight on his. "I feel so… I'm so sorry. For your loss. I had no idea that's why you left. Her death must have been such a shock."

"And then I suddenly also had to take care of Erik, so—"

"You gained custody of Erik at the same time? Why? That's too much to take on when you're grieving. Couldn't Erik's mother continue to look after him?"

Erik's mother? What? "Erik's mother is—was—Rosalie. And, yes, she wanted me to become his guardian."

Sutton's eyes were wide, her pupils dark and large against her green irises. "Rosalie is… So you're not… Oh my God, Xavier. I can't imagine…"

"You thought I was Erik's biological father?" Which meant… He did the calculations. "You thought I had a child and didn't tell you."

"In my defense, you and Erik have similar mannerisms. And you both jut out your lower lip like so—" she demonstrated "—when you're deep in thought."

Her imitation of Erik was spot on. And of him, he supposed. "You're the first person who has ever remarked on that. Most are surprised to learn we're related."

"Was Rosalie blond, too?"

He shook his head. "No, Rosalie and I looked similar. Erik takes after his father, who abandoned them before Erik was born. He still doesn't want anything to do with us. His loss." The less said about Erik's father, the better.

"I really like Erik. I'm so sorry, but it sounds like he's much better off without his bio dad."

Xavier was still stuck on Sutton's earlier words. "All this time, you thought I had a child and didn't tell you? No wonder you've been…" he searched for words that wouldn't cause her to become a frosty statue "…testy."

Her gaze narrowed, but then her face relaxed into a rueful grin. "No, I only believed that since last night. You ghosting me since graduation, however—" she shrugged "—that might have made me testy."

Right. She said she didn't receive his letter. "Well, now

you know what happened. I didn't mean to ghost you." He loosened his grip, letting her escape if she wanted.

She refused, keeping her fingers entwined with his. "Xavier, I really am sorry. For everything. For your loss. For thinking you would disappear without a word. But…"

"But what?" His thumb began to trace a path along her warm skin.

"But—" she inhaled as he found her sensitive inner wrist "—you know, the gossip back then was that the secretary also had a crush on you. Maybe that's why I didn't get the letter. Still, does it matter? The past is the past. We can't change it."

"No. But we can move forward."

Her gaze flashed. "I do wish I'd read what you'd written, though."

"Dear Sutton." He recited the letter he'd long ago committed to memory, retracing the words a thousand times in his mind, wondering where he went astray, said the wrong thing, put her off contacting him. "There's no easy way to write this. My sister just died. I'm on the next flight to Connecticut. I'm sorry not to say goodbye in person. I meant every word I said last night. But graduation is a big deal. A time of transition. Opportunities will be coming your way fast. You should be free to accept whichever one you desire. I don't know when or if I will be able to return to Los Angeles. So take your time. Take as much as you need. But if you still feel the same way after taking that time, call me. Or email. I don't want you to think you're being pressured, so the next contact is up to you." He couldn't stop stroking her skin. "Not the most romantic note."

"Romantic enough." Their gazes met and held, her eyes

glistening. Her fingers tightened on his and he took a step toward her. Now only inches separated them. He became suddenly, viscerally aware of how easy it would be to lean down and capture her lips with his. Taste the unique sweetness that was Sutton and Sutton alone. Gather her to him, with only their T-shirts and his well-worn sweatpants between them. Cup her luscious ass and bring her fast to him, mold her against his cock, half hard since he first encountered her in the hall.

Finish, finally, what they started ten years ago that sultry Los Angeles night. He had invited his seminar students to a small party at his rented house in Los Feliz the night of graduation, a celebration for those who didn't otherwise have plans. He could almost smell the night blooming jasmine, surrounding the porch where Sutton and he found themselves alone after the others had left, could almost hear the creaking of the porch swing as they sat thigh to thigh arguing over the merits of the latest Tarantino film. His entire being focused on her, transfixed. Like now.

And just like that night, her mouth parted, her pink tongue appearing to wet her lips. Her gaze dilated, her eyelids heavy, and she swayed toward him. Her breathing intensified, her chest visibly rising and falling, and he knew if he asked, she would consent to what was sure to be a repeat of the most mind-blowing kiss of their lives.

Plates crashed in the nearby kitchen, snapping him out of his haze.

Erik. He had responsibilities now that he didn't then. From the moment he held two-year-old Erik and became his legal guardian, he vowed Erik would always know he came first. His nephew and now adopted son would never know the searing pain of being overlooked and belittled by a parent.

He wanted Sutton. Even now, his cock was warring with his brain. But he also needed her help bringing *The Quantum Wraith* in for a smooth landing so he could hopefully have even more power to choose his following project.

Erik would be a teenager soon, and the next few years would be critical for him, both in establishing a friend group and preparing for whatever he chose to pursue after high school. There would be more financial security for him, and their schedules could line up more now that Xavier had a studio film on his résumé.

Xavier dropped Sutton's hand, instantly missing her warmth, her strength. "And I was right," he said lightly, leaning away from her. "Opportunities did come your way."

Her gaze, so open and vulnerable a moment ago, started to shutter. "I worked hard to get them."

"Things turned out for the best. I had to be there for Erik." Erik was his priority and always would be. He owed Rosalie that. He owed Erik that. "You've obviously found your place at Monument."

His heart may not believe their current situation was the best of all possible outcomes. But to finish this movie and achieve his goals, his head would act as if it were.

She folded her arms close against her chest. "I have. In fact, I'm up for a promotion. To take Chester's job. But that depends on delivering the film on time and on budget."

He hated the distance in her expression. He hated even more knowing he put that distance there. "And I want to jump to the ranks of A-list directors. And that depends on delivering the best film I can possibly make." He held out his right hand for a handshake. "Partners in getting what we both want?"

There. That was the best he could do. Because saying anything else—such as telling her, no, he did not want to pick her up and run with her to the nearest horizontal surface where they could finally allow the sparks that always flew between them turn into an all-consuming fire—would be a lie.

But Sutton was nothing if not perceptive. One of her traits that first drew him to her was her ability to read other people, both characters on the screen and in real life. Her gaze searched his and he was careful to keep his expression impassive.

She must have found—or not found—what she was seeking. "Partners. In making *The Quantum Wraith* a success," she said, accepting his hand.

The electricity stung sharply, as always. But this time there were no subtle caresses, not explorations of skin against skin. Her grip was firm, almost painfully so. She meant business.

So did he. He returned her grasp, bone crush for bone crush.

Their hands untangled and dropped. Sutton turned her back on him without a word, her head held high as she disappeared toward the guest bedroom. A voice deep inside screamed to go after her, to not let this second chance slip away.

Then he heard Erik from behind him, chatting with Ilsa as they existed the kitchen, and he stayed where he was.

Eight

"Open. And see."
"My eyes are wide open."
"Eyes are blind. Open your heart."
>   Autarch Zear and Lys Amarga, *The Quantum Wraith*

Jay stood in the doorway. "Got a sec?"

Xavier glanced up from his monitor. They were twenty-two days from finishing the location shoot and moving to soundstages to finish the film, and the last scene of *The Quantum Wraith* still didn't read right to him. He knew what the final image would be: Lys, alone, the camera dollying farther and farther away until she is nothing but a dark dot on the expansive sands, the framing emphasizing her isolation with no one coming to save her. But the dialogue leading up to that image…he sighed and closed the file. "Sure."

"I put together tomorrow's shot list but have a few questions for you. Here, I printed it out, thought it might be easier to look at on paper." Jay shut the door behind him as he entered the office.

Xavier held out his hand for the document and glanced through the order of the shots and the camera positions planned for the next day. "Looks good. I don't see anything that would need my input."

"Oh no, the questions aren't about the shots. They're for you. Number one, have you spoken to Sutton about the new location?"

Xavier shook his head. "Not yet. It's going to be a fight. Monsoon season is approaching, and she's determined we leave Arizona before that happens. Since moving locations will add days to the schedule, I'm picking my time to bring up that up with her."

"Excellent segue to my next question. What exactly is going on between you and Sutton?" Jay dropped into the chair across from Xavier's desk. "I finally placed her. She's from LAU, right? The one you couldn't stop talking about at the time."

There were advantages to partnering with the same crew from film to film. Working with Jay as his cinematographer so closely and for so many projects meant they had built up an easy rapport and trust that freed both men to perform their optimum work. And Jay was one of the best in the business at instinctively understanding light and apertures, shadows and angles.

But there were disadvantages, as well. Such as not being allowed to get away with a bullshit answer like, "Nothing is happening."

Xavier leaned forward in his chair. "Do you remember Mimi Kingston?"

"Who doesn't? She won the Emmy last year." Jay crossed his legs, a sign he was settling in for a long conversation. "Also, I remember a bad breakup."

"I wouldn't say bad—"

Jay smirked.

"Fine, painful," Xavier conceded. "But not for the usual reasons."

"I appreciate this quick hop down memory lane. But what does Mimi have to do with our current producer?"

Xavier got up from his desk and started to pace. The office was small, so he only managed four strides before needing to turn. "Mimi and I broke up because she had a promising career in front of her."

Jay frowned. "You broke up because Mimi only thought of herself and no one else."

"That's not fair. She's a talented actress and we all need to hustle when our careers are hot, or the offers dry up. She did the right thing."

"What does Mimi have to do with—"

"But Erik loved Mimi. She's great with kids, at least when there's a timer on the interaction."

"Man, you're making me dizzy."

Xavier stopped pacing. "Mimi and I knew our relationship had run its course. When the film finished, we ran out of things to talk about. But the breakup meant she disappeared from Erik's life. He still won't watch her series."

Jay's gaze narrowed. "So?"

"Erik has lost too much already." He couldn't wholly protect Erik from rejection. But having braced the cold winds of his parents' neglect for most of his life, he would do his best to shield Erik from the same sense of abandonment.

Jay shrugged. "Again, that's Mimi. I'm asking about Sutton. There could be cash riding on the answer."

"What? Why?"

"There's a betting pool on you two. A third of the crew think you hate each other. A third think you haven't slept together yet but will. And the rest believe you're already burning up the sheets. I'm here for insider information." Jay grinned.

Xavier loved directing. The incessant gossip on the set, however, he could do without. "No hate. But no burning. At any time." Unless one considered his thoughts, late at night in his bed, unable to sleep as he replayed their encounter in his hallway. Sutton's nipples pressing against the T-shirt of his she wore, her soft lips parted and available if he had just leaned down… "We're colleagues. And when the film ends, she'll return to Monument, and I'll go wherever the next project takes me."

"Too bad. I like Sutton. She runs a tighter ship than Pauley. Communication between departments has never been better." Jay rose from his chair and clapped a hand on Xavier's shoulder, his expression turning serious. "There are plenty of people who would welcome being a permanent part of Erik's life, you know. Not everyone is Mimi."

"Again, Mimi did nothing wrong. And I know that. I date. But not while working." He shrugged. "We have a film to make. Keeping my eyes on the goal. No room for anything else."

Jay sighed. "Looks like I'll have to make my best guess in the betting pool."

"Told you. Go with never." Xavier sat again in his chair and reopened his file, signaling the conversation was over on his end.

A knock came at his door. "Xavier? Can we talk?"

Sutton's voice. Xavier didn't dare look at Jay. "Sure. Come in."

"Thanks." She entered his office, her gaze focused on the electronic tablet in her hand, her red-gold curls twisted into a haphazard bun threatening to fall at any moment. Like the rest of the crew, she dressed casually, today wearing formfitting dark olive leggings with an ivory blouse loosely flowing on top. But her posture, ramrod straight with her shoulders pulled back, still screamed, *Hollywood suit!*

"Hey, Sutton," Jay said, before turning to Xavier. "Yeah, never isn't the guess I'm going for. Talk to you later."

"Bye, Jay," Sutton called after him. "What does 'never' mean?" she asked Xavier.

"I have no idea. What do you have for me?" He leaned back in his chair.

"We need to talk about moving these scenes to the soundstage. I emailed this list to you but thought we'd better discuss in person." She handed her tablet to him.

His frown etched deeper into his cheeks the farther down the page he read. "No. No. No. And hell no."

"Hear me out—"

He didn't need to. "You're going to say shooting the scenes with green screen and computer graphics will ultimately be more cost effective, even though I've been clear all along I intend to shoot practical effects—"

"The destruction of the Filloli camp scene went three days over schedule thanks to problems with the pyrotechnics. But if you had filmed on a soundstage, the scene would have taken far fewer takes. You'll have to sweeten the firestorm in postproduction anyway, so why not let the visual effects team handle—"

"Because people can tell when a scene is mostly CGI. There's a weightlessness to the footage, to the acting. The actors are on a climate-controlled stage, surrounded by generic green shapes, reacting to a ball on a stick. Here." He pulled out his phone and opened his photo app, thumbing through pages of pictures. "This is a picture I snapped during rehearsal."

He handed the phone to Sutton, the screen filled with an image of Contessina staring into the distance, her jaw set, her gaze narrowed against the bright sunlight. Yellow-red dust clung to her dark hair, marked her high cheekbones. "Look at Contessina. She feels the heat of the sun, the dryness in the air," he continued. "Her eyes reflect the color of the landscape. She is wholly present in the moment, experiencing what Lys would be experiencing. And, yes, she's a great actress and I could replicate the desert with CGI. But there's substance there. A reality that can't be faked."

Sutton stared at the photo. Her lips pressed together firmly as she handed the phone back to him. "Beautiful picture. But this is a science fiction film. Emphasis on fiction."

"The only emphasis should be on the audience. CGI doesn't allow—"

She cut him off with a quick shake of her head. "Bottom line is you're running out of time. Monsoon season is around the corner, and we can't risk weather delays. Plus, the soundstages are reserved and paid for. It's either move these scenes or...you can move these scenes. Your choice."

Her arms were folded across her chest, her gaze emerald dark. But her cheeks were so rosy her freckles nearly disappeared. He was suddenly glad there was a desk between them, both to hide the reaction his body always had when she was near and so there was a physical barrier to remind him she wasn't his to touch, to caress, to witness that blush covering every inch of her curves...

Priorities, he sternly reminded himself. He wanted her, yes. But he needed his direction of the film to be considered an artistic success, to lead to more assignments, so he could provide Erik with the stable life he deserved.

And maybe he could leverage this situation to his benefit.

"What if," he said, rising from his chair and leaning his hands on his desk so his gaze was level with hers, "I agree to your list—mostly—in return for moving the final battle between Lys and Autarch Zear to a new location?"

Sutton blinked several times. "New? You mean, not using the place now earmarked for the showdown scene, but somewhere else on the ranch?"

He shook his head. "No. Near Yuma."

She did a quick search on her tablet. "Move the company two hundred miles? You can't be serious."

He straightened up. "I know you're seeing nothing but dollar signs. But the site was originally on the schedule. Permits were even pulled. Then, the owners of the land changed their minds. But the location manager was recently informed they're now open again to film crews. This is a can't-miss opportunity."

"Do you know how much a move would cost? The extra days that would add to the schedule? If we push into monsoon season, we risk more delays due to weather. I'm breaking out in hives just thinking about it." She pushed up the sleeve of her blouse. "Angry red marks are going to appear at any second."

This wasn't fair, giving him glimpses of the creamy bare skin he was just daydreaming about. His gaze fell, lingered, powerless to look away. She bit her lower lip, the pink glow on her cheekbones deepening to crimson, and she let her sleeve fall. "Not that I matter. But the budget does. I can't ask Monument for more money. The well is tapped dry."

He held her gaze. Her irises were endlessly fascinating to him, a kaleidoscope of gold and green shards. If eyes were the windows to the soul, then her soul was deep and bright and ever shifting in its beauty. "Come with me."

She blinked at the change in subject. "Excuse me? Come with you where?"

"Come look at the location with me. If you don't agree it's the only place possible to film the confrontation between Lys and Autarch Zear, I will drop the discussion." Three hours in a vehicle alone with Sutton. And three hours back. The trip would be an excruciating test of his resolve.

He found himself desperately hoping she would agree to make the journey.

"If I say no after seeing the site, you'll agree with my decision? And you'll also agree to my list?" She narrowed her gaze. "This is too easy. What's the trick?"

He shook his head. "No trick, on my honor. How about tomorrow?"

"Saturday? Aren't you spending the day with Erik?"

"Erik was invited to go camping overnight with some local kids. I spoke with the parents. It's an organized annual trip with plenty of chaperones. He can't wait." Another reminder of the life he intended to give his family. While he was thankful Erik made friends his own age easily, following Xavier from indie film to indie film meant the friendships tended to be transitory. He wanted Erik to have a chance to form lasting bonds with his classmates. "Meet in the ranch parking lot after lunch? Two p.m.?"

"Isn't that rather late? We'll have a long way to travel."

"Trust me. There's a method to the madness. We can get dinner on the drive back, arriving at the Pronghorn around nine or ten. Well before bedtime."

Her gaze narrowed, but her luscious mouth curved up in a half smirk, half smile. "A method to your madness is what I'm afraid of. But fine. It's a d—" She coughed. "It's a plan. See you then."

Definitely not a date. He agreed, even as he caught himself watching the smooth roll of her hips as she exited his office.

But he was more excited than he should be about their plan. He turned to his computer and clicked on the email with the list of scenes to be moved from location to the soundstage, but he couldn't concentrate. The anticipation of spending time alone with Sutton meant the hours until then would painfully inch by.

★ ★ ★

Sutton spent far too much time choosing what to wear for the drive to Yuma, considering she had a limited wardrobe in Arizona and would no doubt be walking around in sun and sand, two items that did not allow her to look her best. Being a redhead made her and solar rays sworn enemies, and she was not someone who could pull off looking attractive when covered in sweat and grit. She eventually decided on a lightweight long-sleeve top in sage with built-in sun protection and moisture wicking, on top of loose khaki-colored trousers that offered the same properties. A sun hat with a large brim completed her outfit, along with hiking boots.

Not that she was thinking of her appearance because she wanted to appeal to Xavier. No, unequivocally not. Her only consideration was comfort while striking a balance between casual yet still professional.

So what if the green shirt emphasized her eyes?

Xavier was waiting in the parking lot next to a four-by-four pickup truck that had seen more than its share of action, judging by the scraps and dents on the doors and along the side panels. The bed of the truck was covered with a boxlike shell that she assumed was for hauling equipment. "Sweet ride," she said as she joined him.

Her palms were sweaty, and she discreetly wiped them on her trousers. While she'd spent plenty of time with Xavier since that morning in the hallway, even time one on one, the reality of spending the next several hours alone with no one around to interrupt them, no appointments to use as an excuse to run, caused her heart to knock hard against her chest walls.

"I borrowed the truck from Dalip," he said, referring to the location manager. "Hop in. There are waters by the passenger seat. Sorry, all out of energy drinks." He flashed her a swift grin.

Her misadventure with dehydration had become an inside joke to the crew. She returned a smirk. "Too bad. How am I going to stay awake on the drive?"

But as they set out on the three-and-a-half-hour journey, Sutton found staying awake was not a problem. Not with Xavier sitting beside her, his hands moving confidently as he drove, his thigh near enough to brush when she reached for the bottle of water in the cup holder between them, his dark gaze darting over to check on her when traffic allowed, his scent, undefinable but unmistakably him, warm and spicy and clean, wrapping around her. They didn't talk much, and when they did, they stayed scrupulously away from the revelations in the hallway.

She gave him the update on the cautiously enthusiastic reaction to the daily footage from her Monument bosses and filled him on the arraignment for Contessina's intruder. The campaign against the film had died down, in part because the worst offenders found something else to be incensed about in bad faith, while others had been horrified at the break-in and realized the rhetoric had gone too far. He discussed Jay's dream of moving from cinematography to directing, and how he was working on a reel to showcase Jay's talent. They took turns exchanging what they knew about the hunt for Pauley and Hera, who had apparently dropped off the grid for now. But Chester, Sutton was happy to note, was facing embezzlement charges.

They stopped for a snack at a roadside taco stand before

Xavier pulled the truck off the paved highway and onto a dirt road. "Now I see why you borrowed a four-wheel-drive vehicle," Sutton said. The truck hit a bump, causing her to yelp as her butt left the seat. Her grip tightened on the passenger side handle attached to the truck's ceiling. "And now I know why these are usually called 'oh shit' handles. Also, reaffirming my love of seat belts."

"Keep holding on. This land recently changed hands, which is why it is now available to us. The previous owner didn't maintain the road, and the new owner hasn't had time to make improvements."

The pickup bumped down the path for what felt like miles, and then started to climb. Xavier kept his gaze firmly fixed on the vista in front of him, referring to his phone's GPS and the compass on the truck's dashboard to ensure he was headed in the right direction. Finally, he pulled the vehicle over onto what had once been a flat paved turnout big enough for several vehicles, but all that now remained were bits of crumbling asphalt.

"This is it?" Sutton asked, opening her door. The drive had been pretty—she'd grown to greatly appreciate the stark beauty of the desert—but she hadn't seen anything so incredibly different from the landscape available to them at the ranch. Or that couldn't be replicated with computer graphics. At Xavier's beckoning wave, she came around to join him at the rear of the truck.

And she suddenly understood. "Oh," was all she could say, a long-exhaled syllable.

They were parked on an overlook that provided an unobstructive view of the surrounding area for miles. Xavier had timed their trip just right, and they'd arrived at the golden hour, much beloved by filmmakers, the magic period before sunset when sunlight was the most concentrated, intensely gilding the landscape. In the distance, barren sand dunes undulated and swooped into surreal peaks and valleys.

But what caused her to gasp were the shimmering colors filling her vision in every direction. The hills and nearby ground were pockmarked with various holes, some big enough for a man or two to stand, some small and hastily made. The area glowed like Aladdin's treasure cave as the late afternoon sun threw sparks of reds and ochres and the occasional blue and green. "What is this place?"

"A mineral mine. Or rather, a potential mine," Xavier said, his gaze on her instead of the landscape. "Turquoise, wulfenite, vanadinite, quartz, selenite and more are in the vicinity. People came up here to prospect. Then the family who used to own this land ran them off. You're seeing the left-behinds."

That wasn't all Sutton saw. She instantly grasped why this location was the perfect setting for the showdown between Lys and Autarch Zear. "The dunes in the distance…that's the Maro Empyreal. Imposing a sameness, a blandness over all the systems they absorb. The sparkle of crystal and stone in an otherwise arid and harsh environment represents Lys."

"And do you see why this is preferable to CGI?"

She sighed and gave him a lopsided smile. "Yes. The scenery is fantastical but tangible in a way computers just can't replicate, making the point this isn't just a fun escapist film—although it's that, too—but an allegory for real life."

His gaze was warm and full of light, and the sun had nothing to do it. "You get it."

"I get it. In a world that is increasingly reliant on AI for images, using a physical setting makes Lys's story that much more visceral for the viewer." She squeezed her eyes shut so tight they wanted to protest. "I get it. But I don't see *how* to get it."

He leaned against the truck's tailgate, his arms loosely folded. "I'll agree to your list of scenes to be moved to the soundstage. You chose well, by the way."

"That gets the original budget to zero. This would be adding a number of zeroes to the debit column."

He nodded, his gaze distant and focused on the far horizon. "What if I cut the detention hold breakout?"

"Maybe." She chewed her lower lip. "I wish I could magic up more budget. I'm sorry."

"I'll see what else I can cut." He opened the driver's door and brought out a small bag containing an SLR camera. "We should get on the road, but do you mind if I take photos before we leave? I want to capture the light."

"That was the second lecture. From your seminar. 'Always observe and record the world around you so you can replicate, enhance or detract as needed in your work. The films that stay with audiences are those that reflect and comment on reality,'" she quoted.

He threw her a tight smile. "Good to see you remember."

"I never forgot," she murmured, but his back was to her, and only the wind appeared to have caught her words.

Xavier should stop taking photos. He and Sutton had a long journey back to the ranch, and they would be driving mostly in the dark as it was.

But the chiaroscuro of tall black clouds forming to the

south and contrasting with the late-afternoon golden sun was too visually stunning to pass up. He played with apertures and f-stops, only ceasing to check the result on the camera's screen.

Sutton explored the area while he worked, stooping to pick up and examine glittering rocks as they caught her interest. The wind increased, turning her red-gold curls into fiery nimbus. A veritable warrior princess in athletic wear, and he couldn't resist taking photos of her, backlit against the light.

Sour disappointment at not being to use this location made a move to take up residence in his stomach, but he did his best to evict the interloper. He knew Sutton was only doing her job, and better than Pauley did. Pauley would have paid his request lip service and then left Xavier to twist in the acrid winds of the studio's disapproval. In her own way, she was as protective of the film as he was. Even if her protection only extended to Monument's dollars and cents.

"Hey! Look at this!" She held up a chunk of wulfenite. He was capturing her delight, her eyes wide and shining as joy appeared to make her glow her from within, when stinging raindrops hit his head and hands. He glanced up just in time to see the last remnants of the sun disappearing behind purple-indigo thunderclouds. "Those showed up quickly," he said.

Sutton dropped the crystal she was examining and stood up. "Monsoon season is still a few weeks off. But that looks ominous."

A crack of thunder so loud his ears rang swallowed the rest of her words.

"We need to leave." Thunderstorms in the desert were no joke. The arid ground was unable to absorb torrential rain, leading to flash floods that could be deadly, which was only one of the reasons why the production team wanted to avoid Arizona's monsoon season.

Xavier steered Sutton to the passenger side of the truck, the wind almost ripping the door out of his hand. The rain intensified, turning from fat droplets to a stinging steady shower as he jumped into the driver's seat. The truck started easily, and he pressed the accelerator as hard as he dared, considering the uneven road. The truck bumped and jostled and even flew for a brief second, all four wheels leaving the ground. The truck landed—

And stopped moving.

Xavier gunned the accelerator. Sutton held on to the grab handle with her biceps flexed. Her face was pale in the reflected light of the dashboard, the storm blanketing all other forms of illumination. The only sounds were the whine of the engine, the hammering of rain and the *swoosh*, *swoosh* of wipers furiously attempting and failing to remove cascades of water.

The back tires spun, trying to find purchase. For a heart-stopping moment, he thought they might be stuck. He finally remembered to put the truck into four-wheel mode and they started moving again, but slower, as if something was grabbing at the tires and not letting go. Something like slick mud.

Almost too late, he realized the poorly maintained road they were on was a former gully and was becoming a gully again, a runoff trench that would turn the water that was falling from the sky into a fast-running stream.

"We have to find higher land." He took the first opportunity he could to leave the road, heading toward a rise he could barely make out between the water and the wipers. He brought the truck to a stop on the crest of a small hill, turning off the engine but leaving the headlights on.

For a few minutes all was quiet, save the steady beat of the rain on the roof and the hard thumping of his heart. Then her hand found his. "I think I've met my thrill ride quota for the year, if not the decade," she said.

"What were you saying about being too early for monsoon season?" he tried to joke. But he was too breathless for the joke to land well. "Sorry. I wasn't thinking. We should have stayed where we were. We'd be safer on the ridge. I thought we had time to get to the highway."

She shook her head. "We would've been stuck on the ridge and unable to return to the ranch tonight."

"Sutton, I hate to point this out. But we're still stuck." He indicated out the windshield at the headlights that revealed only raindrops against pitch blackness. "We need to stay here until the sun comes up to ensure we're not driving into a flood. Or worse."

Nine

"My entire life has been a lie."
"Then tell yourself a new story."
                    Lys Amarga and Con Sulley, *The Quantum Wraith*

Sutton blinked at Xavier. "I'm sorry. I must have misheard you."

No, she heard him perfectly. Of course she did. He was sitting next to her, his thigh just a brief grasp of her hand away, an action that had been primary in her thoughts as they bounced across the desert. She shifted in her seat, drawing tighter against her door. "I thought you said we had to spend the night here. But that's ridiculous."

"Your ears work fine." Lightning lit up the sky in the distance. She braced herself. She knew what would follow, but still she jumped when the crack of thunder followed several seconds later. Her hand went flying, seeking his reassuring warmth on instinct. He grabbed her fingers, drew them into his, warming them between his palms. "The storm is in front of us. If we stay here, it should keep heading in that direction," he said.

She nodded, her jaw aching with tension. "I know."

"You okay?" He shot her a glance. "You seem jumpy. If it's about staying in the truck tonight, you can have the back seat. I'll stay here."

She glanced behind her at the seat piled high with camping gear and other items she couldn't identify and decided the front seat would be far more preferable. "It's not that. I don't like thunderstorms," she said, thankful the lights were off in the truck cab so he couldn't see the terror on her face. "Childhood phobia. Growing up in Orange County, thunderstorms were rare. The first time I heard thunder, I was… three or four? I was on a trip with my parents. I woke up in a strange place and couldn't find them. Turns out they were in the hotel bar. But I guess I screamed so loud the other guests called security."

"You must have scared your parents. I hope that taught them not to leave you alone as a young child."

"In a way. That taught them to leave me at home with my grandparents. They were embarrassed, not worried. They thought they had raised me to be more self-sufficient."

Another bright burst of electricity lit the clouds, and she tightened her hold on his hand. His fingers closed over hers, offering warmth. "You were a baby," he said. "I remember that age. Erik was two when I was granted custody."

"You obviously take age-appropriate development into consideration. My parents expect more. Their current embarrassment is that I'm not a vice president yet. And since I'm not, I should come home and work for the family real estate business, where I'll be kept safe from disappointing them."

"At least your parents have expectations of you. Unreasonable ones, however." There was an odd note in his voice. She pulled back, intending to search his expression, but an impressive burst of forked lightning caused her to squeeze her eyes shut instead.

"Not unreasonable according to them," she said after the accompanying thunder passed, trying and failing to hide the shakiness in her voice. "My father was a senior vice president when he was my age. Of course, he works for his uncle." She plastered a smile on her face. "Yours must be proud of you, however. Award-winning movies, Sundance selection, now directing a major studio film. And I've seen you with Erik. He can't ask for a better parent."

"Hmm," he said, a noncommittal low rumble. She glanced at him, but his face was still, his gaze fixed on the storm in the distance. They listened to the rain rattling on the roof, the blackness beyond the windshield absolute save for another distant display of lightning, more faded strobe than angry gods throwing bolts of energy. A camera flash compared to the megawatt brightness of the earlier strikes.

"You were right," she said, knowing she should pull her hand from his but enjoying the gentle pressure of his skin against hers too much to follow her brain's wise advice. "The storm's moving away from us."

"The sound and light show portion, definitely," he agreed. As if in response to his words, the velocity of the rain started to lessen to a steady thrum. "But…"

"But it's still too chancy to drive to the ranch in the dark, so we need to stay here until morning." She knew where he had been headed. "How far do these seats recline? I've seen the back seat, I'll take my chances here."

"Sleepy?" He quirked an eyebrow at her.

"Not in the slightest." Her heart was beating as if she'd just finished a triathlon, the adrenaline from the storm still spiking her blood. Winding down to a point where she might get some rest was going to take hours. Combine that with sharing the same six-foot space at Xavier and she doubted she would blink all night, much less grab some shut-eye. She wriggled in her seat, and if Xavier's gaze threw sparks, well, that was a bonus. "Not the most comfortable chair." The cushioning had passed its prime sometime in the last decade. "But beats trying to sleep during a red-eye on a budget airline."

Xavier gently untangled their fingers. "Wait. Stay here. I have a better idea." He had his door open before she could react.

"Where are you going?" But he had already left the truck.

What the…? Sutton relaxed in her seat, flummoxed. He wasn't abandoning her, was he? But even as the thought appeared on her brain's scroll, she dismissed it. There was nowhere for him to go.

Then the pickup rocked, followed by thumps and bangs, and then a sound like an air compressor. She turned to look out the rear window but only saw an occasional slash of light, as if Xavier was moving around with a flashlight. By the time he returned to the cab, his clothing dark from rain and his hair slick, her curiosity was nearly bursting. And she could swear he was trying to hide something. "What were you doing? You're soaking wet."

"It's not that that bad. The deluge is slowing." He grinned, his gaze bright. "Your palace awaits, madam."

"My *what*?"

"I remembered Dalip has a pop-up tent on the truck's bed. He uses it to camp when scouting remote locations. I set it up. Took a little longer than I expected, given the weather. But you have a bed. Well, air mattress."

"You set up a tent?" Sutton blinked at him.

"You didn't seem too thrilled about sleeping in the cab. Can't say I blame you." He glanced out the windshield. "Seems to be a sprinkle now, if you want to go check it out."

"There's a tent. On the back of the truck." She still couldn't wrap her head around the concept.

"You don't go camping much, do you? It's a common setup."

"I only camp in hotels. With hot and cold running water. And room service."

"Can't do anything about hot water. But…" He pulled a plastic bag from behind his back and took out two bottles of water and a box of protein bars. "Room service, courtesy of Dalip. There are more bottles in the tent. You're not allergic to nuts?"

"Not at all."

He held the box out to her, taking a bar for himself. "Dinner is served. Sorry we aren't stopping for shakes and burgers as we originally planned."

She tore the shiny wrapper off. She'd thought she wouldn't get to eat until they returned to the ranch, and her stomach growled to remind her how empty it was. Protein bars weren't on her list of favorite foodstuffs, but the first taste was heavenly. "That place had great reviews, but right now this is a five-star meal."

He nodded, swallowing. "Only the best."

"You do know how to show a woman a good time," she agreed. Then her words hit her and she sat up, her back straight and her shoulders frozen around her ears. "I mean… not like…before. Or like a date. I didn't think this was a date. I'm just, y'know, making conversation."

"We both previously established this is not a date."

"Right." She took another bite. "No date."

"Nope."

"Just work."

"Always."

Always? She turned toward him. "What does that mean?"

"I'm sorry?" He polished off the rest of his bar with one bite.

"Just work. Always."

He waited until he had finished chewing to answer. "Means we work together."

"I know, but…" Her bar began to taste like peanut-flavored wet cement, and she wrapped up what was left. "Always. Sounds so…infinite. And yet finite."

"When did you become hung up on semantics? It's just a word."

"That's the thing." She swung around in her seat to face him. "We work with words. We tell stories with them. It's never 'just'—" she made air quotes with her fingers—"a word."

He regarded her. "I'm missing subtext. And that's not a new feeling. Been going on since you arrived."

"'Always' indicates you think we'll always be work colleagues.

He frowned. "And that's not a good thing, judging by how you're fixating on this."

She huffed. "I'm not fixating. I find it…revealing."

"Sutton, I'm not implying you should work with me forever."

But once he did imply that. He more than implied that, he outright said they should collaborate on films—and more. She told him, standing in his hallway, that the past could not be undone. She continued to stand by what she said. But why did his words hurt so?

Even as she asked herself the question, she knew why. Because "always" also implied they would only ever be work colleagues. Nothing more."

"I do want to continue to work together to make *The Quantum Wraith* a success." He threw her a sideways glance. "What do you say? Partners in reaching our goals?"

Her promotion. Cementing his status as an A-level director. Those were the terms they had set and to which she agreed.

There was indeed nothing more.

"Of course. Partners. On this film." She held out her water bottle as if making a toast. "Here's to long and healthy individual careers. For both of us."

"Cheers." He tapped his bottle against hers. "Glad we got that settled."

"And if I get Chester's job, I might be able to make that a reality."

"How's that going?"

She shifted in her seat. "Good." She shifted again. "I think."

"You think?" He moved to face her. "Any trouble with the production?"

She shook her head. "They're happy with what they've seen so far. Although they reserve the right to change their opinion at any time."

"Of course they do. So, what is wrong?"

She shifted again. "This seat, for one." He narrowed his gaze at her and she sighed. "I'm not the only person they are considering. And my competition…let's say he's better connected than I am." Ugh. She did not want to think about Zeke Fountaine. Not tonight.

Xavier regarded her, his expression unreadable. "Is that your dream? To be Chester?"

"Without the larceny and the sexism—Contessina told me about her encounters with him—yeah, sure." The little ball of anxiety that was omnipresent in her stomach kicked into high gear, bouncing off the walls, riding the rising waves of acid. She almost missed the storm. As terrified as her limbic system had been, at least she hadn't been thinking about work and the situation at Monument Studios.

"That doesn't sound very convincing."

"Of course I want Chester's job. It's the next step on the ladder."

"The ladder to what?"

"To being the president of the studio. And then CEO."

She folded her arms over her chest, trying to tamp down annoyance at the obvious questions.

He looked at over the rim of his water bottle. "Was being CEO always your dream?"

The passenger seat was supremely uncomfortable. She couldn't find an agreeable position. "What if it wasn't? People change. Dreams change. Doesn't mean I don't want that job now."

Her tone dared him to challenge her. He cocked his head as if considering taking up the dare, but after a beat, he dropped his gaze. Crumpling up his energy bar wrapper, he placed it in the plastic bag and then held the bag out to her. "Trash?"

She shook her head, placing what was left of her bar in her tote. Slinging the bag over her shoulder, she grabbed her water bottle from the cup holder. "You said there's a tent on the back of the truck?"

"Yes. I'll show you."

"I can find it. Sounds like it's hard to miss."

"There are some tricks—"

"To getting in a tent? I can handle it. I also need to… find a friendly bush." One thing about working on location, she'd learned, was to not be squeamish about asking about the available bathroom facilities.

"Ah." Xavier turned and reached into the rear seat, coming up with another plastic bag, a packet of biodegradable wipes, and a water bottle with what looked like a large squeeze top. "Here. We should practice not leaving a trace."

She juggled the items. "Hence the bag for the used wipes."

He nodded. "And water for washing up. Plus this." He

handed her a flashlight, keeping one for himself. "Also might be handy."

"My compliments on the accommodations. Almost all the comforts of home." She saluted him the best she could with her hands full and exited the pickup.

The rain was a light drizzle now, but she had to splash through some deep puddles, testimony that Xavier had been wise not to chance being caught in a surprise flood. After completing her business, she made her way to the rear of the truck. An aluminum ladder led to the tent perched above the bed, and she climbed up, noting an electric lantern hanging from a hook so she wouldn't be reliant on the flashlight or her phone.

The floor of the tent was an air mattress, as Xavier had promised. A fleece blanket was folded at the foot, and there were even two pillows, small ones, like the kind given out on airlines for long-haul flights. Better than she'd ever expect when stuck in an uninhabited stretch of Arizona desert.

She kicked off her shoes, and there was no way she'd be comfortable enough to sleep in her bra, so off it came, too. Then she wrapped herself in the blanket and settled in, turning off the lantern before closing her eyes.

And then opened them immediately.

There was no way she was going to be able to fall asleep.

Not with his words ringing in her ears, bounding across her brain like a kitten high on catnip and chasing a laser pointer. She sighed, pulled her socks and hiking boots on, and descended the steps, coming around the rear of the truck to the driver's side.

Xavier had the chair reclined and the hood of his sweatshirt pulled low over his eyes. She could make out the blackness of his beard and the fullness of his lips, those utterly maddening, kissable lips—

She banged on the window with her fist. He jumped, sitting up with the flashlight clutched as if it were a very short baseball bat and he was about to swing for a home run.

"It's me!" she said, holding up her hands on the universal sign for surrender and trying not to laugh at his murderous expression. Which was also really hot, she had to admit. Protective Xavier was a turn-on. "Just want to talk."

He rolled down his window. "Sutton? What the hell. Are you okay?"

"I'm fine. Were you sleeping? I'm sorry."

"No, I wasn't. What are you doing out there? Is it still raining?"

To be honest, Sutton hasn't noticed. She took stock. "More like misting, I'd say."

"Get inside the truck. Is there something wrong with the tent?"

She stayed where she was. "The tent is great. And this won't take much of your time."

He leaned out, putting their heads at a level height. "Then how can I help you?"

"Why did you ask if this was my dream job?"

His gaze narrowed in confusion. "You're standing in the rain—"

"Mist."

"—to ask me that? We have a long drive tomorrow in which to talk."

Tomorrow would be too late. Tomorrow they would be back to director and producer.

"I can't sleep," she said, leaning on the truth. "I need to know."

He glanced at his phone. "You've been gone only twenty minutes. You haven't tried to sleep."

"Why did you ask me that? As if I've…disappointed you in some way.

He sighed, pushing his hood up so he could catch and hold her gaze. "I thought you would be a filmmaker. Or a screenwriter. Someone creative."

"Ha!" She couldn't control the outburst, and it was loud. "And I am creative."

"I admit, you can do things to a spreadsheet that are highly original."

"And legal. Don't forget legal. That's not the creativity I meant."

"Stipulated. But…" He shrugged. "You have a gift. I thought you would use your talents to tell your own stories."

"I have a *what*?" Her jaw dropped to the desert floor. "You never thought that."

Now it was his turn to gape at her. "I did."

"You did not. You gave me a C on my final screenplay."

"And?"

"And?" She stared at him. How did she ever think he was attractive? Even though he was. But still. That had been a lead bullet that had torn through the deepest depths of her soul. "How was I supposed to think I had 'a gift' when you handed me one of the lowest grades in the seminar?"

He crossed his arms on the window ledge. "Sutton. You

half-assed that screenplay. You leaned on stereotypes and used clichéd tropes. The world-building was nonexistent. The dialogue on the nose. C was me being generous."

She couldn't speak for a minute, her entire body trembling as her mind tried to process his words. "Well," she finally said, "good to see my work made an impression on you."

"It made an impression because your earlier work was superior," he said. "You're one of the most gifted natural storytellers I've encountered. I told you that."

His face wavered in front of her as if underwater. Then something hot ran down her cheeks and she realized the wetness on her face was not mist but tears. "Oh, come on. We both know you were just being nice, saying things I wanted to hear because I, y'know, chucked myself at you. I don't blame you—"

He cut her off. "You think I… Seriously, what the hell, Sutton?" He stopped and then threw back the hood of his sweatshirt, the better to hold her gaze with his. "'They make us study algebra and calculus even though I have yet to meet a body who needed to find the coefficient in their daily life. But they never teach us the math of loneliness, how sometimes five hundred can be more isolating than one.'"

Her heart raced, then slowed. Time became meaningless as she stared into his warm dark eyes. "That's from the short film screenplay I turned in as part of my application for your seminar."

"I don't say things I don't mean. Ever. Not even to screenwriters who refuse to believe in their own talent. And who think people are nice to them out of ulterior motives."

Their gazes continue to tangle until water beaded along

Sutton's nose and fell with a drip, causing her to break contact to wipe the moisture away. She glanced up, and got a raindrop in her eye. Either the storm had been taking a hiatus, or another one was on the way.

"So," he continued, "you can tell me being a studio executive is your dream. But I'm damn sure it didn't used to be."

And damn him for being right. "Maybe. But it's my job now and I'm good at it."

"You are. But—"

"No buts. Remember our earlier conversation? We're going to work together to get what we want now." She blinked, willing the tears still threatening to fall to disappear.

The other dream had been buried long ago. Knowing he really did believe in her talent poured some salve on her wounded psyche, but in the end, did his validation truly matter?

She'd chosen the correct path. The entertainment industry could be mercurial and there was no such thing as job security, but she was proving her parents wrong and demonstrating she could climb the corporate ladder. And without being related to the company's owners. "I think I can sleep now, so thank you. I need to go."

"Sutton," he called after her, but if he had anything else to say, she didn't hear him over the shower gathering velocity again. She made it to the tent before the deluge started in earnest, taking off her wet top and leggings to wrap herself in the blanket. She put all thoughts of Xavier and her career firmly out of her head. Really, what did it matter what she wanted to do when she was in her early twenties? People change their minds all the time. His words about her gift, she didn't dare dwell on. She let the white noise of the rain lull her into a fitful slumber.

Until a strike of lightning turned the tent's darkness into daylight, followed by a rumble of thunder that shook the pickup. She bolted awake, fear crowding her mind, disoriented by the unfamiliar surroundings at first.

Another burst, another reverberation. The scent of ozone was overpowering. The storm was on top of the truck, bringing wind that tugged at the tent, causing the sides to heave in and out as if the structure was hyperventilating along with Sutton. Her heart raced, her palms were damp, and… air. She couldn't get enough air. She was suffocating, the canvas walls closing in, there was no escape—

"Sutton. You okay?" Xavier was near. Just outside the tent.

She couldn't speak. It took everything she had to wrap the blanket around her before crawling to the tent opening. Trembling, she unzipped the flap.

Xavier appeared, concern creasing his face. Wordlessly, she opened her arms.

He understood her request. Warm hands grasped her shoulders and held her as she shook. He guided her away from the opening and the wind and the rain, back into the sheltered warmth.

A white-blue burst of light turned the atmosphere from night to noon, accompanied by a shaking rumble. She fell into his lap, pressing her face against his shoulder, not caring his Henley was soaking wet. He cradled her as if she were infinitely precious.

She knew he was offering comfort out of pity, the bare minimum a decent human would offer to another person in distress, but she'd take it. She'd take whatever he had to give. Later on, when the primal terror subsided, embarrassment might set in. Or shame. Or anger at herself, for allowing a natural weather phenomena to turn her into a terrified child. But she stored up these minutes regardless, to be taken out and examined, treasured, held close like he held her now.

The past could not be changed. But in the future, she would always remember that when she needed him, he appeared.

"Three seconds." His low voice rumbled against her ear.

"Three?"

"The time between the lightning and the thunder."

The canvas of the tent was lit by a bright flash as if in response. She squeezed her eyes shut.

"One. Two. Three." He stroked small circles on her back. "Four. Five. Six."

The thunder boomed.

"The storm is moving away," he said into her hair. "It'll be over soon."

Her nails were clawing into his shoulders. She commanded her fingers to relax. They reluctantly agreed.

"Thanks," she said, pulling back so she could catch his gaze, despite wishing she could stay where she was into the next week, if not into the next century. "I'm sorry."

"For what?"

"You might have bruises in the morning. Or scratches. Or both. I wasn't paying attention."

"Didn't feel a thing."

"Good." She relaxed, a shuddering sigh. But when the next strike came, she dug hard without thinking.

"Except for that one." His laugh was more felt, a vibration against her cheek, than heard. "But you're worth a little pain, Sutton Spencer."

She turned her face into his neck, breathing in his scent, her lips a whisper away from tasting the warmth of his skin, the soft bristles of his beard brushing her skin. "Thank you," she said. "Thank you for being here."

They sat listening to the wind and rain buffet the tent. She'd have to congratulate Dalip for his choice of gear. The canvas shimmied and shook, but the overall structure was sound. Here, in the dim light of the lantern surrounded by blackness: it was easy to imagine they were only two people left in the universe. No distractions, no interruptions, just them.

He cleared his throat, and discretely adjusted his lightweight khaki trousers. "The storm is subsiding. It's been several minutes since the last lightning strike. I should leave, let you get some sleep."

Her arms trembled, the adrenaline and fear that had flooded her system draining away. She was suddenly tired, so tired. But not sleepy. No, she was tired of the rules and strictures by which she lived her life.

Those principles kept her parents at bay and, above all, kept her professionally and financially secure as possible. But tonight, Xavier prioritized her emotional safety. He ensured she wasn't alone and terrified. She could more than take care of herself, but having someone volunteer to be her shield when her defenses were down…

No one else had ever offered to do that for her that she could recall.

"Stay here," she said. "There's enough room for two."

His gaze lowered, flashing darkly, and she realized her blanket had slipped to reveal the top curves of her breasts. And to also reveal she had removed her shirt and bra, leaving her bare under the fleece.

Heat began to spiral and coil low in her belly. "My clothes were wet."

"I get that," he said. "Which is why I need to go." But he didn't move, his arms draped around her.

She licked her suddenly dry lips, and his loose grip on her shoulder tightened. "Silly to do that when there is a comfy mattress here."

Their gazes tangled in the dim light, and she found herself holding her breath, wishing harder than she wished in ten years. Then his hands fell, leaving cold air where his warm touch had been. "It's better for the both of us if I leave."

"Don't be a martyr. You're not going to get any sleep in that seat."

He swung his head to catch her gaze and the feral intensity caused her to fall back, just a little. "Neither of us will sleep if I stay here, and you know that. But you've had a traumatic evening. I understand you might not be thinking clearly, so the gentlemanly thing to do is stay in the truck cab."

Oh, no, she was thinking clearly. Maybe with the most clarity she'd had in years. "I don't want to be by myself right now, true. I'm still a bit shaky. But—" she scooted closer to him, placing her hand on his bearded jaw, loving the tickle of the soft bristles against her skin "—I also want to be with *you*. Not any warm body. You."

He was still. Only the rising and falling of his chest indicated he had not been magicked into stone. "We have a deal, Sutton. I need *The Quantum Wraith* to work."

"So do I. But we're not at the ranch. We're not on the set. We're in a…time-out."

A faint smile appeared. "Like a toddler?"

"Like…a hockey box penalty. Once we're out of the box, normal gameplay can resume." Not her best simile, but the heat bubbling in her veins, reflected in his gaze, was starting to take over her synapses.

Ten years ago, she and Xavier had been on a porch swing, chatting about recent films and Sutton's plans for life after graduation. Then an errant push of his foot had sent her tumbling against him and the simmering attraction that had been present since she first set eyes on him in his seminar burst into a raging conflagration. She couldn't remember who kissed who first now, but seared forever on her brain were the firmness of his lips, the taste of his mouth, their tongues exploring and licking and sucking until he carried her from the porch to his living room sofa. She hadn't been a virgin, but she hadn't been very experienced, and just a few strokes of his thumb underneath the soaking fabric of her panties made her fall apart in his arms, shuddering and crying with joy that she was finally his.

Then a blur in her mind of hands scrambling, unbuttoning, unzipping, even ripping in the case of her underwear. Hopping on one foot to kick a shoe off, their mouths somehow remaining connected even as he lifted her T-shirt over her head. Her sigh as her breasts spilled into his palms, her nipples so tight that one slight brush of his finger caused her to quake with pleasure-pain.

His erection, hot and heavy and hard, his gasp loud and guttural when she rubbed the beading moisture over his tip, his hips jerking as her fingers traced the prominent vein, moving lower, loving how his eyes rolled back in his head, this oh so carefully controlled man powerless in her hands, begging her—

Then her phone ringing. And ringing. And ringing. Her parents demanding to know where she was on graduation night, insisting she stay the night at their hotel so they could make sure she stayed safe on a night when her classmates were undoubtedly drunk and otherwise disorderly. His insistence that she go, spend this time that would never come again with her family. The two of them now would be able to explore the world, and each other, at their leisure. Making plans to meet the next day in his office.

The letter she now knew she never received.

She tried to move closer to Xavier, but her limbs tangled in the blanket. She kicked it away, not caring she was clad only in her utilitarian white cotton underwear. "Besides, we never finished what we started all those years ago. I don't like leaving a project unfinished."

The storm had removed what had been left of the day's heat. She should be shivering, bare to cool air. But his gaze burned hotter than a July noon in the desert. If she wasn't careful, she would incinerate.

But what a way to go.

Ten

"The best thing about storms? They clear the air, bring a fresh start."
"The best thing about storms is they end. Eventually."
    Con Sulley and Lys Amarga, *The Quantum Wraith*

"Hockey penalty box, you said." Xavier's raspy tones made Sutton shudder. She had to swallow a few times before she had enough moisture in her mouth to answer him.

"Yes. When the time ends, like, say, the sun comes up, we go back to our usual activity as if nothing happened."

"You don't have to do this. I'm not expecting anything. If another storm arrives, I promise I'll come back." His arms remained by his side, but his fists clenched and unclenched.

"This isn't a transactional obligation." She took his right hand in hers, kissed his knuckles, and then turned his hand over to place a kiss against his now open palm. "Here's how much I want this." She led his hand between her legs, to the soaked fabric of her panties. "This is how much I want you."

His eyelids fluttered, and she literally pressed her advantage, guiding his palm to cup hard against her demanding, aching core. "Any additional objections about my possible motivations?" she murmured in his ear.

He shook his head, a knowing grin appearing on his face. His expression made her melt ever faster. "No, ma'am. Did I ever tell you I like hockey?"

"No." She mock frowned. "You didn't."

"Maybe that's because I didn't know I appreciated the sport until now, when I learned about this box concept." His hand no longer needed her assistance. The heel of his palm pushed into her, retreated, rubbing and pulling the fabric of her panties against her aching, demanding clit. His fingers pressed into her, one, two, and she could only gasp and hold on to his shoulders as she rode his knowing, insistent touch. She wanted to slow down, savor this twice in a lifetime night. But she was also greedy for more, harder, faster…

And just like that night, she broke and then flew without barely any warning, her orgasm leaving her shaking and shuddering and mindless, the pleasure so exquisite she saw constellations whirling around her.

"I love watching you do that." She opened her eyes to find him gazing at her with a smug smile on his lips, still stroking her but gently, softly, allowing her to descend safely back to earth.

He earned the smugness, she supposed. But now it was her turn. "And once again, you're still dressed. I call foul."

There was far less room in the tent and he helped her push his khakis off, his erection tenting his boxers, promising to be as bold and breathtaking as in her erotic daydreams of the last ten years. But when she reached out to remove that final barrier, he captured her hands in his. "I don't suppose you have any condoms. Because I don't."

She shook her head. "No, sadly. Also, assuming no test results I should know about? Nothing to tell you on my part."

"No."

"Good. Because if we are redoing that night...." She freed him from his boxers, her eyes closing at having his silky hard length in her hands once more, hers to survey and learn anew. "This is what comes next."

She ran her fingers up and down, encircled him, rediscovered which spots elicited a moan, what strokes caused his hips to buck. She played with timing and speed, with pressure and movement, and when his eyes began to roll back in his head, she stopped and gently pushed him back on the air mattress.

He leaned up on his elbows, his eyelids heavy, his jaw clenched in what she knew was an effort to keep his control. "Had your fun? Good. My turn again."

"Fun hasn't even started," she whispered in his ear, before sliding down to take him in her mouth, wanting to moan at the feel of him, the heat, the harness and tension, finally.

This was new. The intent had been there, but the phone call from her parents kept the action from happening. She loved his taste, salty bittersweet and uniquely Xavier. The way he moved, the way his hands tangled in her curls, the way he muttered encouragement and praise with words low and rasped and profane.

The way he looked at her, his gaze wild and dark with physical want, but also something deeper, more hallowed.

His fingers twisted in her hair. "Sutton, stop..."

She didn't stop. Her fingers found the sensitive ridge of his cock while her tongue worshipped the satiny smooth head, drawing him deeper, exulting as she played with suction, wetness, speed, learning what made him gasp and his hips buck. And when he shouted and tensed, muscles rigid, she didn't let go but stayed with him, holding him fast with her mouth and her hands until his tremors subsided and his eyes fluttered open. "Hey."

"Hey." She placed on last kiss on his lower stomach before shimmying up to join him, curling into his side. He drew the blanket over them both, tucking the edges around her.

"That was..." His voice trailed off in the dark.

"I know." She kissed his cheek. "It was."

"We should probably talk, but—" he yawned "—words... won't form."

"Penalty box," she reminded him. "No talking necessary. Get some rest."

A light snore was her only response.

She smiled, snuggling closer to his warmth. Not that she would be able to sleep, despite the blackout-inducing orgasm earlier. Thoughts and impressions tumbled through her head: his gasp-moan when her fingers found the sensitive ridge along the length of his cock. The dark fire in his gaze when she pressed his hand against her wetness.

His arms, cradling her, as she shivered with fear. Those same arms holding her as she let go and flew apart. Keeping her safe. Not because he thought she couldn't protect herself but because he wanted to. Because he cared. About her.

If she wasn't careful, she was going to convince herself he did care.

Or maybe…she was projecting her feelings onto him.

Penalty box, she repeated to herself. None of this would matter once they returned to the Pronghorn. Or so she lied as she fell asleep.

She woke to the first tentative rays of the day streaming through the tent's mesh window. Xavier must have opened the covering after the rain stopped. The air was cool but promised a hot day ahead, the skies wide open and endlessly blue as if the storms never happened. She stretched out her leg to find Xavier's to make the most of the time they had before returning to the ranch.

But she encountered only an empty mattress. For a split second, she worried that he had left her, old wounds popping to the surface, until her synapses came fully awake and reminded her she was on top of the truck. Unless he felt like trekking miles through the desert, he was close.

She found her now dry leggings and top and got dressed, and then zipped open the tent opening. Only to pause, struck dumb by the beauty that was Xavier taking photos of the sunrise. He wore only his khakis, slung low on his narrow hips, outlining that glorious ass that had been her privilege to caress and cup. His back muscles rippled under his skin as he hoisted the SLR, framing and the firing one shot after another. The pink-gold light created chestnut highlights in his tousled dark hair that narrowly missed his shoulders. The desert in the early morning was spectacular, the rocks even richer shades of terra-cotta, red and ochre than before, the saguaro cacti standing sentinels against a crisp sky. But Xavier… Xavier was magnificent.

He turned around, a grin appearing when he saw her. She waved, a bit self-conscious, aware she must look far from her best. She enjoyed the front view as much as the rear, her gaze lingering on his chest with its thick mat of crisply curling hair, leading to the dark trail disappearing below the waistband of his pants. He lifted an inquisitive eyebrow at her frankly objectifying stare, even posing for a brief second like a Greek statue with his camera instead of a slingshot before swinging the SLR up to his right eye and clicking off several photos…of her sitting cross-legged in the opening of the tent, her arms folded in her lap, and her eyes—she didn't want to know what he might see in her eyes. Lust. Want. Oh, she wanted him. Now. Still. She squirmed with want for him.

But she was also afraid she might want more from him. And that scared her.

"Stop!" she laughed, bringing her hands in front of her face in the universal "no photos, please" stance. "I was reliably informed there would be no paparazzi."

"Sorry," he said. "Photographer's law applies. When one sees a captivating subject, one must capture it."

She looked to her left, then to her right. "The truck? I guess the tent is interesting."

"Funny." He lowered the camera and played with the settings, then rapidly popped off several shots before Sutton could react.

"Hey! I demand photo approval."

"You won't want to delete." He strode to the pickup and handed his camera to her. "Take a look."

The camera weighed more than she expected, and she balanced it on her lap, bringing her right leg up and putting her foot on the ladder's top rung to act as a brace. Turning on the screen, she started to swipe through the images.

His landscapes were stunning, playing with angles and lighting, depth of field and focus. A shot of the rising sun between the arms of a saguaro took her breath away with its composition and use of color.

Then she came to the photos of her. And she almost dropped the expensive equipment.

"Careful," Xavier said, his hands brushing hers to steady the expensive equipment, and she almost lost her grip again. "That's my favorite camera."

She stared, transfixed, at the woman on the screen. The Sutton he captured looked confident, happy. She glowed, the morning light casting a halo that outlined her against the blackness of the tent, her cheeks flushed, her eyes sparkling. She looked like a woman in love. A woman who was loved. But cameras lied, as she well knew. "I can see why it's your favorite. The lens flatters the subject."

"The subject needs no flattery." He took the camera and began packing his equipment for the drive back while she found a convenient bush and freshened up for the day ahead. They met back at the rear of the truck, and she offered him what she hoped would read as a bright smile. "Time to leave?"

He frowned. "Is everything okay?"

"Great, why?" Damn him for his usual perception. Seeing his portraits of her had thrown her, reminded her of the images that had chased her into sleep and embedded in her dreams, where Xavier held her tight and whispered how much he cared against her ear.

He regarded her. "Do we need to talk?"

"About…? Oh, you mean the morning-after talk. We're good. Aren't we?"

"I asked you first. You seem a bit off."

She laughed. If there was a note of artificiality in her mirth, so be it. "I'm great. Because last night was in the—"

"Penalty box."

"Right." She nodded. "And you?"

"In the box. All good."

"Awesome. Then…" she cast about for a change of subject "… I guess we should start putting away the tent—wait! My hat. It's inside."

If there was a sign her brain was still jumbled from the activities of the night before, forgetting to wear sun protection in the desert was one. She scrambled up the ladder and found her hat where it had somehow gotten wedged into a corner. A quick run of her fingers through her hair told her she had a tangled mess on top of her head, and she sat in the tent's opening, feet dangling, while she tucked as many errant curls as she could up into the hat.

But when she went to move her legs, intending to turn around and descend, Xavier used his large palms to hold her thighs in place. She looked down at him. "Pretty sure the tent can't come down if I stay here."

"I was wondering." His tone was casual, but his hands started to trace suggestive patterns on the fabric of her leggings, moving from her outer thighs to inner in lazy sweeps and swirls. "When does the penalty time expire?"

The molten heat that was never far away when he was near began to pool as desire stabbed her deep and low. A shuddering sigh escaped her. "I thought we said in the morning."

His hands traveled higher, causing her nipples to pebble and her hips to squirm. "It's still morning," he pointed out with impeccable logic.

"But shouldn't we get back to the ranch?" Her legs fell open as his gentle urging and he put to good use his recently learned knowledge of her personal geography, which ultra-sensitive spot to whisper his fingers over and which spot to avoid.

"Soon." He cupped his right hand hard against her, and she whimpered. "I never leave a project unfinished."

"I'm positive you didn't—oh!" He deserted her aching core to find the waistband of her leggings. Together they tugged them off, his palms warm on her belly, her ass.

Finally—*finally*—the fabric barrier was gone, leaving her bare and open to his sight and touch.

"Not enough light last night," he murmured, his gaze dark and liquid and hot as he took her in. He found her clit, a gentle flick that caused her hips to buck, and then pressed a finger deep inside, her pussy clenching without thought around the welcome invitation. "You're so wet," he said with something like awe in his voice.

She laughed, both at his expression and for the sheer pleasure-joy of the moment. "For you."

She'd never been this exposed outdoors, never skinny dipped, never even stripped in a private backyard. She hadn't showered in a day; she was wearing yesterday's clothes. And this was the most erotic experience of her life to date.

He lifted his gaze to hold hers. Pinning her in place. Not letting her escape. "You're gorgeous, Sutton. The camera has no idea."

Her breath was gone and with it her words. But if anyone deserved to be captured on film, it was him. Xavier, his dark gaze blazing, his beautiful lips in a half smile, his warm-toned olive skin burnished by the morning sun and looking at her as if she were everything he could ever want.

Her heart hurt.

Her future wouldn't hold Xavier. They'd made their pact. They were colleagues with mutual goals, nothing more. But this moment, this connection, this hot burning flame threatening to consume her and leave nothing but smoldering ash—this moment could never be taken away from her. She could no longer hold herself upright and she fell onto her elbows, her focus solely on him and his exploring hands.

His fingers paid homage to her clit, at first gentle, delicate. Then the rhythm that sent her over the edge began to build. They might not have much time, but she didn't need much, the spiraling pressure building and building until—

He stopped.

Her eyes flew open. What was wrong? Did something…? Was he not…?

He caught her gaze and he smiled. It was not a nice smile. His expression was devious and dirty and told her he knew exactly how near the precipice she was and what would send her over. Her pulse, already racing, began to beat in staccato rhythm as he held her there, his thumb lightly brushing over her clit, his fingers pressing deep whenever she started to back away from the edge. Just when she thought she couldn't take the provocation any longer, he lowered his head, kissing her stomach, tasting her thighs. "This is the project I didn't get to last night."

He replaced his fingers with his mouth.

She dissolved into pure flame, her world reduced to heat and wetness and the rasp of his beard against sensitive, sensitized skin. His mouth worshipped her small bud of nerves, paying persistent attention as his hands gripped her legs, holding her still when she would squirm from so much pressure, so much suction, a whirlpool of desire and want she could not escape, would not be allowed to escape. His tongue dove and laved, licking, sucking, commanding she be present, here, focused only on him and her and the fire demanding she give herself over, fly apart for him in broad daylight, outdoors, no pretense, nowhere to hide—

She screamed, the flame consuming her, the tension releasing in a burst of energy so bright, so powerful she lost all sense of reality, lost somewhere in distant galaxy of pure sensation. He hummed appreciatively against her, his ministrations slowing, bringing her down from the enormous peak she just summited. She leaned up on her elbows, her hazy gaze slowly focusing on the sight of Xavier's tousled dark hair between her thighs. This. This would be the memory that sent a thousand vibrators to their graveyard in her future.

Xavier raised his head when her limbs went completely lax. He smiled at her and her heart, already overloaded, could no longer muster the defenses for her walls. She was falling in love with Xavier. And it wasn't the crush-on-her-talented-professor kind of love, the first love of a young adult who was testing her boundaries after a restrictive childhood. This was true, honest, deep.

And hopeless.

Still, she mustered a smile for him. Made it seductive, knowing, as she slowly sat up straight and rearranged her clothes, her nerves still thrumming even as delicious entropy set in, her arms and legs heavy. She carefully made her way down the ladder, coming up flush against him. The heavy bulge in the front of his khakis demanded her attention and her hands cupped, stroked. "Turnabout is fair play."

But when she would coax the zipper of his fly open, his hands grasped hers, stilling their movements. "Believe me, there is nothing I want more," he said. "But we should get going." He gave her a crooked smile. "You seem less…glum."

If only he knew. She hugged her recent revelation close, so it wouldn't escape. "Hard to be glum when you're still seeing stars on the inside of your eyelids. I could offer you a rain check?"

Too late, she realized the concept of rain checks were not compatible with the time sensitive penalty box pretense they were using. "Or not," she continued airily. "How do we put the tent away?"

In the end, taking down the structure took only a matter of minutes, Sutton admiring the ingenuity of whoever decided pop-up tents for trucks needed to be a thing and then creating one. They silently ensured they left no trace at their impromptu camping site, securing their trash to deposit in civilization. Before the sun could move much further above the horizon they were in their seats, the sky serenely blue, with only the odd remaining puddle serving as evidence of last night's storm.

Xavier put the truck into gear, and before Sutton knew it they were on the main road that would take them back to the highway and then to Pronghorn. He looked over at her. "Tired?"

"Not really." She stared out her window, watching the landscape flash by.

He gripped the steering wheel, his gaze fixed on the road. "When I took custody of Erik, I made a vow. He would come first. I'd raise him with all the care and love Rosalie had planned to give him."

She shot him a glance, curious as to why he brought up Erik. "And from what I can tell, you're doing just that."

"I knew he would have to grow up without Rosalie. And his dad…his dad is a real piece of work."

She touched his thigh, a brush of comfort. "You've said."

"My parents…well. They never left me alone in a hotel room when I was three. They have that going for them. But they're not what people would call involved. Or present."

Xavier and Sutton were on a straight stretch of the highway, with few other cars out so early on a Sunday. This time she let her hand rest on his leg. His left hand remained firmly on the steering wheel, but his right hand found hers, squeezed tight.

"I didn't want Erik to grow up like I did, with parents who were more emotionally absent than not. And Erik's bio parents either couldn't or wouldn't be with him. It was up to me to ensure he had stability and security. It was the least I could do for him. Him and Rosalie."

"I'm glad he has you," she said softly. "I like spending time with him."

"About that." He shot a glance at her and brought both hands to the steering wheel. "I've had my share of relationships, some serious. One, I thought was maybe heading toward marriage."

Her heart gave an unexpected, painful thump. "Was that Mimi Kingston?" she asked in what she hoped was a light tone.

"You know about Mimi?"

"Keep your eyes on the road, please," she teased. "And, no, not really. Contessina said something about how you don't do showmance hookups, and she implied Mimi was the reason."

"Contessina said something?"

"You know how crews like to gossip."

He shook his head. "Anyway, Mimi and I eventually realized we weren't meant for the long haul. But Erik took the breakup hard."

"I'm sorry. That must have been difficult."

His hands tightened on the steering wheel. "Erik's had too many people leave him. I won't bring anyone into his life who doesn't expect to stay."

Apparently there was no escaping a morning-after talk. "We're work colleagues who took a time-out, and now we're returning to work. And I don't picture diamond rings and weddings dresses after one night of sex, Xavier. No matter how amazing it was."

"I'll take the compliment." He shot her an unreadable

glance. "So. I've been thinking. I wouldn't mind if we had more time in the penalty box."

Her pulse started to two-step, but she tamped down her hopes. "Wouldn't mind? I just said the sex was amazing, but you, quote, 'wouldn't mind'?" she teased, affecting a light tone.

His hands relaxed their tight grip. "Let me rephrase. I want to spend more time with you. Beginning with that rain check."

"I see." Her hopes refused to stay subdued. "And you told me about Erik because…"

"This stays between us. Nothing has changed as far as the others on the set know." His glance at her was questioning, as if unsure how she would take the condition.

That was more than fine with her. "I'd have to insist," she said. "It's hard enough being a woman in this industry. You can have a consensual fling on location with whoever you want when it comes to public opinion, but I'll be judged and found wanting of, oh, so many things. Morals, sound reasoning, the ability to control my emotions, the list goes on."

He nodded. "Good ol' double standard."

"Yep. And if I want my promotion…" Acid splashed in her stomach at the thought of Zeke Fountaine discovering she was sleeping with Xavier. He would leverage that knowledge against her, however he could.

"Then maybe we shouldn't." He glanced over. "I don't want to cause trouble for you."

The concern in his voice caused her heart flip over.

Sutton didn't do risk. She made her choices as strategically as possible. to maximize her opportunities to build her career and maintain her financial independence. She lived in fear of proving her parents right and failing, forcing a move back to Orange County and a life working for the family real estate empire like her father.

But she'd be damned if she let worries about Zeke or anyone else at Monument keep her from Xavier. Even if their relationship was only for the duration of production. Even if she knew their futures would always be separate. "As far as I'm concerned, we have ten years of rain checks to make up for and I intend to cash in every single one."

Eleven

"You wear a disguise."

"And you're a master of the obvious."

"I do not speak of your outer appearance. You are in disguise from your heart."

        Autarch Zear and Lys Amarga, *The Quantum Wraith*

Xavier rubbed his aching neck and sighed. The production day had been a long and brutal one involving Contessina and Roberto Madeira, who played Lys's loyal friend and would-be love interest Con, running across the sunbaked landscape in full warrior gear. Xavier was careful to give the actors breaks from the action, ensuring they stayed hydrated and as comfortable as possible, but the desert was the desert.

He was sweaty and covered with dust and grime from a day spent exposed to the elements. He wanted a cool shower and a hot meal, and he wasn't picky about the order.

As a rule, Xavier kept his personal and professional life separate. He meant what he said to Sutton. Erik's life was disruptive enough, growing up on film sets where intense family-like communities form but then dissipate and disappear after several months as everyone headed off to their next project, sometimes never to communicate again. Maybe that was why he messed up his first chance with Sutton. When she didn't respond to his letter, he placed their strong but still unsure connection in the bucket of "intense but temporary production relationships" as a way of sublimating how deeply he felt about her.

Now their relationship was explicitly in that bucket. But the more of Sutton he had, the more he needed. And his need wasn't confined to the sex, amazing as it was.

He wanted *her*. Her smiles, her frowns, the way her eyes crinkled in the corners when she couldn't make a spreadsheet behave to her specifications. Her ease with the crew, settling units that had been at war with each other since day one—like Costuming and Props, who'd had a running battle over control of Lys's battle sword and scabbard—with softly worded suggestions. The way the Arizona sunshine couldn't compete with her smile when it came to lighting up a room.

Not that he'd had much opportunity to slake his thirst. Once at the Pronghorn, they'd separated, and he found himself swept into the hectic maelstrom that always occurred at this point in production, when the newness had worn off but the cast and crew realize they still had multiple weeks to go, working on the same old project. Creative choices became narrower as continuity took over and they had to adhere to decisions made earlier, even if those decisions weren't optimal in hindsight. And the grind of twelve- to fourteen-hour days—especially for the PAs and assistant directors, who were the first to arrive on set and the last to leave—sapped energy and could turn even the most good-natured crew members into grumblers.

Normally Xavier relished the challenge of maintaining morale on the set, finding new ways to engage and inspire the team, to continue pushing them to deliver their best work. But his inability to be with Sutton was sorely testing his patience. In the last two weeks, they'd had few hurried encounters in her office during a meal break—thankfully her desk was sturdy—and once he snuck in and out of her room like a teenager trying to avoid curfew. His right hand got more of workout now than it did when he was a teenager who hadn't gotten up the courage to speak to girls yet.

Thinking of Sutton reminded him she had yet to tell him if the company move to the location they had scouted was feasible. They were running out of time to schedule the equipment and other logistics that would be necessary. He took out his phone to call her as he approached the porch steps of the ranch house only to find her sitting on the porch bench, her head bent over her own phone.

"Hi," he said, ridiculously thrilled to see her even though he had last seen her only two hours ago. Granted, they had barely exchanged three words, as she was on the set to meet the new craft service providers. "What are you doing here? Did we have a meeting scheduled I forgot?"

Her head flew up at his voice, and her mouth curved in a warm smile. "I'd like to think I'm unforgettable. But, no, we don't. I'm here at Erik's invitation."

"Erik?" He brought out his key and opened the front door, indicating she should go first. If the gesture allowed him to discreetly ogle Sutton's luscious ass, delectably outlined by her leggings—well, he always prided himself on his ability to take advantage of visual opportunities whenever they presented themselves.

"He said he wanted to talk comic books, and I'm the only person around who reads the same things he does." She exaggerated the swing of her hips as she walked, throwing him a teasing look over her shoulder. "It's going to be difficult to go back to wearing business casual after this shoot is over."

Right. The clock was ticking. "Nice of you to indulge him."

"I thought I was indulging you." She grinned. "And nothing nice about it. I can't get to my local comic book store to pick up my pull list. Erik is doing me a favor by letting me read his." She stood next to him as he flipped through mail forwarded to him by the studio. Concentrating was difficult with Sutton so close he could count the freckles on her cheeks, marvel at how her red-gold strands formed perfect, tiny ringlets in front of her ears.

She leaned closer to him. "So…are you busy later?"

He wanted to be busy right then, right now. Hoist Sutton in his arms, lock her legs behind his back and take her against the wall; hard, fast, slake the constant fire that replaced blood in his veins whenever he saw her. But he shook his head. "Can't. Family dinner, and then I need to nail down the dialogue for the final scenes. It's now or never."

Disappointment flashed across her expression, wiped away when the front door started to open. She straightened up and put some distance between them. "Got it. You know, we never did discuss the film's ending—"

"Hey, Sutton." Erik bounded through the front door and

came to a screeching halt next to them. "Sorry I'm late. Want to go into the living room?" He turned to Xavier. "You're sweaty and gross. You should wash up before dinner."

"And, hello, how was your day to you, too?" He turned to Sutton. "Am I really...?"

She glanced at Erik. "I'm...staying out of this."

"That's a yes." He sniffed his clothes. Yep, he could be fresher. "Have fun, you two. See you tomorrow, Sutton?"

"Of course." He was learning her smiles, and this was her professional courtesy smile, the one she wore when dealing with recalcitrant department heads. But when Erik moved to lead the way to the living room, she gave him the smile she seemed to reserve only for him, full of sultry promise. "Rain check," she mouthed, and then disappeared after his nephew.

Xavier took as long in the shower as he needed to wash the grit off his skin and out of his hair, and then to relieve the ache Sutton always created. It didn't take long, a few firm pumps of his erection while conjuring her taste on his lips, her throaty gasps in his ear, her slick heat clenched tight around his cock. Sutton sprawled, limbs heavy, her green eyes half-lidded with want for him, a curvy goddess of desire focused only on him. He came with a muffled grunt, his endurance shot to hell. Perhaps it was a good thing he had to turn down her offer tonight.

Nah, who was he kidding. This was a poor substitution for Sutton. But he needed to get used to it. While the production had weeks to go, they were still only weeks. Before long, he'd be off to his next film and so would she.

Keep your eyes on the goal, Duval, he warned himself. *Don't make the same mistake you made with Mimi.*

He toweled off and threw on a clean pair of jeans and a fresh T-shirt. Production days could be wildly unpredictable and often turn into production nights, but on Mondays he did his best to break filming in time for dinner with Erik and Ilsa. Having at least one night a week devoted to family was special to him, something he never had as a child, as his parents were far too busy with their lives to pay attention to the "oops" baby. He pulled a comb through his wet hair and then ran down the stairs, following the scent of barbecue ribs, his favorite. Ilsa had taken classes from a barbecue master when she and Erik accompanied him on a shoot in Austin, so tonight was a meal he didn't intend to miss.

But when he walked by the living room on his way to the kitchen, he spotted Sutton sitting on the sofa, looking at one of Erik's comics. His heart lit up. "Hey. You're still here."

She glanced up, startled. "Hi!" Her smile transformed into a smirk as her gaze ran over him. "Well. You clean up nicely, Mr. Duval."

It was as if his session in the shower never took place. Her effect on him was immediate and hard. "Glad you think so." He cleared his throat. "Where's Erik?"

"I don't know." She threw her hands up.

"What do you mean?"

"We came in here, he showed me this week's haul—I approve, by the way, great choices—and then Ilsa came in and said she needed his help but I should stay here, and he'll be back shortly. And that was—" she looked at the stack next to her—"eight issues ago."

"Interesting."

"I thought so, too, but now that you're here, you can say

goodbye to them both for me. I should probably get going, let you have family time." She rose to her feet, slinging her tote bag over her shoulder.

Ask her to stay for dinner. But asking her to stay would be crossing the streams of his work life and his personal life. And while he liked Sutton, was incredibly attracted to her, was going to miss her terribly when production was over, their relationship had an expiration date. His family did not.

"I'll tell them. But Ilsa is a stickler for manners. She'd never allow Erik to leave a guest alone this long."

Sutton shrugged. "Maybe she doesn't think of me as a guest? Or at least not one who needs to be entertained?" She rose on her toes as if to kiss him, then caught herself. "Damn it, you look so good. I have to go."

"I'll walk you to the front door."

"That's an offer I can't refuse," she said, placing the comic books carefully on the coffee table. She straightened up. "Oh, by the way, earlier you mentioned the final scene and—"

"Ta-da!" Erik appeared in the doorway, startling Xavier and causing Sutton to jump. "Welcome, lady and gentleman, to Chez Duval."

Xavier glanced at Erik, then doubled back for another, longer stare. Was his nephew wearing a…tuxedo? A rather outdated tuxedo with large lapels, but still. Erik loved to perform, and growing up on film sets, he had his share of costumes, both outrageous and otherwise. But a tux was new. "What the hell is—"

"Uh-uh, this is a very refined establishment." Ilsa appeared behind Erik, wearing a black shift dress with a pristine white apron over it. Her accent was now more French than her native Ukrainian. "And in quite high demand. But luckily for you, we have one table for two available."

Xavier didn't budge. He couldn't. He was rooted to the ground. "What are you guys doing? What's going on? Is Erik rehearsing for a play I don't know about?"

Sutton's expression vacillated between amusement and bewilderment. She glanced at her moisture-wicking T-shirt and leggings. "Whatever it is, I have a feeling I am underdressed for this evening."

"But no!" Ilsa tsked. "At Chez Duval, you are always in style. Isn't that right, Erik?"

"Absolutely," Erik said. Xavier was now over his surprise enough to realize Erik had been holding something behind him, and now his nephew revealed a long-stemmed red rose, which he gave to Sutton. "For you."

Sutton took the flower, her gaze still full of bemusement. "Thank you."

"And now, if you would like to follow me, your dinner awaits." Erik made a sketchy bow, then offered his arm to Sutton. She placed her hand in the crook of his elbow, playing along with a straight expression, but threw a confused smile at Xavier over her shoulder as he escorted her out of the room.

As soon as they were out of earshot, Xavier turned to Ilsa. "Now will you tell me what's going on?"

Ilsa dropped her affected accent. "Erik wanted to do something nice for you and Ms. Spencer. This is his plan."

"But what is his plan?"

"You don't expect me to ruin the surprise, do you? But I will say Erik was a champ and he spent a lot of time with

Contessina's younger niece when she came to visit, helping out. They watched many old Disney films. Like *The Parent Trap*. He might have gotten a few ideas."

"Fine." Xavier had known Ilsa long enough to know when he was up against a brick wall. "Where am I going? And there better be ribs, because I smell them."

"You'll see." Ilsa led him not toward the kitchen, as he was halfway expecting, but to French windows off the dining room that led to the backyard and the red-hued mountains in the distance. "And...*voila!*" she said with a flourish, pushing the doors open.

Xavier stayed where he was, struck motionless by the transformation.

Unlike the expansive front yard, where the Friday crew drinks had taken place, the backyard was small and tired. There was an oval brick patio, dotted along the edges with planters containing succulents that could withstand the day's heat, and a few hardy trees with trunks painted white as a form of sunscreen. But tonight, the area was transformed into a festival of twinkling golden lights, strung up and down and among the trees in a haphazard pattern. A circular table for two sat in the center of the patio, set with a cloth tablecloth and napkins. A candle anchored in a jar with sand was in the middle of table, with additional candles flickering on the edges of the patio and in the planters.

Sutton stood to one side of the patio, a filled flute in her hand. "I guess we've found Chez Duval," she said.

Xavier blinked once, twice. "I don't understand," he said slowly.

"You're letting the cold air escape," said Erik from his side.

"My bad." Xavier stepped outside and closed the French doors behind him. "What do you two think you're cooking up? Because we should let Ms. Spencer have her night."

"I've got champagne, I'm fine," Sutton said.

Ilsa approached Xavier with a filled flute for him. He tried to refuse it, but at her frown and Sutton's raised eyebrow, he accepted and decided to play along with whatever game Erik and Ilsa were playing. "Are we all having cocktails?" he asked. "Mocktails for Erik, of course."

Erik shook his head. "Please, take your places," he said, sweeping his hand toward the table, and then pulled one of the chairs out. "Mademoiselle?"

Xavier looked at Sutton. She shrugged at him, and then with a smile for Erik, she sat in the proffered seat. Xavier took the chair across from her and then looked at Erik. "Okay. What's next?"

Erik glanced at Ilsa, who nodded at him. "Siri, play tonight's playlist," she said, and from a portable speaker placed in a nearby planter came a slow, jazzy ballad.

"Enough is enough." Xavier started to stand, but a quelling look from Ilsa caused him to sit down. He snuck a glance at Sutton. Her cheeks were red, but her gaze danced with amusement. "I had nothing to do with this," he said.

"I didn't, either," she said. "In case you thought—"

"I didn't. But I don't want you to think I would—"

Erik appeared before them and handed them each a piece of paper. "Your menus."

Xavier didn't look at his, choosing instead to fix his stare on Erik, the stare that used to be successful in getting his nephew to confess to the broken plate or the missing phone.

However, the stare had started to lose its effectiveness around Erik's tenth birthday. "Okay. I've been patient. But it's a school night, and I have work to do after dinner. It's not fair to keep Ms. Spencer here when she might have other plans."

"I don't, actually," Sutton began, but pressed her lips closed when Xavier turned his stare on her. At least it worked on someone.

He turned to Erik. "Start talking."

Erik rolled his eyes. "I'm trying to do something nice for you."

"I appreciate that. But you can't just—"

"Xavier." Sutton tapped the menu in front of his. "Take a look."

"Why?" He pulled his gaze from Erik. "What does it say?" He glanced at it.

Welcome to Chez Duval

Tonight's Menu

Oysters on the Half Shell
Baby Back Ribs (Xavier's favorite, if you don't like them you don't stand a chance)
Chocolate Dipped Strawberries
Red Wine

"This is a very romantic dinner," she said.

"Good. That's what I wanted," Erik said.

"I did suggest some vegetables," Ilsa said. "But Erik had veto power over the menu suggestions."

"Wait." Xavier held up his right hand, the gesture that could cause a set of three hundred people to fall quiet, but he had a feeling would have little to no effect on his nephew and his coconspirator. "Erik, Ms. Spencer and I work together. I appreciate you've gone to a lot of trouble, but you can't make assumptions about people like this."

Erik folded his tuxedo-clad arms across his chest. "What assumption?"

"You seem to be assuming there is...something...between Ms. Spencer and me."

"But there is, isn't there?" Erik's gaze flicked from Xavier to Sutton and back again. "You know the crew is making bets about you."

Sutton choked on her champagne.

Xavier placed a hand on her back, asking with his touch if she was okay. She waved him off, dabbing at her lips with a napkin while composing herself. He turned to Erik. "What are you doing, listening to gossip? You know better."

"Is it gossip? C'mon." Erik stared him down. His stare was more effective than Xavier's had ever been. "I like Sutton. I know you like Sutton. And I think she likes you, too." Erik folded his arms across his chest. "Stop wasting time."

Xavier pinched the bridge of his nose. Now he understood Ilsa's warning. "Erik. You can't go around trying to... *Parent Trap* people."

"It's just a dinner," Erik continued. "If you guys don't like each other, at least you get some of Ilsa's ribs."

"Well, I for one am honored you thought of me as someone worthy enough to date your uncle. Thank you." Sutton had recovered from her mishap from the champagne. And she'd also recovered her humor. She winked at Xavier.

"You know I can find my own dates, right?" Xavier was starting to see the comedy in the situation, although embarrassment at having Sutton be roped into his nephew's scheme overrode everything else.

"I know you can. But do you? Because I haven't seen many."

Ouch.

"I'm not going to be around much next year, what with going to a new school. And Sutton lives in LA, so she'll be someone there you know."

"Oh?" Sutton turned to Xavier. Any amusement in her expression had fled. "You're moving to Los Angeles? I thought you were based in New York City."

"I..." He glanced at Erik, whose gaze narrowed further with every second he delayed in answering. "That's the plan," he said to her, noting her freckles appeared darker than normal. Or maybe her skin was paler. "You know my goal is to make more studio films after *The Quantum Wraith*. It's easier to take meetings when you're in the same city as the studios."

"And I'm going to go to school. A real school, not being tutored." Erik threw an apologetic look at Ilsa. "Not that being tutored isn't, you know, great."

"No apologies needed. I'm looking forward to retirement from English essays and algebra equations." Ilsa placed her right arm over Erik's shoulder, and Xavier noted with a pang that Ilsa had to reach up to do so. Any day now, Erik would be taller than her.

"I see." Sutton buried her face in her menu, her gaze refusing to be caught by his. "Well, dinner sounds delicious. I can't wait to eat. Thank you for arranging this, Erik."

"Of course." He shrugged out from under Ilsa's arm and ran into the house. "I'll be right back."

Ilsa followed him, closing the French doors he'd left open behind her. "Enjoy the champagne. Hors d'oeuvres are coming up."

The music playing over the speakers switched to something that sounded vaguely familiar. Xavier tried to place the song while observing Sutton, who was still engrossed in the menu as if her life depended on memorizing its contents. He cleared his throat. "There aren't many choices at this restaurant," he attempted to joke. "That will hurt the Yelp rating."

She finally looked up. "Don't worry, I'll eat fast and leave. I know you have work to do and so do I, but Erik has gone to a lot of trouble. I want to honor that."

"I'm not worried. Aside from being worried you would find this to be ridiculous. And overstepping. Which it is."

She huffed. "It's not ridiculous. It's sweet. Erik is obviously concerned about you. It's nice."

He supposed it was. From a certain point of view. "He's a good kid."

"But one who's growing up. Why didn't you tell me you were moving to LA?" Her tone was light, but her gaze would not meet his. No matter how hard he tried.

"I…" He shrugged. "It never came up. I guess I just assumed since you knew I wanted to transition from indie to studio films that meant living in Los Angeles." He was making the move for Erik's sake. Which is why he supposed he never associated the move with informing Sutton.

She nodded, playing with the stem of her champagne flute. "I see. And, I guess, the fact we'll both be in LA doesn't change anything. We already said we'll always be colleagues."

"I'd like that." He missed the Sutton of before. The Sutton who had almost broken out into giggles when she saw his dumbfounded face upon arriving at the patio. And he had no idea what he said or did to make her disappear. "Is there something wrong?"

"Et voila!" Erik bounded out the French doors carrying a silver tray that held a large bowl of shaved ice with twelve oysters on the half shell arranged on top. He looked at Ilsa, who was on his heels. "Did I say that right?"

"You did," she answered.

"I'm learning French," he said to Sutton, placing the bowl between her and Xavier. "Here's the first course."

"Thank you," she said, but her gaze focused on her fingers twisting on the table.

Xavier frowned. "If you need to leave, it's fine."

"I don't need to leave!" Her words erupted. "I've repeatedly said I'd like to stay for dinner. Or…" Her cheeks turned from rose to white. "Do you want me to leave? Is that it? You don't want me here. At your house. With your family."

"No—" Erik started, but when Ilsa put her hand on his arm, he stopped talking. However, his gaze was narrowed in a dangerous expression Xavier recognized all too well.

"Why don't we continue with our plan," Ilsa said to Erik, and then turned to Sutton and Xavier. "We'll return shortly."

Xavier watched his nephew and Ilsa enter the house and shut the French doors before returning his attention to Sutton. "What's wrong? Something is off."

She laughed, a short outburst that had little humor in it. "It's amazing to me how you can be so perceptive most of the time, excel at putting a facsimile of life on film, but when it comes to your life—you know what, never mind. I don't want to ruin this for Erik. Let's have a nice meal for his sake." She took two oysters from the serving bowl, settling them on her plate. "Very decadent."

Her careful smile didn't reach her eyes. As a connoisseur of her expressions over the past weeks, he could tell when she was putting on a polite mask. "Tell me what's wrong."

She pulled the oyster from its shell and let it slip down her throat, making an appreciative hum he felt low in his groin. "Delightful. Have one."

"I'd rather know what's going on in your head."

She put down the second oyster. "It's just…my own stupidity, I suppose. You made it clear that whatever you and I are doing, your family is off-limits. I guess I should have said I have a prior engagement and left, but I…"

"You didn't want to disappoint Erik. You said that."

"Right. Erik." She nodded, her focus sliding to the planters and their flickering candles. "Those aren't real candles, are they? With real fire? Should we be worried?"

He followed the direction of her gaze but wouldn't be drawn off course. "The fire looks fake to me. But Sutton, I don't want you to feel obligated to stay."

"I don't." She finally allowed her gaze to be caught and held. The green depths swam with deep shimmering emotion. His heart leaped, a hard knock taking him by surprise. Air suddenly seemed in short supply. "If anything, I feel—"

"Et voila, encore!" Erik came onto to patio bearing a large, covered platter.

Xavier didn't need the cover removed to know what was underneath. He could smell the smoke on the meat and tang of the sauce from where he sat. Ilsa followed behind with a folding table that she set up alongside Xavier and Sutton. When she was finished, Erik put the platter down. Sure enough, a pile of the most delicious ribs Xavier had ever tasted in his life were revealed.

"Dig in," Erik proclaimed.

Xavier's stomach rumbled. He only had eyes for the ribs, but Sutton's gaze narrowed. "What happened to the tux?"

"Oh." Erik shrugged, looking at his T-shirt and shorts. "More comfortable this way. Besides, Darren would think the tux was weird, so I didn't want to wear it to his place."

"Darren? As in Darren Chen?" Xavier tuned to Ilsa. "It's a Monday night."

"Erik has been invited to join Darren's class for a field trip to Tumacácori. They're leaving first thing in the morning, so it's more convenient if he spends the night at the Chens." She smiled. "They needed an extra chaperone and I volunteered, so the Chens also invited me to stay in their guest room. They live close to the school, so more convenient to arriving on time tomorrow."

"That's tomorrow?" Xavier had been so upside down since that night in the desert with Sutton, it was a wonder he remembered his own name. He rose from the table. "Can I do anything to help you two get ready?"

Ilsa smiled. "Everything is taken care of. Traci Chen called and said they picked up pizza, so we're going to leave now. Right, Erik?"

Erik nodded. "Yeah. So, I think you have everything you need. Oh, and the strawberries are in the refrigerator. We didn't want them to melt."

"Have a good meal," Ilsa said over her shoulder as she guided Erik into the house. "We'll be back tomorrow around dinnertime. If we'll be later, I'll text."

"Have fun," Sutton said.

Erik waved at her. "Take a comic if you want," he called before the French doors closed behind him.

The silence that fell on the patio would be deafening if not for the syrupy music coming from the portable speaker.

"I can turn that off," he offered.

"If you want," she said, that impenetrable shutter falling over her expression again. "So, after we make sure the coast is clear, I should go, right? Let you work."

Go? No. He didn't want her to leave. He picked up the carving knife and fork, intending to cut a portion of ribs for her. His mouth watered at the smell. "You haven't tried these. They're life-changing."

"No, thanks, not in the market for a life change. Tell Erik and Ilsa everything was delicious, and I enjoyed the dinner." She rose from her chair.

He felt as if one of the production trucks had backed over him. Flat and knocked for a disorienting loop. "This night has taken a wrong turn. And I'm not sure where."

She shook her head. "There's no wrong turn. Just…signs I should've paid attention to. I'll see you tomorrow, okay?"

He caught her arm by the elbow as she passed him, more like a brush of his palm against her soft, smooth skin. She stopped as soon as they connected, her chest rapidly falling and rising. Now that his shock at the romantic dinner ambush had started to fade, he could see the advantages in the situation. "Sutton. Stay. I know Erik and Ilsa have left. On the other hand… Erik and Ilsa have left, and we're alone."

She hesitated, her tongue coming out to wet her lips. "Why didn't you tell me you were moving to Los Angeles?"

Was that what was wrong? The thought punched him hard between the ribs. "You're upset because we'll both be in LA. I understand. But we don't have to work together again if you don't want to. Or even see each other. I won't bother you." Rosalie and Erik's father had had a tumultuous relationship, with several breakups before Erik's father disappeared for good. Xavier still vividly recalled how angry and how powerless Rosalie felt when Erik's father would show up at her office or outside her home, unable to take no for answer. He would never behave in that manner, but Sutton didn't know that. "We're in the same industry, so we might show up at the same events. But I promise, on your terms."

"Wait." She stared at him, her lips slightly parted. "You think I'm upset because when you move to LA I might spot you across the room at a film premiere, and that would—what?—ruin my evening?" She clasped her free hand over her mouth. "That is the silliest, most ridiculous thing I have ever heard."

The knot in his throat threatening to close off his airway started to dissipate. "Then, what's wrong?"

She inhaled, then blew the air out in a puff that sent the

red-gold tendrils framing her face flying. "Not telling me you are moving to Los Angeles says to me you don't plan to stay in touch after this production wraps."

He frowned. "How could you think that?"

She blinked at him. "How could I not?"

The song playing over the speakers changed to a tune more familiar to him. "My Heart Will Go On" from the film *Titanic*. Rosalie watched the film on repeat while pregnant with Erik. Appropriate, he supposed, because he sensed there was an iceberg right here in the middle of the Arizona desert, and he was either going to crash on its icy perimeter or maneuver back to smooth seas. "I didn't tell you because I didn't want to presume. I told you. I value being colleagues."

Her gaze searched his. Then her shoulders fell, and she started to laugh. A giggle really, at first, that developed into full body laughter. "It's LAU all over again," she said, her words breathy exhales.

"It is?" He began to chuckle, simply because her amusement was infectious.

She nodded, grabbing onto a chair as if she needed its support to keep her upright. "It is. I'm waiting for you to make the first move, and you're waiting for me, and next thing you know there's an undelivered letter and we don't talk for ten years." She wiped a tear from her eye. "At least your nephew and Ilsa don't suffer from the same paralysis." She inhaled, sobering, then came to stand before him. "Xavier Duval, would you do me the honor of going on this date with me? A real date. Not fake like the candles, not pretending to people's faces we are work colleagues only but sneaking around behind their backs. Just the two of us and dinner."

Warmth spread from the center of his chest to his arms, legs, further out to the tips of his fingers and toes. "I would like nothing more than to be your date, Sutton Spencer."

Twelve

"I'm never lonely when I can look at the stars. Light of the cosmos, avatars of our future, drawing us ever closer to our destiny."
"Stars are hot gas. Like that speech."
                      Con Sulley and Lys Amarga, *The Quantum Wraith*

Although ribs were among his favorite foodstuffs, and he would put Ilsa's barbecue up against the finest pitmasters in Austin and Kansas City, Xavier doubted they would taste as good as they did tonight. Because tonight, the meal was accompanied by watching Sutton's delight. Ribs were messy and involved eating with one's hands, and no matter how many napkins and wet wipes were available, there never seemed to be enough. But Sutton dug in with gusto, her eyes sparkling, their conversation flowing as the pile of bones grew on the plates in front of them. And when Sutton stopped to lick an errant drop of sauce off her index finger… he'd never sat through a dinner in a state of constant arousal before. But the stimuli didn't stop, from her near orgasmic groan at her first taste of Ilsa's artistry to her plump pink lips closing over a rib, sucking the last tasty bits from the bone.

She relaxed in her chair after finishing her final piece, her eyes half closed. "That was amazing. Maybe those ribs really are life-changing."

The oysters were also gone, having slid down their throats at the start of the meal, and the decanted red wine had long been emptied. High above, the round moon threw shadows worthy of film noir, and they ate by the glow of the repurposed Christmas lights and whatever light the battery-operated candles could produce. And he was pretty certain the playlist on the speaker was on its third or fourth go-around. He was starting to recognize songs.

But the date wasn't over yet. "Can I interest you in chocolate-dipped strawberries? Or broccoli? I understand both are in the kitchen."

She laughed. "As tempting as broccoli sounds, I'll pass."

Disappointment hit him, brutal in its unexpected slap. "Ready to call it a night?"

"Depends." Her smile curved with mischief. "You asked me on a real date. Is this the point where you usually say goodnight to your dates?"

He hadn't realized how tight his shoulders had been until they just now relaxed. "We've had dinner. How about a movie?"

"A traditional date activity and yet also an interest we have in common! Well played." She pushed back from the table and began to stack plates and serving pieces to bring them into the house and then followed him into the kitchen. "What film are you thinking of? Should we drive into town?"

He ran water over the dirty dishes and placed them in the dishwasher before turning back to her question. "Better. I have advance screening copies of upcoming releases."

Her mouth made an O shape. A very delectable shape. "Of course you have screeners. I'm assuming Monument set you up with a screening room in this house?"

"There's one. It's where Jay and I watch dailies and rough cuts. But I have somewhere else in mind." He opened the refrigerator and took out a plate with some of biggest strawberries he'd ever seen dunked in thick dark chocolate and drizzled with decorative white chocolate stripes. "Follow me."

"After you." She held up a bottle of champagne she must have taken from the wine refrigerator and their two flutes from earlier.

He led her to his favorite place in the rented house, a downstairs bedroom he had claimed for himself. His heart beat a rapid uneven rhythm as they approached the door, taking him by surprise. But then, few people had crossed this threshold. Erik was welcome, of course. Xavier was always available for him. He would not let Erik grow up as he did, an afterthought who was rarely acknowledged, much less wanted. The rest of the world? He doubted Jay or even Ilsa had spent more than fifteen minutes collectively in what he'd begun referring to mentally as his *sanctum sanctorum*. Erik's comic books had rubbed off on him.

"Here we are." He found himself holding his breath, wondering how she would react.

Sutton stopped in the doorway, her gaze sweeping around, taking in the sofa with its wide leather cushions, the beaten-up desk that was the one thing he demanded be moved to his residences in his contract, the bookshelves crowded with tomes on photography, screenwriting and filmmaking, interspersed with various items he'd taken as souvenirs from his previous films.

Sutton placed the champagne and flutes on the low coffee table in front of the sofa, but she remained on her feet, slowly perusing the books and other items on the shelves, smiling at props she recognized and admiring his latest photo of Erik, a candid taken that fateful night Contessina hosted crew drinks. Then she pulled out a pictorial history of Alfred Hitchcock's films and laughed when she opened the book. "Of course, the spine is cracked at *Vertigo*."

"Because that is the best film Hitchcock made. One of the best films ever made."

She shook her head and put the book back in its spot. "His best film is *Notorious*. We settled this last time we were together."

"The last time we saw each other was this afternoon and you mostly talked about the logistics of securing additional honey wagons for Wednesday."

"Very funny." She sank onto the sofa next to him, tucking her legs underneath her. "I mean ten years ago. And of course we did."

He frowned at her. "I would never rank *Notorious* above *Vertigo*. *Notorious* is fun to watch, but *Vertigo* is a tour de force."

"*Notorious* is brilliantly paced, and the chemistry between Cary Grant and Ingrid Bergman is scorching."

"Hitchcock's mastery of film as a medium is unmatched in *Vertigo*. His use of color. The invention of the dolly zoom."

She waved his arguments away with a flick of her wrist. "And it's a film that leaves people cold. *Notorious* makes us feel. And unlike *Vertigo*, *Notorious* has an ending. A pretty happy one, in fact."

He made a face. "*Vertigo* is a master class in psychological exploration. The ambiguity is a feature, not a bug. The film subverts—"

"Traditional Hollywood cinema," she finished for him, laughing. "I'm familiar with your thinking. But the ambiguity *is* a bug, at least for me. When I'm sick or sad, *Notorious* is one of my comfort films. That's why audiences love a happy ending. They leave people with a sense of optimism and hope. I think I've seen *Vertigo* twice, maybe? Because I don't want to be depressed."

"And you call yourself a cinephile. I'm going to ignore you said that." He opened the champagne with a muffled pop and poured a flute for her before taking the second one for himself. "Cheers. Here's looking at you."

"I appreciate you leaving off the 'kid.'" She clinked her glass against his and smiled, warm and generous. "To infinity and beyond."

He could spend all night staring into her those dark green eyes. *"Toy Story?"*

"'You've got a friend in me' didn't seem romantic enough." She cupped her right hand to his left cheek. Her touch was cool and tender. "I like this," she said, stroking his beard. "Adds some needed gravitas to your face."

"Needed?" But he didn't pull away. If anything, he leaned into her palm, gave her hand permission to explore more.

"You looked too much like you were a fellow student then." Her other hand came up to cup his right cheek. "No wonder I had trouble respecting the boundaries."

His phone beeped with a text, and he broke out of the haze induced by Sutton's eyes to glance at his screen. Erik and Ilsa were safely at the Chens and scarfing pizza.

Right. He had obligations to go with the beard now. He was pleased Erik liked Sutton—she was infinitely likable—but tonight only underscored his apprehension about mixing his professional relationships with his family, setting expectations that had no chance of being fulfilled.

If only life could be controlled like his film set. But he would continue to do his best to ensure Erik was surrounded by people he could count on.

"Anyway, I'm glad we're having this date now," she continued, drinking deeply from her flute. "And speaking of, where's the movie you promised me? I appreciate a cinema without the sticky floors, but the lack of popcorn could be a problem."

"Afraid you'll have to make do with these." He offered the plate of strawberries to her, and the subsequent sight of Sutton Spencer licking chocolate off her fingers rocketed to the top of his personal top ten most erotic images. The pressure building in his groin demanded to know if her mouth still tasted of ripe fruit, but he knew if he started to kiss her, there would be no movie watching. He reluctantly pulled his gaze from her and picked up the remote.

"I could put on the new Gordon Michaeux film. It's supposed to be quite good. An early contender for awards."

"There appears to be a missing 'or' at the end."

"Or... I received the first rough assemblage of *The Quantum Wraith*." His palms were suddenly sweaty, and he had to put down the remote before he dropped it.

His contract stipulated he didn't have to show edits to the studio until much further in the process. But Sutton was the acting producer. She deserved to see what they had filmed so far.

And he wanted her to see what his team had pieced together, but what if she didn't like the direction he was taking? Or if she thought his vision was flat or hackneyed? The realization of how much he craved her creative approval was scary.

Her face lit up. "Are you kidding? I would love to see the footage."

He switched the screen on the television to the file-sharing service he used with his editing team in Los Angeles. "It's rough," he warned.

"You said that. I'm not expecting a completed film. I know we're still shooting. I'm part of the production, remember?"

"No special effects, no sweetening, no color correction, temp music tracks," he continued, his heart beating faster and harder with each word. He shouldn't have mentioned it. "I haven't seen it yet."

"Xavier." She placed her hand over his and turned so she could catch his gaze. "I appreciate this is an early edit. And I am so very honored you trust me with this."

He squeezed her fingers, took a deep breath and then brought the file up on the TV screen. Contessina's face appeared, the image frozen, her brown eyes dark unreadable pools. "Here we go."

The edit was everything he said it would be. The story skipped key moments that hadn't been filmed yet. The explosions lacked power and sound. The scenery missed the computer graphic elements that would be added in postproduction to make the desert appear more otherworldly. In the scene where Autarch Zear materialized to Lys, the sun was shining brightly while Contessina delivered her lines, but when the camera switched to Raul, the sun was behind clouds. All of that could and would be fixed in postproduction.

He took out his electronic tablet and began making notes on his first impression. Later he would pay closer attention to the framing, the shot sequence, the angles chosen. And he would take another pass to concentrate on the actors' performances, to ensure their most powerful takes were included. But for now, he let the scenes wash over him, viewing the edit as an audience member might.

Or at least that was his intent. He was acutely aware of Sutton beside him. His gaze was on her as often as the screen. She bit her lower lip when Lys was being interrogated. Her hands clenched when Autarch Zear taunted Lys with the knowledge she was now a known traitor, and her home was forever forbidden to her. And when Con sacrificed himself for Lys, moisture shimmered at the corners of her eyes.

"Well?" he asked, his breath held, hoping the tears were a good sign.

She was silent for a moment, her face turned from him. His spirits, which had been soaring so high they joined satellites in orbit, plummeted hard.

He was confident in his work. The film was solidly crafted, thanks to his handpicked crew and Jay's cinematography. Contessina was luminous even in a rough cut. The film would cement her as a major star, he was sure.

But if Sutton didn't connect with the film, if the scenes left her cold or worse, bored her...

"Xavier." His name was an incredulous whisper. She turned to him, her gaze still shimmering with moisture. "The film is amazing."

Relief was sweet and felt like his veins had been injected with champagne, bubbles popping and fizzing. "So, better than *Notorious*."

She laughed. "No, *Notorious* is still the one to beat. But I'd put it above *Vertigo*."

"I can't believe you have a degree in film." The champagne sensations continued and he poured himself a fresh flute of the real stuff, taking a heady sip.

"Hey, I acknowledge the artistry of *Vertigo*. But the rough cut is leaps and bounds beyond a decades-old film, admitted masterpiece or not. I can't wait to see the final product." She turned toward him, tucking her legs underneath her once more.

"I appreciate your faith."

She shook her head. "It's not faith. Well, I guess there's a component of it. I have faith the finished film will be amazing. But I've always known you were talented. It was why I fought so hard to get into your seminar." She flashed him a knowing smile, and his heart flipped. "Anyway, thank you for reminding me why I wanted to be in the film industry in the first place. To tell stories that move people."

"You were moved?" Damn if that didn't make the champagne sparkle even more.

She took his flute from him and placed it on the coffee table. "It's going to be a great film," she said, catching and holding his gaze with hers. "And I see now why the confrontation scene needs to be filmed where we visited near Yuma. The story is truly enhanced by how you use the natural scenery for the planet scenes. You'll lose that if you move to a soundstage."

"Does that mean you're approving the new location?"

She nodded. "The paperwork is already in. But now I'll make sure it happens. The budget is going to be an issue…" Her voice trailed off as her gaze turned distant.

"Will Monument make your life difficult?" he asked.

"That's my concern, not yours."

He regarded her. The new location would indeed enhance *The Quantum Wraith*, make the final confrontation more cinematic and richly textured. But he would still be satisfied with the film if he had to recreate the setting on a soundstage and use visual effects. "I don't want you to do anything that would jeopardize—"

She leaned over and kissed him, hard and swift. The kiss was much wanted, but the surprise stole all his words from his brain. He blinked at her. She half smiled, half smirked at him, rising to kneel on the sofa cushions as she faced him. "As the dinner and the movie portion of the date are now concluded, I thought maybe we should move to the rest of the night? Since we have this place to ourselves. If you're amenable, that is."

He gathered his scattered thoughts. "More than. But the budget—"

She placed her right index finger on his lips, then leaned down to cover his mouth with hers for a lingering kiss, hot and wet, her clever tongue giving and receiving while promising much more to come before she broke contact and pulled back. "I'm the producer," she said. "Leave the spreadsheets to me. You direct the hell out of this film."

She went in for another kiss, but with an extreme exercise of will he managed to hold her off. "Aren't you up for a promotion? Don't jeopardize your career."

She sat on her heels. "Right now, I'm up for something else. But if you're not…"

No. He did not say that. In fact, *up* was an accurate description. "Are you using sex to get me to stop talking?"

"Only if it's working." She nuzzled the skin behind his ear, a particularly sensitive spot she'd discovered when they were in the tent and continued to use to great effect. "Is it?"

Oh yeah. Working real well. He'd have to remember to ask her about any consequences from her decision to authorize the new location in the morning. Or at least he would remember if his blood wasn't headed straight south, thanks to Sutton's lips performing their magic on his.

Three mind-blowing orgasms later—he was more than happy to keep the ledger tipped firmly in her favor—his hands made swooping circles on the soft satin of Sutton's back, tracing the gentle knobs of her spine and the curve of her hips. She stirred, raising her head to look at him.

"Hey," he said.

"Hey," she said back, her smile slow and deeply satisfied.

"Want to move to the bed?"

She hummed, a pleasant vibration he would swear he could feel in his soul if he felt like being poetic. "I don't think I can move. I'm comfortable here if you are."

He was. His bed was nice—the mattress was just the right amount of firm, and he had learned over the years not to skimp on the quality of his sheets—but this room was him in a way the bedroom, with its rented furniture and generic Western artwork on the walls, never could be. There was a reason few people were invited into his study. But he wanted Sutton to be here. The intimacy was even more, well, intimate.

"So," she said, her index finger drawing abstract patterns on his chest, "I can't stop thinking about the film."

"Oh. Great. That's not a blow to my male ego."

She laughed. "It's not the only thing I'm thinking about. I'm a very talented multitasker." She whispered kisses along the path her fingers forged.

He closed his eyes, relishing in her touch, enjoying the luxury to just be with her without worrying about being spotted by a member of the production or his family. Not that apparently his family would be all that shocked, judging by the stunt Erik and Ilsa pulled earlier. "Multitask away."

"Mm," she hummed again, leaving off her exploration of his chest to press herself against him, tangling her legs with his before raising her gaze. "So, the edit ended with Lys escaping after Con's apparent death. And I know the confrontation with Autarch Zear is the next big set piece. But you know—" she pressed hot, open mouth kisses along his neck and throat "—you still haven't told me the ending. I think you know you can now trust me not to go running to the internet with spoilers."

"I'm still writing it." He could lose himself forever in the sensation of Sutton's soft curves in his arms, the way she shivered when he found a particularly sensitive area, the pink flush that suffused her face when he explored further. He supposed she might find it tiresome, being a redhead whose light skin made it difficult to hide certain emotions, but he was endlessly fascinated. "But Con's death. That's not apparent."

Sutton lifted her head, abruptly leaving off what had been a systematic progression of kisses from one side of his jaw to the other. "What do you mean, 'not apparent'?"

"Con dies. It's a death. Not an apparent one." His hand drifted lower.

She shifted and rolled away from him, denying him access to his target. "Con can't die."

He blinked. Unlike Sutton, he did not claim to multitask well. "He does."

She sat up. Normally he would be appreciative of the view, but the thunderclouds gathering on her expression demanded his focus. Not to mention she crossed her arms over her chest, barring his gaze from admiring her delicious curves. "Con is who keeps Lys going. He's her support, her rock. And, I admit, I am heavily shipping them."

Con's story was so clear to him. How could his arc not be evident to Sutton? "And that's why he has to die."

Her eyes widened. "Because I ship them?"

"No, of course not. Because Lys needs to stand on her own. She learns she can't rely on anyone but herself."

Sutton blinked at him. "What kind of a message is that? Con loves Lys. He supports her because he loves her. She *can* rely on him. Con and Lys, that's a healthy relationship to put on film."

Xavier narrowed his gaze. "But *The Quantum Wraith* isn't a rom-com. Structurally, it doesn't follow a romance arc."

"Characters fall in love in other genres, you know." She pulled the blanket around her, ensuring most of her was now hidden from his gaze.

"Sure." Now he found himself crossing his arms. "'And they lived happily ever after' is fine for Disney animation and holiday flicks but—"

"Oh, so now we're back to dismissing holiday filmss, which, as you know, are extremely popular. And that's what Monument wants, by the way. A popular film that makes money."

"I want *The Quantum Wraith* to not only entertain but to provoke thought. Use science fiction to reflect our reality. We come into the world alone, we leave it alone."

Her head shook rapidly, her tousled hair a red-gold blur. "That's really bleak. You don't truly believe that."

Oh, but he did. He would also treasure this time with Sutton. But it had an expiration date. The concept of love everlasting was more fantastical than the universe of *The Quantum Wraith*. Life was hard. The best anyone could hope for was to protect their loved ones from the chaos as best as possible. That's what Rosalie did for him.

He couldn't control what happened to her. But he could take care of Erik to the very best of his ability. "That's Lys's character arc. It's true to the human experience."

"But people go to the movies to be inspired."

"Lys is inspiring. She shows how we can rise above ourselves, to keep fighting when all else is gone."

Sutton huffed. "And people want to be entertained."

"You seemed to be entertained."

"I was, but I didn't think Con was *dead* dead." She folded her arms and slunk against the sofa cushions. "He's alive in the comics. No wonder you're keeping the end a secret. There's going to be riot when that gets out, you know."

He raised his eyebrows. "And? Are you saying I should cater to, quote, 'fans' like the one who broke into Contessina's home?"

She sighed. "No, of course not. Filmmakers need to tell their stories without worrying about catering to bullies."

"Kellen approved my outline," he said. "He understood the film is its own story, separate from the comic. He got it."

"Kellen may be the president of production, but he has the story sensibility of a parakeet. He likes anything shiny that gets people talking."

"And you're still talking about the film, which says it is inspiring. Even if your preoccupation with the film despite all this—" he swept a hand over his bare chest "—right here, just for your taking, is putting a dent in my male ego."

She smirked at him. "Why, Mr. Duval, are you fishing for compliments on your sexual prowess?"

"Depends. Do you have any?" He grinned, hoping to head off what had the potential to turn into a real argument over the film's direction.

She leaned over and kissed him, her mouth insistent and warm, her tongue dancing and tangling with his. He sighed and deepened the kiss, his hands sliding through the silk of her hair and cradling her head close. He could kiss Sutton Spencer until the stars grew cold.

She pulled back and gazed at him, her lips dark pink and swollen. "Consider my mind officially blown when it comes to your performance in bed. Or sofa."

He grinned, stroking her cheeks, tracing those pillowy lips with his thumb.

"But—" and she sat back again, removing herself from his grasp "—I'm less impressed with your performance as a writer-director. You can't kill Con. Change the ending."

He struggled upright. "The film is about Lys's journey to being a leader, but fully alone. It's an allegory on the costs of power. You want the story to be something it isn't."

"My reaction is based on the comic, plus seeing the rough edit and the storyboards." Storm warnings reappeared in her expression. "I'm only reacting to what the story already is."

There. That was his out. "You're right, it's a rough edit. You haven't seen the whole film. And you haven't read the full script." He rose from the sofa and walked to his desk, feeling the heat of Sutton's gaze on his nude back. Picking up a stack of paper, he returned to the sofa and presented the pages to her. "Here. The script. So far. I was going to take a pass at the final scenes when I received a better offer for my evening."

His stomach clenched seeing his work in her hands. He trusted her. He did. But he didn't trust studio executives not to interfere with filmmakers' creative vision.

He took a deep breath and concentrated on how the dim light made Sutton's eyes appear impossibly large and depthless. How she had never looked more attractive to him than she did right now, with her hair tousled in every direction and wearing an old wool blanket that had seen better days who knows how long ago.

She reached up to kiss the curve of his jaw. "Thank you. I appreciate your trust."

"You're welcome." He leaned over for another kiss, a real one, but her focus was wholly on the script in her hands. She was already flipping pages. "You're not going to read that now?"

She glanced up. "I didn't think you'd want me to take the script out of your office, as a guard against possible leaks."

That was a good point. But the hours where they had the house to themselves were slipping by, and he was self-aware enough to admit he was greedy and selfish, at least where Sutton was concerned. He didn't want to waste a single moment more than was necessary.

"You could continue reading," he said, his hand finding a gap in the blanket she wore to discover a warm and full breast. Her nipple puckered at his touch and she sighed, shifting to the side so he could better nuzzle her neck. "Or we could move to my bedroom and take notes on what's more preferable: a king-size bed, a sofa, your desk or an air mattress in a pickup truck."

She closed her eyes, her head falling back and allowing

him to kiss the pulse leaping in her throat. "Sounds like a scientific experiment. I like science."

He stood, pulling her up with him. She came willingly, her arms winding around his neck, but the script was still in her right hand. "I'm warning you now, if you try to multitask…"

She laughed. "I'm not that good at it. Not where you're concerned." She let him take the script from her. "Now. Show me this king-size bed, if you please."

Thirteen

"I can't tell you, it's a secret."
"If one wishes to keep a secret, then one must hide it even from oneself. But you, my child, don't know yourself."

Lys Amarga and Autarch Zear, *The Quantum Wraith*

Sutton slowly swam to wakefulness, aware of something warm and heavy draped across her shoulders. She moved slightly, and the pressure tightened as a still asleep Xavier gathered her closer to him, keeping her protected even as he snored. For an all too brief second, she contemplated falling back into sleep, prolonging this connection without her conscious thoughts reminding her this night had been a limited time offer only. But a quick look at the bedside clock reminded her she would only be postponing the fast-arriving inevitable, and she might as well rip the bandage off now.

"Hey." She turned to face Xavier, stroking his beard, adoring the way the soft bristles teased and tickled her fingertips. "Sleepy head. Call time is in two and half hours. You need to prepare and I should get going."

He grumbled, eyes still closed, and pulled her on top of him in an expansive full-body hug. Then he opened one dark brown eye. "What time did you say it was?"

"Too early and yet already too late." She tapped his chest with her open palm. "As much as I would like to stay here…"

He sighed and reluctantly released her. "Right."

Where were her clothes? Oh. In his office. Downstairs. "Um, I don't suppose you have a robe or a T-shirt I can borrow…"

He got out of bed, providing a delectable view of his broad shoulders tapering to one of the most perfect asses it had ever been her privilege to witness, returning with a dark blue bathrobe that she shrugged on. The robe smelled of him, warm musk and undefinable spice, and she resisted the urge to gather the fabric and inhale deeply.

"I hate to get up and leave," he said. "But I need to jump in the shower and run. I have an early meeting with Jay and his unit."

"I understand. As your producer, I insist you put the film first." She smiled. The effort took more than she anticipated.

"Erik and Ilsa won't be home until tonight. You're welcome to stay here longer. There's food in the kitchen. Ilsa insists on getting bagels shipped from Montreal. She says they're the best. Better than New York bagels, but you better not say that in Manhattan."

She regarded him, a genuine smile breaking through. "Xavier. I do declare you are babbling."

His look of affront was almost comical. "I am not." Then he relented. "Maybe. I wish we had more time."

"Me too." More than words could convey. She threw the robe on and left his warm, cozy bed as he pulled on a pair of briefs and started to gather the clothes he would wear after his shower. "I'm going to go downstairs, get dressed and then get to my room."

He hesitated. "You might want to…"

She read his mind. "Make sure people don't see us leaving your house together? Exactly what I was planning to do. Although—" she watched his expression carefully "—Erik mentioned a betting pool."

"Jay said something earlier."

"What? Why didn't you tell me?"

"Hooking up is expected on location. I wouldn't worry about it. Crews gossip."

"But not expected for you, Contessina said."

His gaze became opaque. Then he shrugged. "Rain checks are worth making an exception for. Still, no need to verify the smoke with fire."

Right. Rain checks.

And in cashing them, she was incurring a risk, one larger than she would normally consider. Confirmation of their affair would be juicy currency to be used against her in Monument's offices. But production would be over before she knew it, and per their original pact, they would go their separate ways. The one thing she would never tell him was she feared he would be taking a piece of her heart with him when they parted. "What will you tell Erik and Ilsa?"

He smiled and kissed her, a brief brush of lips she enjoyed

but also felt like he was drawing a line between last night and the days still to come on the production. "That we had a good date, like they planned, and then you went home."

She searched his gaze and then nodded. She wasn't sure what she'd been expecting. He'd already told her that he kept his sexual partners compartmentalized from his family. Part of her had hoped maybe she might be different. That the fact she'd established a separate friendship with Erik that had nothing to do with Xavier might make him reconsider. But like most things when it came to Xavier, her heart was indulging in wishful thinking.

"True that. Okay. Enough talking." The robe was so large she could almost wrap the fabric twice around her. She settled for cinching the sash tightly and pushing up the sleeves when they would fall over her hands. "Catch up with you on the set later?"

"Of course." But when she would have brushed past him to leave the room, he caught her arm and pulled her to him for a long kiss that not only caused sparks to cartwheel through her veins but also sent ripples through her soul. Her heart gave itself over to the moment, although her head warned she was headed for a painful crash and she disengaged away first. "Do you want to—" he started.

"Thanks for last night," she said, managing a carefree smile. "I had a great time. Especially the parts where it was impossible to multitask. And don't worry, we still don't need a morning-after talk—"

"Sutton." God, she loved her name on his lips. "Now you're babbling. I was going to say, do you want to come over tonight and watch the rough assemblage again. In the screening room. With Jay and other department heads."

"You want me there?" A warm feeling blossomed deep in her chest. Warm but also sharp, a knife-edge pleasure-pain. "Even though I'm the suit?"

"You're the producer." His smile was a bright flash against his dark beard. "But if you have other plans, you don't have to come at all."

"No!" In some ways, his inclusion of her in the brain trust he relied on to shape *The Quantum Wraith* meant more to her than his obvious appreciation of having her in his bed. "I'll clear my calendar."

"Okay." Another brief brush of his mouth on hers, but the electricity could power the lights on the set. "Gotta run."

"See you tonight." She watched him disappear into the bathroom, the sound of the shower following immediately after, before making her way downstairs to his office. The last thing she picked up after dressing were the pages he had handed her. She had a long day of meetings and arbitrating various demands and filing reports ahead of her, but that was all going to have to wait.

She had a script to read.

Sutton closed the last page, her unfocused gaze staring at the blank wall in front of her. She'd known Xavier was as talented a screenwriter as he was a director. His double-threat prowess was why she fought so hard to get into his seminar and was also why his critique of her final project had been so hurtful to her ego. The script showcased all of Xavier's strengths: multidimensional characters, moral dilemmas with no easy answers and twists that appeared to come out of nowhere but were cleverly foreshadowed.

And bleak. So bleak.

The Quantum Wraith would no doubt make the list of the top ten movies of the year and would be up for multiple awards. Audiences would flock to the cinemas, she was sure. They would appreciate the artistry. But would they love the film? She was less sure.

"Sutton?" Contessina knocked on the frame of the open door. "Do you have a minute?"

She startled, blinking her way back from the vast reaches of space to the reality of her office at the Pronghorn Ranch. "Of course. What's up?"

Contessina dropped into the guest chair across from Sutton's desk. "Not much. I'm hiding from Tori. She wants me to call my publicist, and I don't want to."

"News about your intruder?"

Contessina shook her head. "His arraignment is set for next week. But neither Juliana nor I have to go."

"So why the avoidance?"

"My publicist thinks I should start making the rounds. You know, get out in public, show up at events and parties."

"It's early to be promoting the film."

"Way too early. People will have forgotten about it by the time it premieres. No, she wants me to get papped and remind directors and studio executives I'll be available for new projects soon."

"You don't have one lined up?"

"No." Contessina rose from the guest chair and started

to pace around the room. "Not every film is a *Quantum Wraith*, you know."

Sutton snorted. "Well aware. I'm employed by Monument, remember?"

"Actually, no. I keep forgetting." Contessina laughed. "Take that as a compliment. Anyway, I'm not excited about going from this film to 'girl in serial killer thriller who motivates the titular hero by dying tragically in the second act, only to be forgotten by the third act.'" She rolled her eyes. "On the other hand, it's work. And a lot of people don't get work. I'm torn between counting my blessings and being angry that the parts I'm offered aren't better."

"I understand." Sutton leaned her elbows on the desk. "I love films and filmmaking, but the industry around them? I do not love. Even though I'm part of it. You're talking about *Lone Sun*, right? That's supposed to be one of my projects as a production executive after I'm finished here. I'd heard they were interested in you."

Contessina clapped her hands to her cheeks and dropped back in her chair. "You won't tell anyone I said that, will you? If I lose the role because I shot my mouth off again…"

"Of course I would never say anything! But, speaking of characters dying tragically, have you read the entire script for *The Quantum Wraith*?"

"Xavier said he is still working on the final pages, but I know the gist. He told you? Welcome to the club. There's a handful of us sworn to secrecy. I'm not sure if Jay knows."

Sutton lifted the script to show Contessina. "How do you feel about ending as it is right now? Lys alone, abandoned, her hope stripped—"

"But her legend goes on," Contessina said. "The ending is brutal. But I get what Xavier is going for."

Sutton made a face. "I get it, but I don't like it."

"I'm sure he'd be happy to explain his thought process to you. Maybe late at night, while sneaking around the ranch."

Sutton's mouth opened and closed. The best response that popped into her head was a weak "I don't know what you're talking about."

"Uh-huh. As a producer, you're a terrible actor. You know, you cost me fifty dollars in the betting pool. I said you two would have a knock-down, drag-out fight on set and *then* have sex. But if you did fight, it wasn't in front of us. Please tell me I lost on a technicality."

Sutton started to issue another denial, then snapped her lips shut. Who was she kidding, aside from herself, when it came to Xavier? "I refuse to answer on the grounds I may incriminate myself."

"I'll take that as a yes." Contessina looked at her phone. "Okay, I have now officially wasted enough time, so when I call my publicist, I will get her voice mail, and I can put off this conversation for one more day."

"Why not talk to her? Be honest with how you feel."

"You work in what industry again? But it's not that you're wrong, it's the timing that isn't right. There are some other pieces I'm waiting to fall into place. Notice I'm stalling my publicist, not my agent."

"Ah. Sounds like you have other irons in the fire."

The grin that launched a thousand online fan clubs during her *Keiko Stowe, CEO* days lit up the room. "And how.

But I don't want to jinx anything by speaking about the future prematurely, so…can I tell you later?"

"Of course. And, um—" Sutton scratched her neck "—does everyone at the Pronghorn really know?" She was asking a rhetorical question. She knew the answer last night, when Erik mentioned the crew gossip.

"To be fair, you and Xavier were kind of a sucker bet. We all saw it coming, although I tried to warn you. Now, Jason in Transpo and Achike in Wardrobe? That one took most of us by surprise." Contessina kissed Sutton's cheek. "See you at crew dinner. Thanks for the hideout."

"Wait!" But Contessina had exited as suddenly as she arrived.

Sutton rubbed her temples, feeling a headache build. She'd learned her lesson about drinking enough water, but the lack of sleep was catching up to her. Her phone rang as she was searching her bag for aspirin. A quick glance at the screen and the pressure in her brain quadrupled. "Hi, Harry."

Her boss didn't bother with niceties like a greeting. "Kellen and Zeke are coming to the set in two weeks."

"Wait. What?" Forget aspirin. She was required a full head transplant to get rid of the pain. "Why?"

"To show off to Monument's investors. Kellen and Zeke are putting on a road show for them. They were going to visit the soundstages, check out the latest *Vim and Velocity* sequel in production, but Zeke came up with visiting your film."

"Okay." This was an extra hassle she didn't need, but she would make the visit work. And if the investors were as enthusiastic about the film's prospects as she thought they would be, this could be beneficial for the film, for Xavier, for everyone involved.

And for her. Her possible promotion was the one lifeline she had to cling to, as the knowledge she was falling in love with Xavier—might even be all the way in love, if she took the time to examine her emotions, which she refused to do—made her future otherwise appear dark and bleak.

"You sound worried, Harry. But *The Quantum Wraith* is going to be amazing. I saw a partial rough cut last night. The investors should come away impressed."

"You authorized an extra company move."

News traveled fast. "I did. For three days. But—"

"I told you, Sutton, you had to be impeccable on this assignment."

Harry's disapproval was almost tangible, dripping through her phone's speaker. "Authorizing the move is within my remit—"

"Investors care about one thing. Money."

"I know that. But," and she crossed her fingers behind her back, as she was still manipulating the spreadsheets, "we're going to make up the overages by cutting days on the soundstage. I got the proper sign-offs—"

"This isn't about your ability to follow protocol. This is about your judgment. And whether it can be trusted."

She took her phone away from her ear and stared at the screen, counting to ten before she said something that might get her fired on the spot. "I am using my judgment. My creative judgment. I saw the location for myself, the scenery is truly amazing—"

"It's a comic book film." Harry's disdain felt like a physical slap. "It's not supposed to be real. The scenes will still require extensive postproduction, so you're not saving any money. You're just costing Monument more."

"But that's the visual language for this film, the genius of Xavier's vision for *The Quantum Wraith*. He's shooting mostly practical effects and filming on location instead of the expected fantastical computer-generated settings—"

"Watch yourself out there, Sutton. That's all I'm going to say." Harry hung up before she could form a response.

What the hell? Harry had never spoken to her like that. She'd heard him be dismissive to others, usually right before they "ankled for new pastures" as the entertainment trade journals euphemistically called being terminated without cause. But never her. She took a few minutes to bring her breathing under control, and then she dialed Nikki. If anyone knew if she had reason to be paranoid about her future at Monument, Nikki would.

"Hey, stranger!" Nikki answered. "I thought you'd gotten eaten by a coyote. Or maybe a Gila monster. They live in Arizona, don't they?"

"Thankfully, wildlife has not been a factor. Everything else you can imagine, yes."

"I guess I'm glad you're not bleached bones in the desert."

Nikki sounded a bit miffed. And Sutton didn't blame her. "I'm so sorry. I thought my previous producing experience would put me ahead of the learning curve, but this production has been…extra, in every way possible."

"Mm," Nikki hummed. "Including Xavier Duval? I've heard 'extra' attached to him. And you. As in 'extracurricular activities.'"

"What?" Sutton sputtered. "How did that get all the way to you?"

"No denial. Very interesting," Nikki said. "Spill the deets. Now."

"Does everyone at the studio know? Great. That's just awesome." For a day that started off so amazingly perfect—snuggled next to the magnificence of Xavier in all his nude glory, warm and satiated—the afternoon was turning into a dumpster fire.

"It's a rumor. That and eighteen bucks will get you a burger in the commissary."

Sutton dug her thumb into the space between her eyebrows, hoping the pressure would help with her headache. Was the rumor of her affair the cause of Harry's curtness? "I'm not so sure."

Nikki laughed. "C'mon. On the scurrilous scale, it's not even a three-point-five. By the time you come back to LA, people will have moved on to something much more scandalous."

"Maybe. But I was just on the phone with Harry and something's up. Do you think he knows?"

Nikki shrugged. "I'm not close to Harry, so I don't know. But you know he disapproves of gossip, thinks it's a waste of people's time."

"True enough." Sutton chewed on her lower lip. "What do you know about the investor boondoggle Kellen is putting together? They're coming out here to the set in two weeks."

"The Chester situation made investors uneasy about the safety of their money, and Pauley being on the lam doesn't help. They're taking investors on a goodwill tour, to persuade them the studio is still in excellent hands with a bright future."

"The feeling I got from Harry..." Sutton sighed. "He's disappointed in me."

"He's under a lot of pressure. Everyone is. Except for your friend Zeke. He seems to not to have a care in the world whenever I see him. Usually with Kellen."

"Not my friend," Sutton muttered. "Hanging with Kellen? That figures."

"Let me put my ear to the ground, okay? I must run to my staff meeting. But you're not off the hook. I want all the gory details, and you better not leave anything out."

"Here's a preview. Pickup truck. Tent. Thunderstorms." Sutton ended the conversation and turned to her own computer screen. She had so much work to do. There were logistics for the company move to plan. Permits to be checked. A new schedule to send.

The weirdness with Harry to straighten out.

Her pulse sped up. She'd already told her parents she was getting the promotion, confident in her ability to secure the vice president role. She'd just have to make sure that happened.

The next hour was spent sending a flurry of texts and emails, setting the most urgent priorities in motion. To Harry, she forwarded a revised budget, including the company move, the numbers now double- and triple-checked, and received a curt but promising "Good work" message in return. But when the immediate fires were out and she had the space to concentrate on larger projects, she bypassed the open documents and spreadsheets on her computer.

And picked up *The Quantum Wraith* script again.

Maybe Xavier was right. Maybe Hollywood endings where the two lovers embrace after overcoming all obstacles were trite and unrealistic. Maybe the final image of Lys, alone and beaten, despairing yet still fighting, would be what cinched awards. Voting members of various film academies and craft associations did disproportionately love movies that were downbeat and "realistic," after all.

Still…

She opened a new document file, setting the template to Screenplay. At the top of the page she typed, Alternate Third Act, The Quantum Wraith.

Staring at the words on the screen brought a rush of feeling. Since starting at Monument, she'd read hundreds of screenplays, given notes on dozens more. She worked with scripts every day. But she hadn't tried to create something original of her own since her ill-fated final project. She'd taken the C grade and Xavier's disappearance as signs her parents were right and she'd never have a financially secure future as a writer, she would fail miserably and have to run home. So she chose to climb her way up the production ladder instead. Still a risk, but at least she had a 401(k).

Her fingers hovered above the keyboard. What if her dialogue was leaden, her plotting cliché? A deep inhale inflated her lungs. Only one way to find out.

She couldn't do anything about the fast-approaching expiration of her time with Xavier. But she could, maybe, do something about the final scenes of *The Quantum Wraith*.

Maybe by giving Lys a happily ever after, she could give herself her own happy ending. Demonstrate that fighting to love and to be loved was a worthy cause not just in Hollywood movies but in real life.

And maybe she could persuade Xavier to believe that, too. She brought her hands down and started to write.

Fourteen

"The scent of fear is on the breeze and the taste of blood is on my tongue. This is a good day, indeed."
Autarch Zear, *The Quantum Wraith*

Xavier exited the trailer provided to him for his use while the company filmed at the site near Yuma. In some ways it felt like he and Sutton had scouted the canyon a lifetime ago, but their adventure had taken place only four weeks in the past. The sky was dark blue and cloudless, the forecast absent any monsoon conditions. Perfect for filming the final showdown between Lys and Autarch Zear.

And then this first and most intricate phase of production, the location shoot, would be over.

"Hey." Sutton came to stand next to him. She wasn't wearing her usual leggings and pullover shirt combination. Instead, she had on a fitted black top worn over slim-cut black trousers, and her feet were clad in low-heeled black leather boots.

He frowned at her footwear. "Not very practical."

"I'm not dressing for the set. I'm dressing for Kellen and the investors," she said.

Her words were clipped. He took a closer look, noticing her clothes bore a resemblance to Autarch Zear's battle suit, her hair tightly swept back as if to wear under a helmet. "You look like you're going to war."

She didn't laugh as he expected. "Nikki texted the war might be over before it began, but I'm still prepared. Want to grab some breakfast while we can?"

He had a million things he needed to do before call time. There were still decisions to be made about the upcoming two weeks of filming on the soundstages. His real estate agent had last-minute questions about the offer he put in on a house in Los Angeles, not a particularly big place but comfortable enough and convenient to Erik's school. And the final scenes of the film…he still wasn't happy with the script. With every draft, the words became even more flat, trite, pretentious.

But time with her was even more precious. Because it was almost over. And he didn't know how to ask to extend it, not when what she wanted out of their arrangement was in her reach.

She would be a great executive. She was smart and savvy about story, and she'd proven her creative instincts to him time and time again.

They walked in companionable silence to where catering had set up for breakfast. Sutton had asked for the spread to be substantial, not only because of their visitors but to celebrate the last day. There would be a celebration tonight, a small one, not as boisterous as the wrap party thrown several days ago to say goodbye to the Pronghorn and most of the company. Today's shoot would involve only vital crew plus Contessina and Raul.

Xavier loaded up his plate and Sutton followed his example. Erik and Ilsa were already seated at one of the long picnic tables underneath the canvas shade. They moved over to make room, Erik keeping his gaze fixed on his comic book while chewing on his bagel.

"Excited about finally settling in Los Angeles?" Sutton asked. "You're flying out tomorrow, right?"

Erik shrugged. "Sure."

"He's overcome with emotion," Xavier said dryly. "Thrilled about the summer program he starts next week to ensure he's ready for school."

"I placed into all the advanced classes," Erik said. "I don't know why I have to spend the summer doing additional work. I want to hang out with you and Sutton in LA. I was hoping Sutton would show us around." He closed his comic and leaned his elbows on the table.

"Um. Well, you see—" Sutton started moving her eggs around her plate but never lifted her fork to her mouth.

"I don't think Sutton will have time," Xavier said simultaneously.

"Elbows off the table when you are eating, please," Ilsa said to Erik. "Speaking of schoolwork, you and I aren't done with lessons. Finish breakfast and let's go."

Erik sighed and slumped over his bagel. "Fine."

"I'll see you tonight at the party, okay?" Sutton said as

Erik and Ilsa rose. "You better not leave without saying goodbye to me."

Erik gave her a quizzical stare. "Sure. But you make it sound like I'll never see you again. It's only a few days."

Sutton's gaze followed Erik and Ilsa as they departed.

Xavier watched her. "What's wrong?" he asked. "You have that crease between your eyebrows again."

"Just thinking about Los Angeles." She played with the tater tots, chasing them around her plate.

A persistent drum began beating in his veins. "And?"

"These past months, we've been in a location bubble. But LA… LA is reality. It's paying rent and running errands and going to appointments and…" She stabbed a hash brown with her fork.

He hated the shadows in her eyes. "I thought LA was mostly traffic," he tried joking.

"That too. Remember, you must put 'the' in front of the freeway number, or we'll know you're an imposter."

"Because freeways are so important, they need an article?"

"You got it." She stirred her scrambled eggs but still didn't take a bite. "So, I…" She looked up at him, her green gaze wide and open and shimmering. "I wanted to let you know the past several weeks have meant a lot to me. But if you don't want me around Erik when we're in Los Angeles, I'd like to say I understand, but I don't. But let's just say I'll respect your wishes."

Now the beat was a metronome, ticking furiously. "You want to see each other in Los Angeles?"

She blinked at him. "Are you making a joke?"

"I want to be mindful of our original agreement—"

She burst into laughter so loud and hard that tears formed in her eyes. "We have got to do something about our communication. Or rather, I need to remember you require bluntness."

"I wouldn't say bluntness." Although his parents had taught him not to assume people wanted to spend extended time with him, much less sought out his company without an ulterior purpose. So maybe she wasn't wrong.

"Yes, I'd like to still see each other in Los Angeles, if you do. And please don't leave your answer in a letter." She threw him a crooked grin.

The metronome beat so loud, he wasn't sure he heard her. "There's an overabundance of rain checks left to be cashed, if I recall correctly."

Her gaze flickered, just for a second. Then the skies brightened, or perhaps that was just her smile. "I'll take them." She took a big bite of her eggs. "And speaking of the future, earlier this morning I sent you an email with something I wrote. And I want you to know, if you read it, I hope you don't think I'm overstepping, but it's really a way to let you know how I feel and—

"Hey, guys." Contessina ambled over, a plate of fresh fruit in her hand. "Can anyone join, or is this a party of two?"

Sutton hesitated for a split second, but then she waved Contessina in. "Sure."

"Actually, Sutton and I were in the middle of something." He tried to catch her gaze, but she was busy scooting over and patting the bench next to her.

"No, I was babbling. I can babble later. I thought you'd want to eat in your trailer, Conti."

"I have a long stint in makeup ahead, so I'm enjoying fresh air while I can." She side-eyed Sutton. "You look like you've already been to makeup. Quite the bold lip. If I didn't know better, I'd say you're about to play Fierce Female Executive in a boardroom drama."

"Perfect. Exactly what I'm going for." Sutton winced.

Xavier frowned, but Contessina beat him to the question. "Everything okay?"

"Oh, the usual jitters at the thought of entertaining Kellen and a select group of investors. Nothing big."

He squeezed her hand under the table. "They'll watch a scene, I'll introduce them to Contessina and Raul, and they'll take some selfies before getting on the corporate jet. Shouldn't be too rough."

"I know. But it's…it's the president. Of the studio."

"And there's your…thing," he added. "The thing you're hoping might happen."

"Exactly," she said.

Contessina glanced between them. "I'm sensing there's something going on, and for some reason I haven't been informed what it is," she said. "Just let me know if I have anything to worry about."

Sutton shook her head. "You're golden, as always. You're going to blow Kellen away when he gets here."

"I knew I liked you." Contessina threw her arm over Sutton's shoulders. "Hey, you know the irons in the fire we were talking about? Because I tell you things and you apparently don't tell me? One of them might be red hot. But I need to finish this film first."

"I hope it's not *Lone Sun*. Because I read the latest draft and—yikes."

"No." Contessina scoffed. "I've officially turned that down. But if this iron turns out to be what I think it will be? You and I should have a conversation."

Sutton's phone buzzed. "Sounds good," she mumbled, her attention focused on her screen. "Kellen's jet is scheduled to land in an hour. If you two will excuse me, I'm going to check with Transpo to ensure cars and drivers are waiting for him and the investors at the airport."

Xavier caught her elbow as she rose from the bench. "I know you're concerned. But today is going to be great." He stopped speaking when she started shaking her head violently.

"When you're being an optimist, that's when I worry. I'll see you at this morning's safety meeting." She waved and set off toward the trailer that served as the production office for the day.

He watched her leave, admiring as always how she moved through the crowd with a grace and ease he could never affect. He was going to miss this. Miss the early morning conversations, both about items weighty: the production, Erik, them—and items inconsequential such as the weather and ranking their favorite Ryan Coogler films.

But she was right. LA would be real life.

Real life killed his relationship with Mimi. Once they left the cocoon of production, the demands and pressures of two busy lives—plus ensuring Erik had all the time and attention he needed and wanted—the affair fizzled. In fact, he wondered if he and Mimi had been in love or merely swept up in the romance they were creating for the screen.

His feelings for Sutton were different. Deeper. Truer. Honest. And as long as *The Quantum Wraith* was filming on location, they could indulge in their private penalty box—carve out time away from the set.

But once they were in Los Angeles...

He hoped they could make seeing each other work. He wanted to. But life was not a movie. There were no scripted happy endings.

The morning went by swiftly as he, Contessina and Raul, and the fight coordinator staged the scene, coming up with a plan of attack that both actors felt comfortable with. Then the crew went to work, rigging the lights and placing the camera, while Contessina and Raul went to hair and makeup and then to wardrobe before returning to the set for the final rehearsal that preceded shooting. They were nearing the end of that run-through when his peripheral vision caught a red-gold ponytail standing with a group of unfamiliar faces on the far periphery near video village.

Most of the newcomers were dressed for the desert in light-colored pants and either golf shirts or loose blouses, but everything from their fashionable precision haircuts to the expensive athletic shoes on their feet—not to mention the way they ignored everyone but themselves—said these people had money, power and influence. The only exception to the desert casual wear rule was a man who appeared to be in his early thirties wearing a sharply cut suit, who didn't get the memo they would be outside among the sand and cacti or didn't care. He had *studio executive* written all over him—the kind of suit Xavier had once feared Sutton had become.

Contessina followed his gaze. "Time to give an extra performance," she said dryly. "One for the camera and the other for the Monument brass. I should be paid twice for today."

"Are they too distracting? I can get rid of them," he offered. Perhaps not the most political move to make but protecting the actors' performances came first.

"No, you can't," she said. "I mean, you could, but I'd like to see you make more films. And this is nothing compared to having the head of the network in the front row for the taping of a 'very special episode' in which Keiko frets about her first kiss. Which takes place at a pool party. While wearing a bikini. Nothing embarrassing about it at all, especially when that was my first kiss in real life as well."

"You have the best stories," Raul said. "I can't compete. The closest I ever came was forgetting my dagger in a production of *Romeo and Juliet*. That was a rather anticlimactic death for poor Juliet."

"Back to the scene," Xavier interjected. He had only been half listening as it was. His gaze kept slipping to Sutton. Her smile was calm and placid, her posture straight but not rigid. And nothing about her expression or body language read as genuine to him. "Do you want to go again? Or are you comfortable?"

"I'm very confident," Contessina said. She turned to Raul. "You?"

"More than ready to tear you into tiny shards," he said with a laugh. "And to get some water before we go for real."

"Great." Xavier broke the actors for fifteen minutes, allowing for hydration and last hair and makeup looks, and then strode over to the group of newcomers.

He loved the craft of filmmaking. He lived for the artistry, the use of light and shadow and color and texture, the careful composition designed to draw the eye to an item or area of the frame. And he relished the teamwork, working with hundreds of talented craftspeople who cared as passionately about their work as they did, each person contributed their talents to the mosaic of the finished film. That was the *show* in show business.

Business, on the other hand, was not his thing. The constant dinners and lunches, the taking of meetings that usually went nowhere, the need to paste a grin on his face as he slapped the backs of people who were complimentary to his face but then never returned his agent's phone calls. Sutton may play the game beautifully, but he had neither time nor desire.

Still, duty called.

"Xavier Duval," he said, sliding his headset to rest around his neck before holding out his right hand to Kellen, followed by the remaining newcomers. "Good to see you again, Kellen, and welcome, everyone, to *The Quantum Wraith*. We'll start again soon. In the meantime, can I answer any questions?"

"Just pretend we're not here," said the man in the suit, squeezing into the space between Kellen and Xavier. He extended his right hand. "Zeke Fountaine. New vice president of production for Monument."

Xavier's stomach twisted, the words landing a sour punch to his gut. That was the promotion Sutton had wanted. His gaze slid to her and she shook her head slightly, keeping her expression schooled in a calm, placid mask. Okay. He'd talk to her later.

"Real glad to be here," Zeke continued. He put his arm around Xavier without an indication he would welcome the touch, moving him away from the knot of people. Xavier caught the scent of cloying aftershave. "Now, I know you're occupied now, but can I grab you after the day is over? We've got things to discuss about the postproduction schedule."

"I thought you were here for a meet and greet."

"Oh, sure, this is a boondoggle for the investors so they can see we're spending their hard-earned dinero correctomundo. You know, wine, dine, observe the talent at work."

He made Contessina and Raul sound like animals on display in an exhibit. Perhaps Xavier was supposed to be one, too.

"But after that you and I have lots to do, buddy!" Zeke thumped Xavier's back. "And, hey, we must celebrate. Pauley and that assistant of his have been found holed up in Mexico. They're being hauled back as we speak."

Xavier pointedly stared at Zeke until the other man stepped back. "Sure," Xavier said evenly. "There's a small cast and crew party tonight after we wrap location. Sutton and I can celebrate with you then."

Zeke sucked on his lower lip. "Not so fast on Sutton."

That unsettling squeeze deep in his belly returned, sharper and more insistent. "Sutton is the producer."

"Temp producer. I'm taking over to get you across the finish line, and don't you worry, it's how you finish that matters. None of the foolishness with Pauley and Sutton will be held against you."

"What foolishness? Sutton saved *The Quantum Wraith* after Pauley embezzled the money." The sun was climbing higher in the Arizona sky, but Xavier was chilled as if he were in Antarctica at midnight. "There wouldn't be a film without her."

"Look, Sutton did her best, and we all know you were 'close.'" Zeke made air quotes with his fingers. "I mean, you're on location, right? Look at Pauley, he went so far as to run off with his squeeze. So of course you'd stick up for her, you're a loyal guy, that's likeable of you. But we took a look at the footage, and this film is moving up on our priority list—could be an award contender...if you get real support and guardrails during postprod, not Sutton deciding to sign off on extra days willy-nilly, y'know?" He moved as if he were going to throw his arm over Xavier's shoulders, but Xavier turned the full force of his glare on him, and Zeke let his hand drop. "We're going to have fun together, buddy, and in the end *The Quantum Wraith* will turn out to be a film Monument is proud to distribute. You'll see."

His vision was shades of red and puce, his hands forming fists without being asked. He was going to pop Zeke Fontaine square in his pointy nose, and then he was going to demand Kellen promote Sutton as she deserved—

"Hey." Sutton's soft warm hand on his right bicep brought him back to the set. "Jay is signaling for you."

He tried to search her gaze, but her shutters were firmly in place. "Kellen said—"

Her attention was caught by someone over his shoulder, and she nodded at whoever it was. "I have to go. We'll talk later?"

"Sure." Xavier watched Sutton join the tight knot surrounding Kellen. Despite his best attempt at psychic communication to make her look at him and give him an indication she was okay, she did not turn around.

"You have got to start answering your walkie." Jay appeared at his side. "I volunteered to come get you and to save a PA's legs in this heat."

"Sorry." He pulled his headset over his ears.

Jay's eyes narrowed. "Monument meet and greet not go well?"

Xavier once more tried to attract Sutton's notice, to no avail. "It was a meeting. Not much greeting."

"Oh?"

"Yeah." Sutton remained standing with her back to him. He wanted nothing more than to take her aside and discover what had happened, to ensure she was fine after this Zeke person showed up and announced he had the vice president job, but time didn't permit. "Let's get this scene in the virtual can."

Fifteen

"You can't hurt me. You can't break something that's already dead."

Lys Amarga, *The Quantum Wraith*

In the end, the shoot couldn't have gone better. Contessina and Raul received standing ovations from the crew for their intense dedication to the confrontation. The otherworldly beauty of the canyon only enhanced the drama. The team performed their roles expertly with little to no mishaps or delays, and the martini shot was completed and the production wrapped in plenty of time for everyone to clean up and change their clothes for the celebration. The investors departed for the airport, chattering excitedly about their enthusiasm for the film, and Kellen had given Xavier an especially hard back thump of congratulations as he left the set.

Xavier should be basking in his well-earned triumph, but his inability to connect further with Sutton kept him from enjoying the sincere congratulations and celebratory hugs. By the time he made his way to the small hotel ballroom with Erik and Ilsa for the party, his skin vibrated with concern.

"What's up with you?" Erik asked. "You haven't answered me at all."

"Sorry. What was the question?"

"What time are we leaving for LA tomorrow?"

"Oh. The flight is at eleven a.m., I think?" He looked at Ilsa for confirmation, and she nodded.

"Cool." Erik bounced on the balls of his feet, a rather uncharacteristic motion.

"Anxious or excited?" Xavier asked.

"Both."

"Me too." He followed Erik's gaze to the table set up with assorted sliders, from hamburger to pulled pork to portobello mushroom. "Go eat. I'll be right behind—"

His breath caught. Sutton had entered the ballroom, her hair loose around her shoulders in a fiery halo of curls, clad in a simple blue dress belted at the waist. She'd never looked more assured, more confident. And absolutely gorgeous.

"Yeah, no, you won't be behind me," Erik said with an eye roll, tempered quickly with a grin. "Have fun. See you later."

By the time Xavier could reach Sutton, she'd been joined by Kellen. He arrived just as Kellen said, "This doesn't seem like a cheap party."

The same smile Sutton had on her face all day continued not to falter. "You'd be surprised at what we were able to get at cost."

"Sure, sure. That's what you said about the film's budget. And now I'm somewhere near Yuma."

"And the location made the scene," Xavier interjected,

stepping into the space between Sutton and Kellen. "We wouldn't have gotten the same impact, the same performance from the actors if we filmed that on a stage. We needed to be on location."

Kellen nodded. "It looked great on the monitor. But there's still to be seen what post—"

"Listen, I'll be the first to admit the production was in disarray. I didn't…" He inhaled. Admitting he ran a less than a tight ship in front of the president of Monument Studios could be fatal to his goal of receiving more studio directorial assignments, but this was important. Sutton was important. "I should have paid more attention to what Pauley was doing. I trusted him too blindly. Sutton took a demoralized team and accounts that were out of control, and she turned the entire situation around. If the film is a success, it's due to her hard work and dedication. She deserves Monument's thanks. I know she has mine."

Kellen's look of surprise was almost comical. "Sutton has done a good job, but—"

"No. Sutton has done an excellent job. She's the beating heart of this unit—"

"Oh, is this the part where we praise Sutton?" Contessina joined them, glamorous in a silver silk dress cut to drape just so over all the right places. "I couldn't have gotten through this shoot without her finding a way for me to go home and be with Juliana. Lys may not break, but I would've."

"Guys." Sutton stepped forward. Her mask slipped, emotion welling in her green gaze. Xavier's chest squeezed, hard, and he found himself reaching for her hand before he remembered a public display of affection in front of Kellen wasn't the best idea. "I appreciate all the kind words, but I think there's a misunderstanding."

"The misunderstanding is Zeke saying he'd be overseeing the rest of the production," Xavier said.

Kellen's face hardened. "That was premature. But not a misunderstanding."

"I am not allowing Sutton to be pulled off this film when she's the best thing to have happened to it." Xavier's voice cut through the hum and noise of the ballroom.

Chatter stopped in their immediate vicinity as the other guests shot questioning glances in their direction.

Sutton touched his arm. "Can we talk? Privately?" She looked at Kellen. "If you will excuse us."

Kellen gave her a half shrug. "Sure." He turned to Contessina. "What about you? Have a minute?"

"For you, I have all the minutes." She flashed her smile and led Kellen to the bar on the other side of the room.

Xavier watched them only long enough to make sure they were out of earshot before turning to Sutton. "I've been wanting to ask you all day if you're all right."

"I'm fine," she said with a smile. "Especially after that defense. That was so sweet. And wonderful. Thank you." She leaned up and briefly brushed her lips across his cheek. "You've been a knight in shining armor throughout this production."

He held her gaze, searching the green depths. "But Zeke Fountaine—"

"Is an ass. And he shouldn't have said anything to you. Not yet."

"What do you mean, not yet? Sutton, he introduced himself as the new vice president of production. And he implied you're off *The Quantum Wraith*. What's going on?"

She sighed. "Zeke is a sore winner."

"What he said is true?" Lava erupted in his veins. "Let me talk to Kellen—"

"No!" Sutton grabbed his hand and squeezed his fingers before dropping the connection. "Everything's fine. Honest."

"But if Zeke is the winner—"

"He's the winner in a manner of speaking. But that doesn't mean I lost." She squeezed his hand.

"I don't understand." His confusion was complete. As for his emotions, they couldn't be more jumbled if they'd been put in a blender set to terminal velocity."

"First things first. It's true. Zeke was given Chester's job. Did you meet the older man among the investors? Silver hair, tall, dark blue polo shirt?"

"What does the investor have to do with Zeke?"

"That's his father."

"Oh." He thought the information over for a beat. "Zeke is still an ass."

"Can't disagree." She shrugged. "But in the end, it was never a contest. My boss Harry thought I had a chance if I proved myself on this film, and he was furious when he discovered the promotion was never going to me. But the writing was on the wall once Zeke's father put his money in the studio."

"I'm so sorry." His gaze locked with hers. He hoped she could read all the things he didn't dare say in public.

"I won't deny it stings."

"I'm going to tell Kellen where he can stick Zeke, and

it's not on my film." He started to move past her, but she grabbed his arm.

"No! Don't do that. There's more."

"More?" His stomach squeezed at the warning look in her gaze.

She steadied herself. "I'm not getting the vice president job. But Kellen was truly impressed with today. Thinks Contessina is going to be a big star. And he agreed the location was the right call, matched the grittiness and reality of the scene but also the otherworldliness."

"That sounds like good news. So why are you—"

"Because it is good news." Her smile turned brighter than the crystal chandeliers above them. "Kellen offered me an even better position, overseeing Monument's productions in Europe. They're expanding their overseas coproductions, which is part of the new investment deal. And Kellen thought my experience on *The Quantum Wraith* made me the perfect candidate for cutting through barriers and communication problems."

Xavier broke into a grin, relief that caused his knees to go weak. "Sutton! That's amazing. And well deserved."

"Well, I doubt I can use the same methods of communication on them that I use on you." She briefly touched his cheek.

"They're pretty effective, I will admit." His lungs could take in air again. "Good thing there's already a party happening, because we need to celebrate." He signaled for a passing waiter with a tray of freshly poured flutes of champagne to come by and offered one to Sutton before taking one for himself.

She accepted the flute, but her fingers were tight on the stem. "There's one thing more."

"Oh?" The champagne was crisp and cool, the bubbles matching the fizzing feeling in his veins her nearness always caused.

"They want me to start tomorrow. In London. They're already working on an expedited work visa. The director and the two stars are in a tense standoff on the latest *Destiny's Dragons* film, and, well, I don't need to tell you how that can affect morale on the set—"

"Wait." The champagne turned to battery acid. Turned out, the shoe just hadn't fallen yet. And this was a hell of a shoe. A steel-toed boot, in fact. "London? Tomorrow?"

"I know, but I'm already packed thanks to my time here, and Nikki said she'd continue to look in on my apartment. Although, I guess I'm going to have to buy an umbrella and dump my year's supply of sunscreen."

Whiplash didn't begin to describe what was happening to his emotions. "What about *The Quantum Wraith*?"

She bit her lower lip. "That's the worst part about this. But the film is in great shape. There's only two weeks of principle photography left on the soundstages and then you'll be going into post. You won't need me—"

"What do you mean? Of course, the film will need you."

She folded her arms across her chest, the excited light in her gaze fading. "Just the film?"

The sounds of the ballroom faded away, replaced by the dull thumping of his heart.

He'd always known losing Sutton was inevitable. The relationship would fade out eventually once they returned to prosaic reality and the excitement of making the film was over. She would have left him anyway, once the glamour wore off. Like Mimi. The only thing that should come as a surprise was that the day arrived even quicker than he anticipated. All her announcement did was speed up the process.

At least Erik hadn't become too accustomed to having Sutton be a constant presence in his life. He did that right. Although Erik would still miss her.

He would also miss her. So much. More than he dared admit to himself.

"You're a vital member of the team. I respect your judgment. Of course, I would welcome the opportunity to still work with you. Hopefully we will work together again in the future."

Hurt flashed deep in her emerald eyes. But in the end, he was being kind. To both of them. No need for protracted goodbyes. "So, it's my judgment you like," she said slowly. "You can't possibly need me for any other reason. Like, say, ten years of rain checks. Or anything more."

"We had a deal, Sutton. You get your promotion. And you said Kellen is pleased, which mean I'm delivering a film that will allow me to move into the ranks of top tier studio directors. Looks like we got what we both wanted."

Confusion chased anger chased dismay across her expression. "The last few weeks…us…it was just a deal to you? I don't believe that. I think you're trying to push me away." Her gaze searched his until he could no longer take her scrutiny. He glanced around the ballroom to see if they had attracted any attention. Sure enough, interested glances were being thrown their way.

"This isn't the right time—"

She huffed. "Time. It wasn't the right time at LAU. And it's not the time now. When will be the right time, Xavier?"

"You just told me you're going to London tomorrow."

"London doesn't matter! Yes, we'll be in different cities. But there are phones, video calls, texts, email, planes... It's not like we can only communicate by letters sent by ocean voyage. And even when ocean voyages were the only thing possible, people still managed to have long-distance relationships."

"That's not the issue—

"It *is* the issue. It's the only issue." Red suffused her face, obscuring her freckles. "We just spoke about continuing to see each other in LA. The only thing that has changed is that I will in London instead. Why does that make such a difference? Tell me."

He knew what she was really asking. And he wished he had faith. That he believed in a world where "love conquers all" wasn't a shopworn cliché, where happily ever after wasn't merely a trite ending for a popcorn flick meant to be consumed and then forgotten. That he could sweep Sutton into his arms and hold on her to forever, to wake up with her breath warm on his cheek every morning and to go to sleep with their limbs entangled every night.

But the world wasn't popcorn and rainbows and riding off into the sunset. Life was chaotic and complicated and hard, hard work. His parents never gave him much, but the one lesson he took from them was a firm appreciation for ripping off bandages and facing immediate hurt instead of prolonging the agony. And he knew her. Her optimism and desire to never give up even on hopeless situations meant she would never be the first one to call quits in any given situation.

Therefore, it was up to him to do the right thing for both of them. And let her go to her bright future without any encumbrances, any assumed obligations.

Free from inevitable future resentments and painful regrets.

He fixed his gaze on a distant point over her shoulder. "LA would have been a continuation of our time here. And we had a good time. A great time. I will forever be thankful you walked onto my set and back into my life. But you have an amazing opportunity now. You need to take it."

"I'm going to take it. That was never a question. But I don't have to choose between you and London. *We* don't have to choose. I don't understand why you're… I don't…" She took several gulping breaths. "Wait. I do know. This is *Vertigo* versus *Notorious* all over again. All of our conversations about storytelling, from film school to today. Why you so hated my final project."

Her voice, thin at first, gained power with every word. "I recently reread that screenplay, for the first time since seeing your grade. And you know what? You were right. I did half-ass the writing. But you're wrong about the emotion. I poured my heart into that script because I had such an enormous crush on you. That happy ending wasn't a tired, unrealistic cliché. That ending was hope. Hope and a promise for the future. But you…you're scared to ask for a future. You scared to demand what you want. You leave it up to fate, other people. You left our future up to a letter—*a letter*—ten years ago."

His feet were rooted to the floor. He was cold, cold as stone, a statue of marble and metal. His heart screamed to tell her she was wrong, that a future with her was worth fighting to the death.

His head wouldn't let the words come out. There were no fairy-tale endings in real life.

"And the thing is," she continued, her brilliant emerald gaze pinning him in place and allowing him no escape, "we could have a future. A great one. You're thoughtful and caring and smart and you…you make me feel treasured. You took care of me when I needed you, and you take care of Erik and Ilsa and everyone on set. You're a good man, Xavier Duval."

Something started to tear deep inside his chest.

"But I offer and offer myself to you, and you won't accept. I understand why when I was your student. But that's not the case now. And yet I still had to practically beg to get you to go on a date with me, and now you're outright refusing to consider a future only because I'm going to be in another country."

His mouth finally agreed to form words. "I'm being realistic. One of us has to face reality."

She nodded, her head bobbing rapidly. "Right. Realistic. Of course. You think realistic is Kim Novak jumping to her death at the end of *Vertigo* but Cary Grant realizing he loves Ingrid Bergman and saving her life in *Notorious*, that's unbelievable, correct?"

"Films are not real life—"

"I know that! But news flash, Xavier. Sad endings are not realistic. They're just tragic. And I know tragedies have happened to you, but good things would happen, too, if you would only allow them. Allow me."

His heart hurt. His head was beginning to ache, too. "Go to London, Sutton. Be amazing. I know you will be."

"I love you." She searched his gaze, her gaze open and pleading and shimmering.

And he loved her. Her words caused the rift in his heart to widen enough to now fit the entire solar system.

But he'd learned long ago people who loved him left. People who loved him died. If Sutton stayed, if they tried to continue dating, she would gradually pull away like Mimi did. The light in her gaze would fade to indifference, and while he quickly got over Mimi, witnessing the same from Sutton would devastate him.

He was doing her a favor. He was keeping Erik from another loss. He just had to keep repeating that to himself.

She fell back, her shoulders slumping. "Tell Erik I'm sorry we didn't say goodbye after all, please? I'll text Ilsa as well. He needs to know if he wants to talk comics, I'm always available for him. Always. I mean that." She took another step before turning around again. "Oh. I almost forgot. About that email I sent you earlier today. Go ahead and delete it."

"Why?"

"It's a collection of hackneyed clichés. Disregard. See you in the movies, Xavier." And with that, she was gone.

She took all the light and warmth and music of the room with her. But he was doing the right thing.

He was saying he loved her by letting her go.

Sixteen

"Love makes the universe spin."
Lys Amarga, *The Quantum Wraith*

Six months later

The unrelenting Los Angeles sunshine came as a welcome surprise after six months under London's nearly perpetual gray skies. Sutton fumbled for her sunglasses in her purse with one hand while gripping the handle of her suitcase with the other. The sidewalk in front of the international terminal at LAX was crowded, and although she was exhausted thanks to the eleven-hour flight, she still needed to keep her wits about her long enough to find the designated pickup place for her rideshare and then brave the traffic until she could collapse in her apartment.

"Excuse me, miss, but I think I'm supposed to take this." Someone grabbed the handle of her suitcase and Sutton whirled around, prepared to scream for help, when she recognized Contessina's smile under the Dodgers baseball cap and curly blond wig.

"What are you doing here? And what are you wearing?" She hugged the actor.

"I wouldn't let you come home without a real welcome!" Contessina tugged on the bag, and this time Sutton let her take the handle. "As for the wig, *Keiko Stowe* recently started airing in reruns on ScreenNet. I can't tell you how many ten-year-olds I've disappointed by being a grown-up now. The blond hair throws them off." She led Sutton to a waiting town car, where the driver deposited the luggage in the trunk before helping both women into the back seat. "So. Tell me all."

"There's not much to tell." Sutton ran her fingers through her hair, trying to put life into locks left limp by the dry recycled air on the plane. "You know London. The food is delicious, the history is stimulating, the shopping unparalleled and the theater awesome."

"Yeah, yeah, three cheers for Old Blighty. You know what I want to hear. Last time we spoke—"

"Yes. I quit Monument."

"You did?" Contessina's grin was brighter than the sunshine outside the car windows. "So, does this mean…?"

"Yes, I will be the head of production for your new startup company. Which you already guessed, or you wouldn't have shown up at the airport."

"This is true. I like you a lot, but not enough to brave the hell that is LAX arrivals unless I thought there was something in it for me." Contessina rubbed her hands together. "So, do you have to serve out your notice to Monument or can you begin right away? We really need you. I'm drowning in scripts, and my partners are eager to start spending their money."

"I already served my notice. Truthfully, I gave it right after you and I ended our call. The London gig was great, but I realized I wasn't happy being an executive at a big studio." Sutton realized her mistake almost as soon as her plane touched down at Heathrow. She gave the job her best effort, but after the collaborative atmosphere of *The Quantum Wraith*, shepherding other people's projects from afar for a paycheck, no matter how steady, was no longer fulfilling.

Her experiences in Arizona also caused her to recognize how she'd stunted her own growth by being afraid to follow her creative dreams because of the risk. While her gamble to secure Xavier's heart didn't pay off—even the thought of his name caused her to wince with how much she missed him—she'd decided the time had come to throw off the corporate golden handcuffs and test her own wings. Contessina's offer was the perfect launching pad. "I'm so excited to be part of your company's mission. Thanks for your trust in me."

"I have zero concerns. Not after how you turned *The Quantum Wraith* around. Now, here's our short list of potential first projects. They're all from first-time screenwriters or directors." Contessina and her backers were determined to provide opportunities for voices and visions who had previously received nothing but Hollywood doors slammed in their faces. She handed an electronic tablet to Sutton, and together they scrolled through the pitches until Sutton's gaze started to swim. She glanced out the window to see how far they had traveled from the airport and was surprised to find herself in the neighborhood of Los Feliz.

"Where are we going? I live in the Valley, near Encino. Opposite side of town, other side of the hill."

"Oh, didn't I tell you? Your timing is impeccable."

"Tell me what?" The car was slowing, turning onto a tree-lined residential street filled with one- and two-story houses of various styles, from colonial to mid-century, set back from the street with expansive yards and flowering bushes. "Is this where you live?"

"Me? No. Juliana and I are in Laurel Canyon."

"So, where..." The car pulled to a stop in front of a white two-story Spanish revival home, and the driver opened the door on Contessina's side before coming around to open Sutton's door. "You realize I just got off a transatlantic flight, right? I'm not in any shape to meet new people?"

Contessina tsked. "Good thing you're meeting old people. Well, not old in age."

Sutton suddenly had a bad feeling about who lived behind the heavy wood front door. "Conti, this isn't funny now. I'm not big on ambushes."

"Wow, your face is so white! No, no ambush. We're here to see a rough edit of *The Quantum Wraith*. Well, it's pretty close to a final edit. There's some sweetening left to be done and the music is still a temp track—they haven't added the score yet. Like I said, your timing was impeccable. I was going to come here anyway, only I picked you up first."

"So, Xavier is..." Sutton couldn't bring herself to finish the sentence, a half hope, a half fear.

She hadn't talked to Xavier since that night in the Yuma

ballroom, although she and Erik texted about comics and comics only. While she kept tabs on *The Quantum Wraith*, the surveillance had been from afar, mostly abetted by Nikki and occasionally Harry. Her stomach folded into various origami shapes and she regretted her overly salty airline meal.

"Not here. Honest. I meant it when I said no ambush. He offered up his house when the original venue fell through, but Jay is hosting the screening." She searched Sutton's gaze. "I thought this would be a fun surprise for you, but I appear to have overstepped again. If you want to go home, the driver will take you."

"No, it's okay. I want to see the film." Her trembling hands and feet warred with her curiosity, and the latter won. If by any chance she did run into Xavier, at least this time, only six months had passed and not ten years. She was an adult; she could manage her emotions.

She hoped.

The screening room was at the rear of the house, so Contessina led the way through a side gate into the backyard and around the patio to a back entrance. Sutton couldn't help but notice that while this patio was lusher and greener than the one at the ranch house at the Pronghorn, there were still miniature lights and battery-operated candles strewn around the area. She briefly wondered if Erik had pulled off a Chez Duval dinner for another unsuspecting date. The subsequent stabbing pain caused her to almost trip on the flagstones.

The screening room was filled with familiar and much-missed faces—except for one. Sutton greeted various department heads from the crew of *The Quantum Wraith*, from Transportation to Camera to Luisa. When she finally got up the nerve to ask Jay if Xavier would join them, she got a headshake in return. "He wanted to be here, but he had meetings he couldn't miss, and then Erik has a game."

Sutton wondered which sport, but before she could pose the question the lights dimmed and people started finding seats. She sat in the last row, where hopefully no one would spot her if she succumbed to jet lag. But any thoughts of sleeping dissipated, starting with the opening frame. *The Quantum Wraith* was even more riveting, with most of the scenes now completed, than when she saw the initial rough edit with Xavier. Her tears fell thick and fast when Con died, now knowing he was indeed dead and Lys's heart would be buried with him.

As the minutes ticked on toward the end of the film, her neck and shoulders began to tense. All would soon be lost for Lys: physically beaten, her spirit broken, her heart brutally ripped away. Aware the film would end with only Lys's name surviving, the legend of her exploits a rallying inspiration for future generations, Sutton crafted a plan for a quick getaway so she wouldn't have to watch Lys's devastating defeat.

But the moment never came.

Lys confronted Autarch Zear…and lived. Hurt, in pain, damaged both in body and soul, but she lived. And the lines spoken by Contessina…

Sutton knew those lines.

She'd written those lines.

The buzzing in her ears made it difficult to understand what was being said on the screen. She leaned forward in her seat and concentrated. Not every word was hers. The dialogue had been polished, the subtext clearer, the wit more biting. Some scenes had been tightened, others had been cut for something more resonant and affecting.

But overall, this was her alternate third act. Including the revelation that Con had survived to assist Lys's escape so she could fight, and love, another day.

The lights came on. Excited chatter filled the air around her as everyone in the room jumped up and began to mill about the room, back slaps and animated hands attesting to the overwhelmingly positive reaction.

Everyone but Sutton, who remained still and silent in her chair, her mind trying to process the unbelievable.

Xavier used her ending. An ending that promised love and hope and optimism. An ending in which she gave Lys everything she desired for Xavier and herself.

He. Used. Her. Ending.

She needed air. Fresh air.

Contessina was deep in conversation with Raul and Jay, and if the past was any guideline, the three of them could happily talk for hours. She wouldn't be missed.

Retracing the steps she took earlier, she found herself on the patio. Daylight had faded and the tiny twinkle lights in the bushes were making their presence known. She was suddenly craving ribs, and she started to laugh, pacing the length of the patio and then turning to pace in the other direction—

Xavier stood in her path.

His beard was a touch longer, as was his hair. His jeans hung low on his narrow hips while his white shirt was open at the neck, revealing that triangle of chest air. He appeared tired but content, his hands carrying what looked like a hockey stick and helmet. He looked mouth-wateringly delicious, and Sutton pressed her lips together on the off chance this was a hallucination caused by jet lag and she would wake up in a pool of her own drool at any moment.

But if this were a hallucination, it was a lifelike one. Sounded like him, too.

"Sutton? What are you doing here?"

Xavier blinked. And blinked again.

He'd had many vivid daydreams about Sutton in the past six months. His dreams were even more visceral, Sutton by his side, in his bed. His heart happy, his life full...only to wake up with empty arms and the space next to him cold. Now his fantasies were seeping into reality because he could swear Sutton was standing on his patio.

"What are you doing here?" he repeated.

Maybe it wasn't her. Her hair was shorter than he remembered, the red-gold curls cut into a messy shoulder length bob. The casual leggings and tops of the desert were gone, replaced by well-cut jeans that emphasized her long legs and curvy hips, and a boxy dark green sweater that brought out the roses in her cheeks and the emerald in her eyes.

Her pink plump lips—lips that haunted his thoughts—opened and closed a few times before she spoke. "I... Contessina brought me here to see the rough cut of *The Quantum Wraith*."

"But you're in London."

"Apparently, I'm not."

"But you have to be in London." His mind stuttered on that fact. She had to be there. Everything depended on her being on British soil.

She frowned at him. "Are you…are you holding a hockey stick? And a hockey helmet?" A small smile came and went so fast he wasn't sure if he saw the expression. "Watch out for the penalty box."

Penalty box…he took a step toward her, but the stick banged against his leg. Right. Erik's game. Seeing her had completely wiped his short-term memory. "I need to leave."

No. Wait. What was he doing?

When Erik learned Sutton had left for London, he had read Xavier the riot act in the way only a twelve-going-on-thirty-years-old kid could do. God help him when his adopted son became a teenager in reality. "I mean, I need to drop this off for him. But I'll be back." His phone vibrated with a text. "This is probably him, wondering where I am."

She nodded, her expression continuing to read as shocked as he felt. "Say hi."

The text was indeed from Erik. Who'd sent a selfie of himself wearing an identical helmet and carrying an identical stick with the message: **You can miss the game. Tell Jay I owe him. Tell Sutton welcome home.**

Xavier stared at his phone. What the…?

"Is everything okay with Erik?" Sutton asked.

"He's fine." He had to laugh. "Erik sent me here on a wild-goose chase. Jay must have told him you were here, so he pretended he forgot his equipment."

"Conti promised no ambush. I guess Jay and Erik made no such agreement." She took a step toward him, and his heart, already racing, took off at a gallop. Her expression was somber, her gaze opaque. But even as he watched, a light glowed in those green depths. A light that caused his breath to stutter even as his chest expanded. "The film. You changed the ending."

"I did." He held her gaze with his.

The light burned brighter. "I told you to delete my email."

"I would never delete anything from you." He thought for moment. "Well. Maybe some of the budget spreadsheets. There were a lot of them."

She laughed, a strangled choke-sob. "Were you going to tell me?"

He was still holding the hockey equipment like a brainless mannequin. "I was going to do one even better. I was going to show you."

"What do you mean?"

"I'm on a flight to London tonight. The first break I had in the postproduction schedule." He frowned. "Didn't you get the email?"

"What email? Xavier, if you wrote me another letter that has gone missing…"

"I spoke to your assistant to make sure your calendar was clear and swore her secrecy. Four weeks ago. Then sent the email invitation to you yesterday. When you didn't respond, I thought…maybe you were still making up your mind."

She blinked. "I don't have an assistant in London."

He didn't understand. "Yes, you do."

"No. I left Monument. Two weeks ago. I'm moving back to LA to work for Conti's new venture. In fact, I just got off the plane."

"What? But that was your dream job."

She shook her head, curls flying. "No. You were right. That wasn't my dream, it was my parents' dream for me. A corner office, an expense account, a steady paycheck. They made me believe failure was the most catastrophic thing that could ever happen to me." Her smile was tentative, but her gaze continued to glow. "But they were wrong. Losing you was."

A dam broke inside him, sending something like hope cascading through his veins. He took two steps toward her. "Sutton, I—"

She waved her right hand. "You don't... What I do need to do is thank you. You helped me realize I want to tell stories I care deeply about, not stories picked solely for the maximum financial return. Stories with vision. Like *The Quantum Wraith*." She peered at him. "The ending... Did Monument make you change it?"

He laughed, the hope expanding in his lungs. "My darling Sutton, how likely do you think that is?"

She scoffed. "Not very...wait. Darling?"

"It's a common form of endearment." He dropped the hockey equipment, closing the space between them.

Twin suns now burned in her eyes. "I know what it is. But you don't use terms of endearment."

"I didn't. I didn't end my films happily, either. Then I read your beautiful, heartfelt, hopeful ending, and here I am. Here we are. Not how I intended." He'd rented a screening room at a posh London hotel, ordered canapés and very expensive champagne to be served. He'd planned to stay hidden, watch her reaction to the film they made together and then surprise her when the film was open. And pray she understood what he was trying to say to her by using her ending.

But life was messy and had a way of changing plans. "And I wouldn't have it any other way. Because you're here."

Her hands found her way into his—how, he wasn't sure—the sparks at her touch as vividly electric as ever. He caught and held her gaze. "I thought I was protecting Erik by limiting his exposure to people who might leave him. But I realize now I was using that as an excuse. In reality, I was limiting myself. Hurting myself. And hurting Erik, too, because he missed out on getting to know some great people. He's still not happy with me for letting you go."

"When you live in fear of the worst that can happen, you also miss out on the best that can happen," she said softly. "I understand some of that. I bought into my parents' framing of the world. They made me afraid to chase what I want. That's why I never contacted you after graduation. But I'm not afraid now."

He cupped her face with his hand, reveling in the satin of her skin. A tear gathered in the corner of her eye and started to fall. His thumb wiped the trail away. "Sutton, I love you. I loved you from the first moment you sat in the seminar, and I fell irrevocably in love with you in Arizona. But I was afraid to admit it because if I did, I was admitting I might lose you someday. It was easier to tell myself all relationships come with expiration dates and to get the loss over with. I'm so sorry for not telling you sooner. But I will tell you every night and every morning for as long we are together, if you want."

Her smile was incandescent, more beautiful than any image he could put on film. "See, this is why happy endings are realistic. You're never going to lose me. I waited ten years for our second chance. I'm holding on to you for another one hundred. Because I love you."

And then she was in his arms, for real, not his imagination conjuring her up. Real and warm, her curves soft and pliable as he pulled her tight against him to kiss her. A kiss of heat and depth, of forgiveness and devotion forever, of passion and white-hot flame.

A kiss for now, and ever.

Seventeen

Two years later

The lights came up in the theater on LAU's campus, revealing a packed house. Every seat in the auditorium was taken, and even the standing room along the walls was crowded with shoulder-to-shoulder students. The host for the evening, the president of the campus film society, approached the podium set up at on side of the stage. "I hope everyone enjoyed tonight's screening of *The Way Fair*, the first film from Contessina Sato's production company Bullish Bear. Tonight, we are privileged to have very special guests for an in-depth discussion, but first I want to remind you of our upcoming events…"

The host continued to speak, but Sutton tuned him out as soon as Xavier enveloped her left hand in his, careful of the solitaire diamond on her ring finger. "Nervous?" he asked.

"Why? Just because this is the first time I've been asked back to my alma mater, and it's to appear onstage before a theater full of critical film students? Piece of cake." Her other hand trembled and she thrust it into her pocket. Not much longer until she had to leave the safety of backstage and go in front of the crowd as one of the panelists for the after-screening discussion.

He kissed her. "The film is a work of art from start to finish."

"Thanks to Jay's direction."

Jay heard his name from where he stood on her other side and gave her a wink.

"Hello. I'm the one who greenlit this masterpiece in the first place," Contessina said from behind Xavier.

"You need to keep reminding people of that, because your performance is all people are going to talk about." Sutton was being sincere. Contessina's star had shot into the stratosphere with *The Quantum Wraith*, and *The Way Fair*—an updated version of *Vanity Fair*—promised to cement her as a perpetual award contender for years to come. But Contessina's true passion was providing others with their first big breaks, like taking a gamble on Jay as a director. Or her co-star in *The Way Fair*, who had been teaching acting for years but never landed a film role with more than five pages of dialogue before.

Contessina shrugged. "As long as people respond to the films we produce at Bullish Bear. That's what matters. Not what they say about me." She kissed the six-month-old baby being held by Juliana. "Right, sweetie? At least when it comes to work. Otherwise, you and Mommy are the only things that matter."

"Well, I'd rather no more intruders show up," Juliana interjected. "But that appears to have been a one-off. Thankfully." She smiled at the infant. "Time to go out front and watch Mama do her thing."

"That's my cue as well," Xavier said to Sutton, with a squeeze of the hand he held. "Break a femur, as Nikki says. She's here, by the way. She just texted. She's with Erik, helping him get reactions from the audience for social media."

Erik had recently started as a high school marketing intern for Bullish Bear. Their social media had never been better—or snarkier. Sutton was so proud of him.

The stagehand signaled at Contessina, Jay and Sutton to get ready to go onstage.

Sutton clutched at Xavier's hand, not willing to let him go until the last second. "What if the audience hates the film? I think I'm looking more forward to my parents' visit next week than I am this."

Sutton's parents had accepted her choice to leave the corporate world for Contessina's riskier venture, much to Sutton's surprise. Of course, they then turned their concern to her matrimonial future, harping on how a marriage certificate would provide her with more security when it came to the future.

"About that. I was thinking. You're leaving for Prague for reshoots on the new film after your parents depart. When you return, I start work on *The Quantum Wraith* sequel."

"Yeah. I'm already missing you." She gave him a rueful smile.

"But right now, we're all together. Jay, Conti, Juliana, Erik, Nikki. We're only missing Ilsa, and that's because she's visiting her sister." Xavier was nearly vibrating.

She searched his gaze. "What are you up to?"

"I know how much stress your parents' visit is causing. So, let's go to Vegas. Tonight. With the people we love. We'll get married, and your parents will lose their last ammunition."

"Xavier, we can't just—"

"We've been engaged for a year. This isn't spur of the moment." He kissed her and she melted. Like the first time. Like she always would.

"I know, but…" She stopped. Why was she protesting? Their schedules were wreaking havoc with planning a big white wedding. "But it's perfect."

He smiled at her, love and laughter lighting his face. "We can always have a formal ceremony later. But I don't want to put off forever one more day. Life is chaotic. Let's embrace the chaos."

"I'd rather embrace you." She pressed herself against him, reveling in his warmth, his strength, his confidence in her and in them, only pulling away when she heard her name coming from the stage. "Gotta run."

"Be amazing. You always are." He let her go.

But only for now.

They would always be each other's happy Hollywood ending.

★ ★ ★ ★ ★

Don't miss Susannah Erwin's next book coming in Winter 2026 from Afterglow Books!

afterglow BOOKS

Looking for more Afterglow Books?

Try the perfect subscription for spicy romance lovers and save 50% on your first parcel.

PLUS receive these additional benefits when you subscribe:
- **FREE** delivery direct to your door
- **EXCLUSIVE** offers every month
- **SAVE** up to 30% on pre-paid subscriptions

SUBSCRIBE AND SAVE

millsandboon.co.uk/Subscribe

afterglow BOOKS

Afterglow Books is a trend-led, trope-filled list of books with diverse, authentic and relatable characters, a wide array of voices and representations, plus real world trials and tribulations. Featuring all the tropes you could possibly want (think small-town settings, fake relationships, grumpy vs sunshine, enemies to lovers) and all with a generous dose of spice in every story.

♪ @millsandboonuk
◉ @millsandboonuk
afterglowbooks.co.uk

#AfterglowBooks

For all the latest book news, exclusive content and giveaways scan the QR code below to sign up to the Afterglow newsletter:

SCAN ME

afterglow BOOKS

Break Point
YAHRAH ST. JOHN

THESE ENEMIES ARE A MATCH MADE IN HEAVEN...OR HELL!

- ♥ Second chance
- 🎾 Sports romance
- ❤️‍🔥 Enemies to lovers

OUT NOW

To discover more visit:
Afterglowbooks.co.uk

LET'S TALK
Romance

For exclusive extracts, competitions and special offers, find us online:

- **f** MillsandBoon
- **X** @MillsandBoon
- **◉** @MillsandBoonUK
- **♪** @MillsandBoonUK

Get in touch on 01413 063 232

For all the latest titles coming soon, visit
millsandboon.co.uk/nextmonth